OPULENCE

Published by Lemon Rose Publishers

Paperback ISBN-13: 978-1-7396955-0-7
eBook ISBN-13: 978-1-7396955-1-4

Printed in the United Kingdom

Cover design and layout by www.spiffingcovers.com

OPULENCE

P A LEWIS

CONTENTS

CHAPTER 1

'Hurry up Sarah, for goodness sake,' Jasper Teasdale snapped at his wife. Sarah teetered on six-inch Louboutin's, trying to keep up with his long strides as he made his way to check-in at the Neptune Terminal at Southampton Docks.

Jasper and Sarah were among the 200 priority embarkation passengers for a 24-night Caribbean cruise on *Opulence*, the world's newest and most luxurious addition cruise liner to the prestigious Purple Cross Cruise Line.

The terminal was fairly quiet, as they'd arrived earlier than necessary hoping to avoid any form of queueing with other passengers. Priority embarkation was all well and good, however, there were another 198 passengers in the same position and Jasper didn't like queues, nor for that matter did he care much for people. Jasper was the son of a wealthy American business magnet who moved to the UK in 1943. His father Edward was very successful, earning his wealth through hard work in the stock market and Jasper had inherited his father's brusque manner, arrogance and business acumen. Jasper was an entrepreneur with a huge portfolio of properties, as well as a success in the international banking industry. Jasper, some would say, teetered on the edge of being a cruel, cold, calculating man who would do anything to get what he wanted. He also exuded charm and sophistication which would not have been out of place in a romatic period novel.

Jasper and Sarah went straight to the check-in desk, their 16 matching Louis Vuitton suitcases having already been taken from them as they exited their chauffeur-.driven limousine at the terminal. It had taken three porters to ensure their luggage's safe transportation to security. The next time Jasper would see the luggage was when it was stored away in the huge dressing room in his suite on board the ship.

'Good Morning sir, may I take your passport and ticket please?' A smiling middle-aged lady wearing a snow-white blouse with purple skirt and cravat, the uniform of the Purple Cross Cruise Line welcomed them. Her name badge identified her as Vivienne.

Jasper handed over the documents with short shrift as Vivienne tried to make conversation about their journey to the terminal. Vivienne, realising her passenger was in no mood to chat, set about checking-in the Teasdales with the utmost politeness and efficiency.

Jasper was irritated and just wanted to get into his suite on board the liner and have his butler open a bottle of Chivas Regal. He'd been up since 4am and had already endured the traffic on the M25 and M3. He should have travelled yesterday and stayed overnight he thought, but that meeting with the CEO of a large American developer was damned important and not one to be missed. His irritation was further exacerbated by his wife's behaviour. Sarah was a raven-haired stunner but according to Jasper she should have been blonde due to her lack of brain cells and education. *This marriage is a joke*, thought Jasper not for the first time, frowning at his exuberant dolly bird wife of five years. *I should have married someone my own age. Twenty-six-year-old models are fine as eye candy but a nightmare as a lifelong companion.* Sarah was dressed top to toe in a hot pink Gucci trouser suit. She carried it well, but Jasper thought she looked ridiculous. *This was a holiday of a lifetime for god's sake*, thought Jasper. *It's cost me hundreds of thousands of pounds to secure one of the best suites on the ship and here I am travelling with a chav.* She may be a stunner to look at, dripping designer labels from her sunglasses to her shoes, but money can't buy sophistication or class, and this was something which irked Jasper.

Jasper conveniently forgot that this was not the sort of cruise which Joe Public could afford and it was highly unlikely there would be any chavs within 500 miles of this ship. *Opulence* was the newest addition to the Purple Cross Line and had cost a cool £1.7 billion to build. Her sisters *Indulgence* and *Decadence* were only a couple of years older and had taken the cruising world by storm for their glamour, sophistication and luxury. *Opulence* was the newcomer, but she was without doubt the world's finest and most luxurious cruise liner ever. Her passengers would pay premium rates for the privilege of travelling on her and there would be no cruise club special deals for this ship, nor the bargain hunters associated with the cheap and cheerful fares.

Sarah's Gucci sunglasses perched atop her immaculately coiffed hair which hung loose over her shoulders while she was frantically searching her hot pink Michael Kors tote looking for her mobile phone.

'Where is it, Jasper?' shouted Sarah. 'I need my phone. I need to take a selfie and post it on Instagram for my followers.'

'For god's sake, Sarah, will you just sit down, calm down and stop embarrassing me,' growled Jasper through clenched teeth.

Sarah ignored Jasper and continued to rifle through her oversized tote. 'Oh here it is,' she announced in a voice so loud it carried to the other passengers sitting in the exclusive waiting area. A few other early-bird passengers turned their first-class heads to look at the gorgeous girl with the loud voice – admiring glances from the men and looks of disdain from jealous women.

There was no escaping the fact that Sarah was a beauty. Her perfect figure enhanced by breast augmentation and a few fillers here and there and her love of low-cut necklines to show off her assets gave Sarah a confidence which belied her failings in the brain department. Jasper knew Sarah was beautiful but he thought she was stupid.

Brought up by a single mother in Braintree, Essex, Sarah knew her fair share of 'uncles' throughout her childhood and early teenage years. Her mother, more interested in her men than whether Sarah was at school, didn't have much to do with her daughter, instead preferring to allow Sarah her freedom from an early age. Sarah's father had been a one-night stand who fled for the hills when Eve told him she was pregnant. He was a soldier based at Colchester. A group of squaddies had ended up having a night out in the notorious Braintree and Sarah was the result.

Sarah's father had been posted three days after his liaison with Eve and despite Eve's best efforts to try and find him, her search was fruitless. The army closed ranks and wouldn't disclose any information. It turned out that he'd even given her a false name. The adjutant was sympathetic but not unrealistic. 'Listen love, this happens all the time. If I were you, I'd jump back on the bus and get on with your life.' Eve did just that and, although happy with her daughter, she felt burdened having to be responsible for a young life at the tender age of 17. Eve relied on friends to look after Sarah while she went out every night enjoying the good life. Sarah was passed from pillar to post and didn't really have a close bond with her mother. Eve was young herself and looked on her daughter more as a little friend. When she was in the mood to play at being mum, she loved dressing Sarah in frills and bows, but these times were few and far between. She did what she could for Sarah and she loved her but maternal guidance was low on the list.

Sarah's stunning looks and immaturity led her to quickly become a plaything for any man who showed her attention. She was sexually active at 12 years old and could easily pass for an 18-year-old. Sarah quickly learned that sex bought her all the designer products she saw in magazines and the more friendly she was, the better the gifts. Sarah wasn't interested in young boys her age. She made sure she was seen on the party circuit where wealthy playboys gathered, guzzling champagne as if it were water. Sarah pored through the tabloids and magazines every day taking notice of the latest fashions, hair styles, hot designers, places to be and who to be seen with. Sarah knew she was pretty and wanted to model or be on television so she made it her goal to get herself noticed. Sarah landed a few local modelling jobs which led to her being discovered by Ray Fuller, a TV producer from London. Ray recruited Sarah for a new reality dating show and she quickly became an icon for young girls throughout the country who wanted to look like her and live the partying lifestyle which she lived. Sarah was in demand and travelled all over the UK for personal appearances. She would turn up to the opening of an envelope if she thought it would benefit her career and she was asked to guest model in some local fashion shows. Sarah loved this lifestyle where, although a pretty small fish, she had visions of her headlining the catwalks in Milan, Rome, New York and London, promoting the top fashion designers.

Sarah lacked education but her business acumen soon started to grow. She wasn't as dumb as people thought when it came to fame and money. She was quickly becoming Z-list famous in her own right and loved being seen on the arm of real celebrities. Sarah hated her own company and had lots of casual flings and one night stands. She was no longer the Braintree Super Slut thanks to her TV appearances but she did have a reputation. Sarah loved being the centre of attention but didn't realise it was for all the wrong reasons.

Sarah quickly gained a reputation for being a good-time girl. Despite her growing wealth and Z-list celebrity status, she was always seen hanging out at the best establishments, wearing designer clothes and expensive jewellery. She was never short of suitors and was often the guest of a professional football player or celebrity rock star. Sarah loved her lifestyle and wouldn't listen to criticism that she would end her career before it began if she continued to party at the rate she did. Sarah was quickly becoming too big for her boots and her infamy was starting to wane. Photographers and magazines were getting fed up with Sarah's failure to show up on time to photo shoots and her tendency to turn up to fashion shows under the influence of something which made her a no-go for known designers. Sarah had a knack of ending up in the tabloids for all the wrong reasons. Falling out of a car, flashing her G-string or sprawled on a pavement, red eyed and smashed after leaving a nightclub at three o clock in the morning.

Sarah was fed up with the strict rules wannabe models had to follow. Why couldn't she have a kebab if she wanted one? She was only size 6 so who said she was too big and needed to lose weight? Who did these people think they were? Sarah had enough of a prospective modelling career and turned her attention full time to a career on television. She sacked Ray and hired Larry Taylor, another agent willing to take on Z-list celebrities and promising them the world, so much so that Sarah was confident that one day she would be fronting the UK's most popular TV shows. Sarah wasn't aware she had little talent and producers wouldn't touch her with a bargepole for serious presenter roles but her agent's enthusiasm and promises had already hooked her and she was no more than puppy fodder for cheap, humiliating TV. She signed on the dotted line with a flourish of her Montblanc Meisterstück pen and a loud giggle.

Jasper had come into Sarah's life quite by accident. They both attended the birthday party of a rather famous middle-aged actor six years ago. Sarah's invitation was as the plus one of a premier league footballer and yet again, with little effort, she looked stunning. The party was held at the London Savoy and Sarah spotted the gorgeous Jasper as soon as she entered the room. As usual, all heads turned to look at Sarah and she was immediately drawn to the tall sultry dark-haired man who was talking to an attractive young chestnut-haired TV newscaster.

Jasper was the handsome dark-haired Mr Darcy to Sarah's young Sophia Loren. Jasper's designer stubble and sexy smile melted Sarah's heart and as she watched him mingle with the guests, exuding a charm and sophistication that she craved, Sarah made it her goal to get this Adonis' attention. Little did she know, but Sarah had caught Jasper's attention also. A renowned bachelor with his own reputation in the circles he moved in, he was a sucker for a pretty girl and his head turned when Sarah walked into the room. His eyes were drawn to the stunning black-haired beauty dressed in a white beaded Chanel gown.

Jasper approached Sarah with the arrogant confidence he was known for and six years later here she was about to board the most luxurious cruise liner in the world, her Adonis now her very wealthy husband.

'Come on Sarah,' said Jasper, grabbing her elbow and leading her towards security. 'It's time to board.' The 'A' star passengers in the executive waiting area watched again as the handsome dark-haired man grabbed roughly at the stunning dark-haired busty beauty and thought what a gorgeous couple they made, although by his obvious irritation with his wife they could question whether or not all was well within this marriage. They made their way as swiftly through security as they could. Even the wealthiest were subjected to security checks and after having removed their shoes and belts and being body scanned they were cleared to make their way on board. Jasper led Sarah up the gangway onto the most magnificent cruise liner in the world.

Long, sleek and majestic *Opulence* rose out of the water, a huge 16 decks' high. Her magnificent pointed bow curved subtly, showing off her gleaming white hull and plimsoll line and funnel with purple and silver trim. There was no mistaking that this was one breathtaking vessel which would live up to her name in the most luxurious fashion. Built to carry 600 passengers and 1,500 crew, *Opulence's* size was deceptive. Despite the relatively small passenger capacity, *Opulence* boasted individual suites of accommodation starting at 1,500 square feet, up to the most ostentatious and lavish suite consisting of 3,795 square feet. Fitted out in only the best and most luxurious fabrics from all corners of the globe, no expense had been spared. Only the best craftsmen had been hired and each piece of fixture and fitting had been handmade. Crystal, granite, marble, leather, wool, silk, jacquard and lace were the chosen fabrics and materials. Each deck was colour coordinated and the ship boasted sheer opulence throughout her very core, hence her name. This was the most expensive ship ever built and even the cheapest suite on board would set you back a cool £150,000 pounds per person for a seven-day voyage. *Opulence* was built to carry only the wealthiest passengers and those with a grace and etiquette befitting this magnificent cruise liner. *Opulence* was designed by the best shipbuilding engineers in the world and built in Italy. Boasting a helipad and helicopter, submarine and garden deck, it had been a challenge for all concerned to ensure the weight of the marble, granite and glass would not destabilise the liner but the engineers had worked their magic to overcome this particular problem with slightly wider decks and additional stabilisers. The ship was huge but sleek and elegant. Her sea trials had been a dream and this was her third voyage. Any teething troubles had been ironed out and *Opulence* was now beginning to take on her own lifeform.

They were met at the top of the gangway by a liveried steward holding a silver tray containing two Baccarat crystal champagne flutes. 'Welcome Mr and Mrs Teasdale.' Jasper ignored the offer of champagne, wishing it was a large scotch on the rocks. However, Sarah excitedly grabbed a glass while giggling and proclaiming that she hoped it was nothing less than Cristal? A man with skin the colour of cappuccino walked forward. He was dressed in a black jacket and trousers, white shirt and purple bow tie. His cuffs were embroidered in silver and purple silk thread with the crest of the Purple Cross Line. His name tag identified him as 'Lewis', their butler.

Lewis introduced himself and led the Teasdales to their suite. *Not bad*, thought Jasper. *The staff know us by name already. They damn well should do given what this is costing me,* he mused. The Ocean Suite was situated on Deck 8 AFT of the ship and measured 2,978 square feet, it consisted of a lounge, three bedrooms, dining room, dressing room, office, toilet, bathroom, shower room, kitchen and gym. The balcony could be accessed from every room within the suite by remote-controlled French doors and was one of the most prestigious suites on the liner with the exception of The Queen of the Seas Suite. This was the biggest and most decadent suite reserved only for the Russian oligarchs and Japanese billionaires of this world. The Queen of the Seas had five bedrooms, five en suite bath and shower rooms, gym, dining room, kitchen, games room, and office located within her 3,795 square feet. The balcony had its own pool and sauna as well as the standard al fresco barbeque area and bar. The suite also offered a daily private chef and concierge for those who just could not be bothered to mix with mere mortals and required a completely secretive relaxing getaway, a regular home from home. On this voyage, the Queen of the Seas was playing host to a Japanese businessman from the world of electronics. He and his wife paid a handsome sum to occupy the most luxurious of luxury accommodation.

Sarah gasped when she entered the foyer of the Ocean suite. It was magnificent and would not have been out of place at the Burj Al Arab in Dubai with the preference on *Opulence* being pastels rather than bold colours. The foyer's magnificent oak-panelled doors and white marble floor led into a sumptuous lounge carpeted in the softest white deep pile carpets. Two large white Italian leather sofas accessorised with purple and silver cushions dominated the room. Crystal glass tables with ornate white marble legs supported beautiful crystal and marble lamps with white silk shades edged in delicate silver and purple. A white silk swivel rocker sat in one corner and arrangements of fresh flowers and candles with only purple and lavender colours adorned every surface. The smell of freesia wafted through the suite, adding the scent of summer to the start of this Caribbean voyage. Jasper normally hated frills and fluff, as he found this decor too ostentatious for his liking, however this was a holiday and he supposed he could put up with it for a few weeks. He lived with Sarah after all and had to reign her in to stop their homes looking like something from a Barbie movie. Jasper took in the overflowing fruit bowls in crystal containers which were displayed throughout the suite and contained every fruit anyone could possibly wish for.

An 80-inch curved smart TV hung from one wall, while beautiful contemporary art specifically commissioned for *Opulence* by the renowned American artist Michael Godard was displayed throughout the suite. A huge white unit ran the length of one wall and secretly housed a state-of-the-art Bang & Olufsen BeoSound 35 music system. Heavy white silk drapes trimmed in purple and silver adorned the French doors and these too were controlled by a small remote controller.

A champagne bucket on a stand contained a bottle of Cristal Brut 1990, suitably ice-chilled and a bowl of fresh raspberries and strawberries sat beside the champagne flutes. A platter of canapes and chocolates also awaited the Teasdales. Purple Cross liked to ensure their passengers had an appropriate glass to raise and toast 'Set sail!'.

Sarah was excitedly tottering around the suite finding her bearings and gasping with an affected 'ooh lush' when something took her fancy, while Jasper barked at Lewis to pour him a large Chivas Regal on the rocks. *At least there's a decent complimentary bar in the suite*, thought Jasper as he settled himself on one of the plush sofas to read the leather-bound welcome pack and told Lewis to unpack the luggage when he'd attended to his drink. Lewis merely smiled and said, 'Of course, Mr Teasdale.' Lewis had come across arseholes like Jasper Teasdale before. A forty-something rich kid with an arrogance the size of Mount Everest and his token dolly bird wife. Designer tits and no brains.

Many of Lewis's passengers were lovely people. He had been with Purple Cross for 17 years and achieved the lofty ranks of senior butler. He had dealt with the rich and famous, the crazy, the deluded and the no-marks. The fact that they were wealthy did not necessarily make them treat the crew like shit, however there was always one and it looked like Teasdale would be the one on this voyage. Lewis was paid reasonably well. However he, like all crew, depended on the generous tips to make up their wages, so once again Lewis would smile and kowtow to his passengers until the end of the voyage to ensure a good payday.

'Jasper, you have to come and see this!' shrieked Sarah. Jasper, still irritated by his wife's earlier behaviour, strode purposefully into the bedroom as Sarah grabbed his arm and pulled him into the master bathroom.

'Look,' she said excitedly as she pointed to the huge whirlpool spa bath that sat in the middle of the sumptuous marble bathroom. 'Shall we have a spa bath now, Jasper?' shrieked his tipsy wife as she called to Lewis to bring her a third glass of champagne.

'Leave it out, Sarah and pull yourself together. You're embarrassing me. Remember where you are and try and act with some decorum, for fuck's sake.' Sarah had already managed to polish off a bottle of Veuve Cliquot in the limousine on the way to Southampton. Sarah, too tipsy or too excited to realise she was again being chastised, ignored Jasper and set about cooing and shrieking at the variety of complimentary Ferragamo products provided for their voyage.

As well as the usual shampoo and conditioner, the products

also included anti-ageing face masks, shower gel, body lotions, facial mist, bath soaps and bath tablets, lip balms, hand cream, eye cream, face cream moisturiser, shaving gel and shaving emulsion. Hanging on all the towel rails in the bath and shower rooms were the most gorgeous Egyptian cotton soft white fluffy towels with the purple cross crest hand embroidered with purple and silver silk threads. Sarah was in her element.

Jasper was secretly impressed with the suite and its accessories, however, his wife was annoying him so he stalked out of the bathroom and went out onto the extensive balcony which encased their suite. *At last, some peace*, he thought as he stood against the rail taking in his surroundings. A warm gentle August breeze fanned his face as he looked out over the port. Tugboats and container ships were docked along the numerous berths in Southampton. The noise from huge cranes as they lifted large containers and transferred them expertly onto the empty container vessels rang throughout the docks. Buoys bobbed on the water, guiding safe passage to the vessels which used the shipping lanes. The warm midday sun glistened on the water and the Isle of Wight was clear to the naked eye.

The drop from the suite to the quayside would be enough to kill someone, Jasper thought as he imagined a crushed skull, broken and shattered bone and blood and matter oozing from a twisted and tangled corpse lying on the quay. Jasper held that thought as he turned to take in his outdoor surroundings. He noticed the interior colour theme of the suite continued on the balcony furnishings with the six large sunloungers, four tables and umpteen chairs which made up their outside living space. Huge exotic green plants and ferns stood proudly in pots around the balcony, breaking it up into a relaxing and entertaining outside living space. During rough seas, all outdoor plants were moved into a storage unit carefully hidden away on the balconies. Every last detail was thought of. The small private pool and hot tub was a welcome addition to the balcony. Even the parasol umbrellas were white, purple and silver. Jasper had to admire the barbeque grill area also. *You can't say they skimped on amenities or facilities*, thought Jasper. *I have everything*

I need here. I think I'm going to enjoy this holiday.

Jasper sat down and called for Lewis to bring him another scotch but this time to bring the bottle and leave it with him. He needed as much of the golden nectar he could consume to mellow his mind from his loud and in-your-face wife.

CHAPTER 2

Three decks below, an excited cry of 'Oh my god, have you seen this?' echoed around a penthouse suite from Chris Bailey to her best friend Denise Patterson. 'I can't believe how we've landed on our feet!' Denise said, greedily finishing her second glass of champagne. 'Who would have thought little old us from a council estate in the New Forest would end up on this bugger of a ship?' Denise and Chris had been friends since school and grown up in ordinary houses with ordinary parents on an ordinary council estate near Lymington. They had never been wealthy but their parents made sure they always had food in their stomach, clean clothes and a clean and tidy home. Their parents worked hard to provide them with a decent upbringing, something which was sadly lacking with many of the neighbours on the estate.

The majority were council tenants, who didn't work, relied on benefits and had no inclination or intention of improving their lives. The Baileys and the Pattersons were different and wanted more for their children and this drew them together. They kept themselves to themselves and socialised only with each other, gaining them the name of being the posh ones and the butt of most of their neighbours' jokes.

They'd lived on the estate for years, in the days when everyone was proud of their property and where they all kept clean houses and pretty gardens. Through the years, many had moved on and the new-age council tenants had moved in. Unfortunately, they did not hold the same standards as the Baileys and Pattersons and were somewhat scorned by the newcomers which made them keep themselves to themselves. They were now surrounded by properties with gardens which looked like scrapyards, screaming neighbours, loud music, revving vehicles and flytipping. This upset the Baileys and the Pattersons who spoke to each other but kept their distance from the newcomers. They were intimidated by the louts and obnoxious youths and were pretty much at the end of their tether about living on the estate. They wondered how it could have turned out so badly when it had started so well. Both the Baileys and Pattersons worked hard and had done for most of their lives, apart from when Brenda and Eileen gave up work to bring up their daughters.

Both sets of parents longed for the day when they could earn enough money to move away and perhaps buy their own home on a nice private estate. They had the option of buying their two-bed council houses but both knew that unless the area changed drastically they would never be able to sell the properties so they made the best of a bad deal. They were desperate to move.

Their fortunes changed one day when Denise and Chris won the lottery. The girls had dreams of the WAG lifestyle and their only hope was to win the lottery or somehow meet a rich and famous celebrity who would take them away from their dreary lives and catapult them into the lifestyle they could only read about in magazines. Denise's job as an admin assistant at the local council offices and Chris's dental receptionist job wouldn't get them the lifestyle they craved so each week they invested in a European Lottery Ticket and a British Lotto Ticket. One Friday evening their European ticket numbers came up and they found themselves winning a jackpot of 47 million euros. Their winnings were life changing and the first thing they did was to resign from their jobs and buy their parents their dream homes away from the shabby council estate that had been home for 22 years. Both families moved to the beautiful countryside near Romsey, home to the late Lord Louis Mountbatten and his huge estate, Broadlands.

After splashing out on designer clothes, shoes and handbags and treating themselves to relaxing spa breaks at the plushest hotels in the south of England, and securing a fabulous penthouse apartment overlooking the Solent, the girls decided the only way to meet the celebrities they craved to mingle with was to cruise on the most expensive ocean liner in the world. Despite being a relatively new liner, *Opulence* had already gained a reputation for being the top choice for actors, rock stars, reality TV stars and television presenters and personalities to get away and be with their own kind without being stalked or harassed by fans desperate for selfies or paparazzi and journalists who wouldn't leave them alone. Denise and Chris had looked forward to this cruise for months and now they were here. They were finally somebody as they took in their glorious surroundings in one of *Opulence's* penthouses.

The furnishings were in keeping with the white, purple and silver theme of the company colours and the beds and sofas were sumptuous. The girls had never experienced luxury like this in their lives and they were going to make the most of it. Denise threw herself, giggling, onto her king-size bed and sank into the soft down duvet. 'I could get used to this, Chris. Let's hope we find a couple of fit blokes on this cruise as it would just put the icing on the cake for us. Think how happy we could be for the rest of our lives.'

'I wonder if Ed Sheeran is on board?' mused Chris. 'He'd do for me.' The girls rolled about on Denise's bed, giggling like schoolgirls.

The foyer of the ship located on Deck 2 was buzzing with embarking passengers, all eagerly anticipating the voyage of a lifetime. Most cruise ships during embarkation appeared to be chaotic, however the crew of Purple Cross were so highly trained and professiona,l the buzz was from the atmosphere of excitement and not the chaos.

Liveried stewards and bellboys personally met all embarking guests and accompanied them to their suites. The Pursers Office staff watched closely to see what the newest batch of passengers would bring. They never knew whether they would have an easy voyage or a difficult one. It depended mainly on who the passengers were.

'This could be an interesting trip,' said Chloe Simpson. She was looking at the passenger list which read like a Who's Who? Chloe scanned the 'A' star passengers and smiled to herself as she recognised all of them.

The Jackdaws, Michael and Michelle Benson, Louisa Hudson,

Kurt Robbins, Mia Manzo, and many more. *Mmmm not bad*, thought Chloe. *Wait until I tell my friends about this little lot, they'll be so jealous.* Chloe's attention was interrupted by raised voices from the other side of the plush foyer.

'Jenson, stop that and come back here!' The voice belonged to a large tattooed man. 'Diana, do something will you?' boomed Sam Jenkins to his wife. Diana Jenkins was looking harassed and gripping the hands of two small boys aged about four and six years' old who were screaming and throwing tantrums as they tried to wriggle free of their mum's grasp to run and copy Jenson, the errant nine-year-old who was currently jumping from one inter-matching purple and white velvet club chair to another, located throughout the area, tearing off large leaves and fronds from the beautiful shrubs, ferns and plants which decorated the lavish foyer.

'Jenson, get back 'ere now, you little shit!' screamed Diana, who was racing after her uncontrollable nine-year-old and now dragging his equally uncontrollable brothers along for the ride. 'Jenson, so help me I'll fucking kill you when I get hold of you, showing me up like this!' screamed Diana.

'Jenson!' boomed Sam as he grabbed his son's arm. 'You are a fucking little moron and if you carry on like this I'll drop you overboard, do you understand?' he said as he sent a blow crashing to the back of Jenson's head. This elicited loud screams from Jenson who now matched the screams of his still struggling younger brothers.

'Oh dear god,' thought Chloe as she took in the scene unfolding before her. Lotto Losers by the looks of it. No way could those chavs afford a holiday like this unless they were members of the Lotto Losers club – fondly nicknamed by the cruise industry to label passengers with no class or manners who somehow managed to find themselves on board beautiful ocean liners but sadly lacking any social etiquette or grace. The ones who knew the standards before booking but then insisted they wouldn't be told what to do. *It wouldn't be tolerated on this ship*, thought Chloe as she tried to imagine how the Jenkins family could afford to cruise on *Opulence* and thought that this family would probably elicit a few complaints from other passengers about their behaviour and language before the voyage was even underway.

Embarking passengers were looking aghast at the Jenkins family and their antics. Couples hurried away from the scene unfolding in front of them as they followed their liveried stewards to the lifts. John Bensimon, the on-duty chief purser went to the Jenkins family to try and calm the situation. Chloe checked the passenger list and saw that the Jenkins family's suite was forward on Deck 5. *It shouldn't be too bad for the big bucks*, thought Chloe as she pictured the suite's location nestled between service areas. Out of sight and hopefully out of mind.

Chloe sniggered to herself, feeling sorry for the suite steward who would have the unfortunate task of tending to this family for the voyage. Just then the door leading to the back office opened up and David appeared. Tall, blonde and drop-dead gorgeous, David sauntered over to the counter and with a flounce, deftly snatched the passenger list from Chloe's hands. 'So let's see what delicious celebs I have the pleasure of attending to this voyage.' Chloe told David he'd be lucky as the list contained all known heterosexual passengers. David's smile disappeared and he moodily threw his arms down against his thighs in an exaggerated motion which totally highlighted David's sexuality.

'Damn, how am I supposed to get out of this shithole of a job and live the life I was born to live?' whined David.

'If you don't like the job, then go find something else,' said Chloe, fed up with David's constant whinging about how he was born for better things and just waiting for his dream man with a large pay cheque to come along and take him away from all this drudgery.

'Don't be such a bitch, Chloe, you know I'm only working for Purple Cross as a bolthole until I can make my mark. Passengers love me, I'm hot, sassy, funny and extremely polite. I can get any guy I want but I've had enough. I've worked in the hospitality industry for eight years now, bowing and scraping to customers and passengers who think their shit don't stink. I'm sick of being treated like something on the bottom of their shoe. It's my time now and I want to be on that side of the counter anyway, Mia Manzo is travelling with her personal assistant and I hear he's just my type, so just watch this space, sweet cheeks.'

David smiled and gesticulated to the bustling foyer where happy and excited guests were still embarking and a still screaming Jenkins brood were being swiftly escorted to the lifts away from the other passengers. David looked out wistfully over the beautiful foyer with its light oak panelling and sumptuous purple and white decor and silently took consolation that one day it would be him being shepherded to his suite with the love of his life. 'Oh yes, one day it will be me,' smiled David broadly, as an elderly gentleman approached the Pursers Desk.

CHAPTER 3

The Calypso Club was heaving. Situated on Deck 11, the Calypso Club was a stunning indoor/outdoor venue created for deck celebrations such as Set Sail Sounds. The resident Caribbean band, Rum Punch, belted out lively tunes as white-gloved and jacketed waiters served lavish cocktails, glasses of champagne and canapes to the passengers who gathered for the Set Sail Sounds party.

It was 5pm and the weather was hot and the sun was shining. The glass roof had been retracted and the Calypso Club was jumping. Passengers were smiling and the crew were equally happy in this vibrant atmosphere. The ship's funnel sounded once as the ropes holding the gigantic vessel were released. *Opulence* silently slid away from the quayside with a sideways motion until she was far enough from the quay to be accompanied by two tugs displaying huge waterfall plumes as she was gently escorted out into the Solent. The band of the Royal Marines on the quay playing 'We are Sailing' faded, as *Opulence* majestically sailed smoothly out past the Isle of Wight towards Spain.

The majority of passengers who didn't partake in the Calypso's hospitality toasted their Set Sail party in the comfort and privacy of their own suites and waved from their balconies.

'Have you been to look at Zone One yet, Todd?' asked Rocky Fallon, lead singer with the number one rock band on the planet, The Jackdaws. The band had booked for a well-deserved holiday but had been asked by the chief executive officer of the Purple Cross Line, Marcus Thompson, to play a gig in the ship's nightclub, Zone One, during the voyage. It was also the perfect opportunity for the boys to let loose and let their hair down away from the ever-present paparazzi who followed them everywhere.

Todd Fitzpatrick, bass guitarist, laughed as he told Rocky, Ed and Terry about Zone One. 'Fuckin' hell dudes, you need to see it. It must hold about 400 people and it's got an amazing dance floor. The stage is massive and will easily hold our equipment and Ed's 60-piece drum kit.' They all laughed as Ed good naturedly threw a Nike trainer at Todd.

'Go to hell. Todd!' shouted Ed. 'I need these drums and cymbals, you know. Our sound would be crap if I only had run-of-the-mill gear, you asshole.'

'Seriously though guys, the club is awesome. Hopefully there'll be enough decent totty on this gig to keep us satisfied,' grinned Todd as he regaled his bandmates with the obligatory rock star image of what he was going to do to them.

Terry O'Brien, electric guitarist with The Jackdaws, laughed with the others but secretly he wished Todd would wind his neck in and appreciate what he had rather than what he could do because of who he was. Despite their phenomenal success, Terry and Rocky were the only two who remained relatively normal and unaffected by their status. Todd and Ed, on the other hand, lived for their fame and all the trappings that came with it. Rocky, Terry and Ed were schoolmates and found music at an early age. Rocky's family were all musically talented and sang every week at Sunday mass. They also sang at weddings and funerals when requested. Rocky had been born Liam Fitzmichael but quickly gained his nickname from an early age when learning to walk. Liam was not as steady on his feet as his parents would wish and spent most of his time upright, rocking back and forward on his heels. It was the source of amusement for the Fitzmichaels and their friends and Patrick Fitzmichael named him Rocky. Ed and Terry were also talented. The boys used to practice in their rooms emulating their idols Boyzone and Westlife. At 14 they formed a band which they named The Jackdaws. The name came from Rocky's love of corvids, ever since he found a tiny chick which had fallen from its nest eight years before. He called it Jet and managed to successfully raise and release him. The chick, at first mistaken for a blackbird, turned out to be a jackdaw and his love of all animals and birds developed from there. Jet returned to Rocky's bedroom window two or three times a year for a few years to say hello to the boy who rescued him, and from there a long-term friendship and bond had been created. Jet brought his mate and his chicks to meet the human boy who was part of his murder. As time went by, Jets visits became less regular until one year they stopped completely and Rocky feared that Jet was no longer alive. How he grieved for that little bird, at least he'd never forget him. One day, the boys from Dublin had entered a national TV competition to find up-and-coming talent, and to their surprise they had won. During the audition process a music producer connected with the show suggested they take a new member into the band. He knew just the lad to enhance their look and sound. Todd O'Reilly was auditioned and welcomed into the band and they hadn't looked back.

They were not the stereotypical boy band, with floppy hair and cute faces who sang in harmony about lost love and broken dreams. The Jackdaws were a rock band. Soft metal, gravel vocals and tons of personality propelled this mix of Meat Loaf and Bon Jovi to overnight stardom and a plethora of platinum albums and world tours.

On the whole they were good boys, but Todd and Ed had been tempted by the perils of celebrity trappings. They had become arrogant and egotistical whereas Rocky and Terry kept their feet firmly on the ground. Despite Rocky's laid-back, congenial manner, he was the leader of the band and the boys knew this. They had a quiet respect for the 24-year-old with dark brown hair which hung past his shoulders, deep blue eyes and designer stubble. Rocky was lean but muscular and he looked awesome in jeans and leathers.

'I'll take a look later, guys. I want to look round this magnificent ship first,' said Rocky as he made his way to the door of their four-bedroom suite.

'Hang on and I'll come with you!' shouted Terry as he leapt over a duck egg blue satin pouffe and made his way to familiarise himself with his new surroundings. The duck egg blue and gold decor which decorated their suite wasn't really in keeping with the rock star image but the boys loved it. It was elegance like they had never known and they were going to make the most of it.

The 16 passenger lifts situated forward, aft and midships were busy. Passengers eyed each other curiously as they made their way around the ship, taking in the glamour and opulence which the ship was named after. Fake smiles covered jealous glances as the haves and have-less all mingled together in the lobby areas, each one looking to outdo the other with their particular designer brand of shoes or handbags. *Opulence* dripped diamonds, tanzanite, rubies, emeralds and every designer worth a mention. If you wanted to be seen, this was the place to be.

Voyage PCOP03 to the Caribbean was underway and the ship had the beginnings of life being breathed into her luscious fabrics and furnishings.

Back on Deck 8, the Teasdales were enjoying their early evening on the balcony. Jasper, mellowed by half a bottle of Chivas Regal, was pumping into his tipsy wife from behind while she was bent over a sunlounger. Even in the throes of passion and with half a bottle of whisky in his system, Jasper could not be labelled anything other than brusque. He was cupping Sarah's enormous breasts and squeezing as he fucked her. Sarah was oblivious to Jasper's selfishness and willingly pushed back against him as he continued to ram his stiff rod into her.

'Oh Jas, harder, you feel so good,' whimpered Sarah as Jasper stiffened, bit his lips and released his seed into his willing spouse. Sarah shrieked and gasped as she too reached orgasm and dripped sweat all over the plush wooden floor of the balcony. Sarah turned and straddled her now seated husband as she thrust a large pink nipple into his mouth.

'I love you so much, Jasper Teasdale,' said Sarah.

That was good for starters but now it's time for the main course. Jasper let his fingers work Sarah's wet pussy as he sucked her nipple and massaged her other breast while his flaccid member recovered and started to become erect again. Sarah smiled at him as she pondered over what expensive gifts she would receive on this trip, knowing that the more she fucked him and the more alcohol he consumed the better the gifts. He had a bad temper and she didn't particularly like him but she loved their lifestyle and would suffer this moody arrogant prig as long as she needed to enable her to set herself up without him one day.

I quite fancy a villa in Bermuda this time, thought Sarah. Sarah was not completely oblivious to her husband's disdain of her and she was fed up being chastised and berated. Sarah had plans for her future which didn't include Jasper and they were coming together nicely. Jasper was oblivious to his wife's manipulation and congratulated himself on having a stupid young wife with pussy on tap. At times like this, Jasper couldn't think about his wife's faults. His thoughts were only on her awesome body and what he could do to it.

'Darling, where are my diamond studs?' drawled Mia Manzo. Cosmo, her male assistant, came running from the dressing room with a box containing 18-carat white gold studs with 1 carat of diamond in each earring. 'Here you go, Mia. Oh my but you look stunning,' gushed Cosmo.

'I know darling,' drawled Mia in her Texan accent as she studied herself in the full-length mirror separating the bathroom from the dressing area. Her tight-fitting long black Dior sheath highlighted her hourglass figure. *Not bad for a woman of 50*, thought Mia as she straightened her 18-carat white gold, 8-carat diamond pendant over her enhanced bosom, courtesy of Dr Lance Giovanni, the best plastic surgeon in Los Angeles. Her blonde hair piled high on her head was held in place by diamond clips and her heavy make-up made for a striking sight and enhanced her natural beauty. Mia was a huge A-list American actress who had starred in a number of blockbuster movies. At 50, Mia was still very popular. She was being chased by up-and-coming starlets but was still considered to be Queen of the Screen. Mia had a global following; she was the modern-day Audrey Hepburn.

Mia had just divorced her fifth husband, a 39-year-old Texan oil magnate who had grown fed up with his spouse. Grant Macy was under the impression Mia was only five years older than him when they met and married 18 months earlier, however Mia had been lying about her age since she was in her teens and when Grant accidentally came across her birth certificate he was shocked to see that she was in fact 11 years older than him. This was the final straw for Grant and he divorced Mia and generously gave her a $2m dollar fortune as settlement.

Mia was a wealthy woman in her own right. Along with her own earnings and four previous marriages, her net worth was in the region of $120m. In addition, she owned six properties, from Europe to the British Virgin Islands, and spent most of her time at her $25m mansion in Beverly Hills. Mia had been shrewd from a young age and took her father's advice to invest in property. Mia's wealth had accumulated throughout her career and she would never want for anything, except maybe lasting happiness with a partner who loved her.

Mia was supported by her faithful assistant Cosmo, who knew what side his bread was buttered. He had happily worked for Mia for two years and learned a long time ago that if you wanted to keep in Mia's good books then you told her constantly how beautiful she was and never disagreed with her. Working for Mia Manzo far outweighed his previous jobs working for large TV companies in the most menial of roles. Cosmo's dream to be a top wardrobe designer would have to start small, taking roles as a runner, assistant to the set designer and so on. Cosmo was eager and willing and this had got him noticed among producers, directors and celebrities. He had a dream but he was prepared to live the nightmare to make it. Cosmo met Mia when she was filming a sequel to one of her blockbusters. Mia was quite taken with the polite, funny and bold young man who knocked on her dressing room door one day and handed her a bunch of blood-red peonies. Cosmo would fast become Mia's favourite and she would call on him for everything. The TV company had to let Cosmo go as Mia commandeered him for herself. Their relationship worked well and surprisingly Mia had grown very fond of Cosmo and his eclectic dress sense which today consisted of multi-coloured hair, wire spectacle frames with no lenses, black lipstick and skinny jeans. Cosmo was on duty 24/7 but it was a small price to pay for his magnificent salary, being more or less his own boss and other perks of the job that came with his position such as his luxurious suite on the world's most prestigious cruise liner and a free holiday. Cosmo would still be working but it would be a doddle compared to being at the mansion.

Mia straightened her sheath, slipped into her diamond-encrusted heels and wrapped her silver mink stole around her neck as she rallied herself for her search for husband number six.

The Atlantis Suite was located midship on the port side of the ship and for the next three weeks was to be home to Michael and Michelle Benson. The Bensons were the golden couple of British television. With popular shows like 'Coffee Morning', 'Britain Awakes' and 'Bedside Manner' (a popular hospital reality series), Michelle and Michael Benson could at last kick off their shoes, remove their masks and be themselves for a while. This pearl wedding anniversary trip was much needed. The media's Golden Couple image was merely a front. In reality, Michelle and Michael despised each other. Both in their late 40s and equally attractive, the Bensons met 30 years earlier when they presented children's TV shows. They were instantly attracted to each other and were passionately in love in the early days, however over the years they had grown to hate each other with the same passion as they had once loved. Consummate professionals, in public they retained their on-screen chemistry and continued to grab the hearts of the nation.

Television work was lucrative but presenters had a shelf life. The Benson's had been lucky to still be working 30 years after they had met but Michelle was aware their careers could be cut short at any time with the rise of a shining new starlet with Hollywood white teeth and a perfect figure. Michelle was the driving force behind the relationship. She was desperate to crack the USA and land some dream presenting job which would propel them to global heights.

The Bensons had spent time in the USA over the last five years filming documentaries for British TV and appearing on low-rated American talkshows. Michelle dreamed of hitting the big time and would stop at nothing to get there.

Michael was feeling a little tired and not in the mood for dining in The Oyster restaurant. Dress code on *Opulence* was formal every night which meant tuxedos for the men and evening dresses for the ladies when dining in the restaurants and traversing public areas.

'Why can't we just eat in our suite tonight, Michelle?' asked an irritated Michael as he fought with his bow tie.

'Because I want to see who else is on board and enjoy the experience, that's why,' spat Michelle, also irritated by her husband's demeanour.

'You know I'm tired. I spend ninety per cent of my time dressing up when attending red carpet events and award ceremonies. I come on holiday to relax, not to dress up within three hours of boarding,' Michael replied sulkily.

'STOP WHINING will you!' shouted Michelle. 'I'm sick to the back teeth of your pathetic whining. We're on this holiday so you better make the most of it and if you dare to let me down in public, so help me, I'll make you wish you'd never met me.'

Michael was fully aware of his wife's temper and her threats and he knew he was on the back foot. Yet again he would acquiesce, put on his fake smile and gaze lovingly at his darling wife of 30 years to keep the public happy, but underneath he was seething and trying to find a way out of this sham of a marriage without her exposing things he'd prefer to remain private. Secrets like his could end their career so he needed to keep her sweet.

Opposite the Benson's suite on the starboard side of the ship, Louisa Hudson was in her suite putting the finishing touches to her make-up. Louisa was an established British actress. At 29 years old, Louisa was single, mainly due to her heavy workload, however she was never short of suitors. Louisa had a string of successes to her name and this opened many doors for her in the USA where she had just returned from a nine-month stint filming a new movie. Louisa was the epitome of an English rose. Long silky blonde hair, huge round piercing blue eyes, full lips and a gorgeous figure. Her looks were only matched by her lovely soft personality. To the public, Louisa had never given herself over to the glitz and glamour of the thespian world and celebrity status although it came with the job. All her pictures were of her at home surrounded by her family and pets. They knew the celeb lifestyle made Louisa feel uncomfortable. Step and repeats were really not her thing but she would smile sweetly and give the photographers what they wanted. The public saw Louisa at her happiest when she was being photographed in her beautiful West Sussex country mansion with her beloved dogs. Louisa had been on TV from a young age. Her career started in adverts then moved to parts in children's TV drama which then culminated in Louisa being the girl next door who made it big.

Nine months in the USA had taken its toll and Louisa had booked this trip to get away from everything. Taking in her gorgeous penthouse, Louisa thought what a lucky girl she was and thanked god above for giving her everything she could dream of. Well there was one thing missing, she thought but was confident enough to know that one day she would succeed in her ultimate goal of finding herself. There was time yet – not much, granted, but time anyway. Turning to take a last look in the mirror before she went for dinner, Louisa allowed herself a little smile as she saw the beauty looking back at her in the mirror. The act must continue.

In the same grade penthouse next door to Louisa, Kurt Robbins was towel-drying his dark hair and drinking his tumbler of Jack Daniels. Kurt was a 24-year-old pop star with an ego far outweighing his talent. Kurt Murray had been excluded from school at an early age and caused real problems for his parents. He was only interested in singing and being famous and to give him his due, he pursued his dream endlessly. The turning point for Kurt was when he was spotted by a music mogul's assistant at an amateur music festival seven years ago. Andy Mason had signed the ambitious young wannabee, given him a stage name of Robbins and moulded him into Justin Bieber's nemesis. Andy knew he was good and he was going to enjoy this break before embarking on a world tour starting in Japan after the cruise. He had grown fond of the trappings of fame, women, drugs and wealth and he abused them with the same arrogance he grew up with.

Kurt fished his tux from the dressing room and proceeded

to get dressed. 'Geez, I am hot to trot,' sang Kurt. As he finished dressing, Kurt recalled his anger at Andy when he was told they were going on a cruise before the world tour. 'A fucking cruise? Who the fuck do you think I am? I'm 24 not fucking 84. What do I want to go on a cruise with all those coffin dodgers for?'

Andy firmly told Kurt that world famous producers and directors cruised aboard *Opulence* and not everyone on this liner would be old. 'This is a very special ship, Kurt, and one which could lead to greater things for both of us. You want to be an actor, right? Well, this could be the break we need to put you on the books. You are at the top of your game in the world of pop but you are nothing as an actor and we need to network. I hear that Manny Dubrow, world famous director, is going on this cruise and I want to meet him. Keep your mouth shut and do as I tell you and you and I will be riding the crest of the proverbial movie wave this time next year.'

Kurt's vision as a world-class actor overshadowed any stuffiness of a cruise and if it meant he had to put up with old biddies for three weeks then he was sure he could manage this. After all, he had a reputation to maintain and it was hard at times to keep his wild boy away from the press. At least he could stay in his penthouse and drink himself into oblivion if he wanted to and the gutter press wouldn't know.

Andy was his keeper. Not only did he sign him, he also looked out for the feckless lad. Kurt had no filter and as his drug habit got worse so did his behaviour. Andy knew Kurt was his retirement fund and as long as he could keep him as the world's number one solo artist for another two years, Andy could then dump the little bastard and let him end up in a drug den, with track marks in his arms. He was expendable and Andy was happy to make the sacrifices he had in order to secure his own future. Andrew Mason had been managing talent from the age of 21. Now at 38, Andy was looking to secure his retirement fund. A good-looking guy, Andy had his share of relationships but he'd never found the one to settle down with. His career and always being on the road saw to that.

Commodore Anthony Andrew Griffiths sighed as he pulled

his braided cuff down. *Here we go again*, he thought to himself. *Another voyage and another round of gushing hospitality to exude to my passengers*. Commodore Griffiths had already made the official welcome announcement over the ship's tanoy system shortly before sailing and at 4pm he had talked the passengers through the mandatory emergency evacuation drill. Now it was on to his next official task of dining. Commodore Griffiths hosted the captain's table and would dine with most of the 400 'B' star passengers throughout the three weeks. 'B' star passengers were wealthy beyond belief in their own right, however they dined together in the Porpoise Restaurant rather than the more exclusive and private 'A' star Oyster restaurant.

I wonder who I'll be dining with tonight? mused Commodore Griffiths. The Commodore had met many a diverse character throughout his 32 years at sea and although he loved people, he did occasionally get a little tired of the constant smiling and handshaking. *Onwards and upwards*, thought Commodore Griffiths as he left his suite to make his way to the Porpoise Restaurant for his first night's dinner.

In the exclusive Oyster restaurant reserved for the 'A' star passengers, all eyes turned to the entrance as Jasper and Sarah and Mia and Cosmo arrived at the same time and were greeted by the maître d'. Jasper looked handsome in his tuxedo, with a flop of loose black curls falling onto his forehead, while Sarah looked stunning in a gold Versace backless flowing gown. Sarah's hair was swept into an elegant chignon and exquisite diamond drop earrings draped from her ears. Mia looked divine in her black sheath and Cosmo, although he kept the trademark frames and black lipstick, looked dishy in his Tom Ford dress suit.

Michelle Benson shot Michael an 'if looks could kill' glare and kicked him under the table then quickly replanted the congenial smile on her face as her waiter Robert waited to take their order. Michael had been captivated by the stunningly beautiful sight before him and the barely audible sharp intake of breath caused him to colour slightly. If there was one thing Michelle hated more than Michael, it was when all attention turned to some trumped-up little tramp of a WAG who used her looks to gain an income yet lived a lavish lifestyle of which she felt they had no right to. Michelle flashed Robert her award-winning smile while exclaiming that she had decided on a hot appetiser of lobster ravioli with escargot in a tomato and basil sauce followed by chateaubriand with a béarnaise sauce. Michael looked at Robert and asked for the wild Alaskan salmon with citrus foam dressing as his appetiser. Even his entrée had been decided for him. Silently, Michael was seething but he had to keep up the public profile of a couple deeply devoted to one another.

The Jackdaws were seated at the far end of the intimate restaurant at a table of four next to the window. When Todd spotted Sarah, he stood up and like the lech he was he let out an enormous wolf whistle. Disapproving looks and tuts emanated throughout the restaurant with the exception of Ed who found this highly amusing.

'Sit down and shut up, Todd. Stop making a show of us will you?' scolded Rocky.

'Look at the rack on that!' said Todd, never taking his eyes off the stunning beauty.

'We can all see the rack clearly enough,' replied Rocky, 'but we are on a six-star luxury liner not in fecking McDonald's so will you behave yourself and stop acting like a prat!' Todd, duly chastised, shut his mouth as ordered but he couldn't keep his eyes off the stunner on the arm of the older geezer who was obviously her sugar daddy.

Ten decks below on Decks 3 and 4 respectively, the Porpoise Restaurant was a hive of activity. Elegantly dressed ladies and their handsome escorts seated at beautifully decorated round tables spanning two floors. The restaurant held 400 passengers while the remaining 200 dined in unthinkable splendour in The Oyster restaurant on Deck 14. Waiters busily served appetisers and entrees while sommeliers uncorked bottles of the finest wines and port. Crystal glasses clinked and silver cutlery gleamed in the low-level lighting. The restaurant was swathed in bowers of white orchids and candles and everyone seemed to be enjoying themselves.

At table 11 on the top floor of the Porpoise Restaurant, Commodore Griffiths was holding court with his adoring passengers hanging on his every word. The loud and bumptious Westons from New Jersey vying for attention with the equally loud and obnoxious Scheindlins from New York City. Both woman in their late 70s, with faces stretched by plastic surgery into cartoon-like expressions, hairpieces badly attached to their own thinning hairlines of dyed hair, each one dripping in jewels with rings on every finger and lips like cherry-coloured trout. Their husbands equally as obnoxious, banging their fists on the table and trying to outdo the other as to who had accumulated the most wealth. Commodore Griffiths smiled politely as he listened to the Americans' banter. They were wealthy people but why did they have to brag about it? Bumptious was the best way to describe people like this. Commodore Griffiths wished that his first officer would come and excuse him from the table under the pretext that he was needed on the bridge.

Two tables away, the Jenkins sat with their three offspring, one young honeymoon couple and a middle-aged couple from Canada. Tommy, the youngest boy, was grizzling. 'I want chips; I don't want this rubbish.' Di Jenkins tried to console Tommy by telling him he could have ice cream for pudding but he needed to behave while everyone had their dinner. Jenson added fuel to the fire by playing soldiers with the cruet set and using the crystal glasses as tanks while Kyle, the middle son, was kicking the table legs and announcing to anyone that would listen that this holiday was crap and he wanted to go on the ship with a flowrider and skating rink.

'Shut it, you three before I slap you!' shouted Sam. 'I wish I'd bloody left you with your nan, if you're going to continue being little shits for the rest of the cruise. Do something with them, Di. Order them chips and shut them up.'

'They don't have chips on the menu, Sam, so do you expect me to go into the sodding kitchen and cook them myself?' hissed Di. 'I can't understand a thing on this menu myself. It's all in some language I don't know with fancy names.'

Sam Jenkins' face was puce, he was in a foul mood and these little bastards were not helping the situation. *Can't that damn woman keep them under control for an hour*, he thought to himself? 'What do you mean no fucking chips? I paid a small fortune for this fucking holiday and if my kids want chips then they'll bloody well have them.' The young waiter attending to the table advised that unfortunately there were no chips on the restaurant menu this evening however there would be fries available in The Lobster Pot.

'Take them to The Lobster Pot and get them chips, Di,' seethed Sam. 'From now on, if they can't have decent food they eat up there. This poncey stuff is not what they're used to.'

'Come on Mum, take us to The Lobster Pot for chips!' shouted Kyle. This was followed by cheering and shouting from Tommy and Jenson. 'Pizza and chips, Pizza and chips,' they sang in unison. Di was oblivious to the looks from other passengers. This food was much too fancy for her little angels so if it was pizza and chips they wanted, then she would make sure that this was what they got. Sam was seething at his meal being interrupted by his kids. Sam was so thick-skinned he didn't realise that his attitude and foul language was as inappropriate as the boys' behaviour and the disdaining looks and whispers were for him as much as his unruly children. The newlyweds glanced at each other as she leant towards her new husband and whispered, 'As soon as we get back, you're going to the doctors to see about a vasectomy.' The middle-aged couple forced smiles onto their faces while Howard declared that, 'Lads that age are full of beans and little tykes.' Mona desperately hoped they would not see this dreadful family again for the remainder of the voyage.

Sam Jenkins got up and forcefully pulled all three boys from their chairs, slapped each one on the face and pulled them out of the restaurant with them screaming and screeching at the top of their voices, and his wife Di bringing up the rear calling Sam all the names under the sun. *Can this get any worse?* thought Bernard, the restaurant's maître d'.

Louisa Hudson, Kurt Robbins and Andy Mason were all seated at a table for three in a little alcove in The Oyster restaurant. Kurt was eyeing Louisa up and down and Andy thought he was making her feel rather uncomfortable in the process. Subtlety was not Kurt's strong point. He'd been bragging about his status for the whole of the meal and most of the surrounding guests also heard all about his adventures. Mia and Cosmo were seated next to Kurt's table and Mia felt a little sorry for Louisa. Here was a beautiful, shy and gentle girl subjected to lewd conversation and innuendo and the girl didn't seem to know how to deal with it. She watched as Louisa shifted uncomfortably in her seat and tried to avoid conversation by staring out into the darkness of the night ocean.

'Louisa, would you like to join me for cocktails?' asked Mia, leaning towards Louisa's table. Louisa gratefully accepted and quickly said goodnight to Andy and Kurt. Cosmo stood and escorted both women from the restaurant. All eyes fell upon Mia and Louisa as they made their way through the ship from The Oyster restaurant on Deck 14 to the Mermaid Lounge at the bow of the ship on Deck 10. All the passengers knew exactly who these women were. Siren of the big screen Mia Manzo and the newest starlet to grace their TVs, Louisa Hudson. The American diva and the beautiful girl-next-door English actress.

Mia and Louisa's presence caused a stir of excitement among the guests. Despite everyone's high profile in terms of being some of the wealthiest people on the planet, they were still starstruck when it came to top-name celebrities. The 400 B-class passengers would not have known who the celebrities on board were unless they met when walking round the ship or in the lounges and bars. Mia and Louisa were approached for autographs and selfies as they made their way through the ship to the Mermaid Lounge and both graciously agreed, despite feeling tired. It took them a good 30 minutes to make their way to the Mermaid Lounge. Appearances had to be maintained.

The two women said goodbye to Cosmo at the lift. Cosmo had other fish to fry and wanted to explore the ship. The Mermaid Lounge was furnished in gold and red with matching seductive lighting. Cocktail bartenders entertained passengers with their amazing synchronised shaking and moving. Expensive inset lights twinkled above the bar and all around the lounge. The engineering on this ship was outstanding.

Once there, the twinkling lights and plush furnishings of the lounge and the beautiful notes of the harpist had an instant calming effect on both ladies. They were shown to a table at the window and offered the cocktail menu. 'Thank you for rescuing me earlier, Mia,' whispered Louisa. 'I was rather fed up with Kurt and his attitude but didn't like to get up and walk away.'

'You are welcome, darling,' drawled Mia. 'I've eaten men like him for breakfast and shat them out an hour later. He's an arrogant prick,' declared Mia, much to Louisa's amusement. 'Have you decided what you want yet, darling? I'll have a Kir Royale,' said Mia.

'I'll have a lemon drop,' said Louisa. She had acquired a taste for the refreshing lemon cocktail in Los Angeles. It was all the rage so she may as well fit in with the luvvies.

Mia thought that, despite being an amazing actress, Louisa appeared to lack confidence and was a shy girl at heart. She only really blossomed when she was immersed in a role and breathing life into a character. Those who met Louisa were quite surprised at her innocence and naivety in general. It made a refreshing change from dealing with the divas and brats manufactured from reality shows. These so-called celebrities had no talent and huge egos. Louisa knew her talent was natural and she was Britain's sweetheart. The roles and invitations flooded in. She was the hottest property on the planet.

The two ladies sat talking avidly for a further two hours and managed to drink another two cocktails each. Louisa learned all about Mia and her five marriages but was totally enthralled by her career in Hollywood and Mia was happy to play mentor to her young protégé.

'Stick with me, darling, and I will ensure you have the best roles in Hollywood,' bragged Mia.

Louisa was in awe of this star of stage and screen and had to pinch herself to check that this was really happening. Oh, Louisa knew she was already a big name and a rising star in her own right, but to be mentored and seen with one of the biggest legends ever to grace the movie industry was an accolade Louisa was more than happy to accept.

'Hollywood is cut-throat, honey, and you need to grow a set and take control. Stick with me, toots, and you won't go far wrong.'

Louisa was grateful to Mia for just being there and for her inspiration. The two women celebrated with another cocktail before making their wobbly way back to Deck 8 to settle down for the night.

CHAPTER 4

The sun blazed down on *Opulence* as she sailed through the serene ocean towards La Coruna in northern Spain. This would be the first port of call on their 24-day itinerary before spending seven days at sea en route to the Caribbean Islands.

Opulence boasted two sun decks. The Terrace for 'A' star passengers situated on Deck 12 and The Sun Seeker for the 'B' star passengers was located on Deck 10. The Sun Seeker deck was packed with designer bathing suits and sun cream. Bodies littered the deep sunloungers and luxury cabanas around the pool and hot tub while the more reserved sat in deliciously comfortable sofas and chairs at the sides of the deck. Waiters in white shorts, and white polo shirts with the ever present Purple Cross logo embroidered onto the fabric, deftly manoeuvred around the obstacles of sunloungers as they delivered delicious ice cold drinks and cocktails on silver trays. Fruit, sparklers, ice, gaily coloured umbrellas and swizzle sticks decorated the dullest cocktail and made it jump out as though it was one which couldn't be passed up. Stewards patrolled the deck offering cool towels to passengers who were overheating in the sweltering 88 degrees heat.

The pool was full of designer bodies cooling down and the crew often joked at how the women would come out of the pool looking better than before they went in. There wasn't a hair out of place and their false eyelashes and lip gloss expertly dodged the water. The Jenkins boys were running amok among the sunloungers, chasing each other with water pistols, squealing and yelling, only stopping to refill their weapons of mass destruction with salt water from the pool. Jenson was shouting to anyone who would listen that he'd seen a ghost walking the deck last night. Sam and Diana ignored their brattish behaviour and the glares from other passengers preferring to partake of ostentatious cocktails and work on their tans. They were laid out on their cabana like two beached whales without a care in the world.

Sounds of lively Caribbean music from the band, Rum Punch, filled the air and lent a party atmosphere to the deck. The Sun Seeker was rocking.

The Terrace, however, was a different matter. Located towards the aft of *Opulence* on Deck 12, 'A' star passengers relaxed in the relative peace and quiet which they craved. Away from the masses, they could be themselves.

The Terrace wasn't too busy. It could comfortably hold around a hundred passengers but was only about a third full on the first morning at sea. The main attraction of The Terrace, apart from the seclusion, was the infinity pool, which fell away from the back of the ship into the ocean. The optical illusion made you feel that you could swim right off the end of the ship. The only thing separating passengers from the ocean was the one-inch-thick reinforced glass which ran the width of the pool.

Following a sumptuous in-suite breakfast, Sarah donned her white two-piece by Melissa Odabash. *If it was good enough for Elle Macpherson, it's good enough for me,* thought Sarah as she checked herself out in her dressing room mirror. Her long tanned legs, small waist and enormous breasts showed the bikini off to its full advantage. Sarah snatched up a matching cover-up, picked up her Gucci sunglasses and bag and shouted to Jasper to meet her on The Terrace when he was ready.

Jasper was sitting on the balcony working at his laptop. Money still had to be made and although he had a fantastic and loyal workforce, he liked to keep his hand in and let them know that he was still in charge. Jasper ignored his wife's ramblings and shook his head. He couldn't understand the fascination of lying in the sun getting hot and sweaty. The only place Jasper was happy to be hot and sweaty was between the sheets with a big busted beauty who was happy to get down and dirty. *I'll go when I'm ready*, thought Jasper selfishly. *For now, I have things to take care of and I don't want to be disturbed.* Jasper reached for the tumbler containing a scotch on the rocks and took a long swig. It was only just gone 10.30am and already Jasper was drinking. The corner of his lips curled upward and if you didn't know any better you would swear Jasper Teasdale just smiled.

Chris Bailey and Denise Patterson were lying on sunloungers on The Terrace sipping Mojitos and recounting last night's events. 'To think we are sitting at the next table to The Jackdaws,' said Denise. 'I can't bloody believe it. Did you see the way Terry winked at me last night when they left the dining room? I wonder why they didn't go for breakfast this morning? Where do you think they went last night?' Denise rattled off all these questions to Chris who was now applying factor 15 sunscreen.

'I can't believe it myself, Denise,' said Chris. 'I think Terry fancies you. I just hope we can get to speak to them without looking like we're stalkers. Perhaps they went to another bar last night? This ship is so big that we could search for an hour and still not find them. Maybe they went back to their suite for a quiet night? Maybe they skipped breakfast or ate in The Lobster Pot?'

Denise giggled helplessly like a schoolgirl and kicked her legs frantically. 'I can't believe it, Chris, I really can't. Little old us from a council estate, now living in luxury and mixing with the rich and famous. This is going to be one holiday we're never going to forget.' Denise didn't realise just how those words would pan out!

The Jackdaws were reccying Zone One while it was quiet and free of passengers. They would be playing their first gig here in a few days' time and wanted to familiarise themselves with the layout and sound systems they would link to. Tirash was a Goan crew member who looked after the technical and sound engineering in Zone One.

Rocky was quite impressed with the facilities and discussed the more technical aspects with Tirash, while Todd and Ed were itching to get out and catch some rays. They were even hoping to go for a wander to search for some 'fit' birds to pass the time with.

'What did you think of the two on the table next to ours, Ed?' asked Todd.

'They seem fit enough,' laughed Ed. 'I wouldn't say no.'

Both boys laughed raucously which brought a glare from Terry. 'Cut it out, you two will you and do something useful or bugger off and find someone else to annoy.' This was all Todd and Ed needed to hear and, suitably chastised by Terry, they ran from Zone One shouting 'Sorry Dad!' and flipping Terry off.

I wish those two would grow up sometimes, thought Terry. *They seem to think that just because we are rock stars we all need to act like morons. Well, I for one won't ever go down that road.* Thinking back to last night Terry glowered as he remembered being woken at 3.49am by his two very drunk bandmates jumping on top of him. Rocky and Terry had gone straight back to their suite after dinner to go through some songs and get an early night while the errant duo had ended up in the Sturgeon Pub on Deck 3, swigging lager and acting like they were seasoned hardcore rock stars. A few glasses had been smashed and their language had been colourful, much to the annoyance of other passengers and the crew. A senior officer had been called to speak to them about their behaviour and it was then that they took up with Jessica and Olivia, a couple of WAG wannabees from Knightsbridge, and spent a few hours in their suite drinking champagne, snorting cocaine and receiving blow jobs. Terry and Rocky had been disgusted by their behaviour and were seriously worried about the band's future.

Michael Benson was swimming in the pool on The Terrace while his bitch of a wife, Michelle, was holding court with Mia Manzo. Mia looked comical as she was covered completely in a stunning floor-length Shahida Parides kaftan and a huge floppy straw hat covering most of her face. Her oversized Versace sunglasses ensured that no sliver of sunlight would blemish her beautiful face and her hair was covered under the hat by a white silk scarf.

Michelle, on the other hand, was happy to soak up the rays. Wearing a low-backed, high-leg red swimsuit with plunging neckline, Michelle's 48 years were swallowed up to those of a 35-year-old. She had a fabulous figure and she knew it. Michelle shook loose her thick red hair which was cut into choppy shoulder length layers and threw back her head as Mia regaled her with naughty titbits from the secret world of Hollywood A listers.

'Oh Mia, we are so alike, aren't we?' gushed Michelle as she revelled in Mia's company. Michelle was a legend in her own right in the UK but could only dream about the trappings a break in Hollywood could bring. Mia could be her meal ticket to greater things.

Michelle drew approving looks from other passengers as she smiled genially and passed the time of day with them. After all, she and Michael had an image to maintain.

Kurt Robbins and Andy Mason were sunbathing poolside next to Louisa, Chris and Denise. Louisa attracted attention like bees round a honey pot. Denise and Chris were delighted to find loungers next to famous celebrities. The lift doors opened and Sarah emerged with Cosmo who had just been to collect Mia's mobile phone which she had left in her suite. Sarah looked stunning. The less she wore, the happier she was and she knew she had an audience when she walked out of the lift. Her beautiful face was plastered in make-up and false eyelashes and her eyes were heavy with Urban Decay Dark Chocolate eye shadow.

Michelle looked over at Michael and was aware of his gaze as he took in the sight before him. Michael was smitten, it was written all over his face but only Michelle registered the look.

Not again, raged Michelle internally as red mist descended, and she marched over to the pool. Stopping at the side and smiling brightly, Michelle shouted out 'Michael, darling, catch me' before launching herself gracefully onto a stunned Michael and caught him a glancing blow to the side of his face. Michael went under and came up spluttering and coughing as he swallowed a huge mouthful of sea water. Michael was frantically scrambling to the surface and took in huge gulps of air. Temporarily winded, Michael could hardly think straight. What the fuck was this stupid bitch doing?

The onlookers had been a little concerned when they saw Michael go under with force. Michelle looked suitably scared and pleaded with the gathered crowd to 'Help him please.' Andy and Cosmo both dived into the pool and grabbed Michael beneath his armpits, ensuring that his winded body did not allow him to submerge again. Between them, they dragged Michael to the side and hoisted him onto the deck.

'Is he OK?' 'Get him a drink!' 'Get a doctor.' Give him space!' were the cries from concerned onlookers. Michelle was now leant over her husband apologising most profusely for catching him when she dived in to join him. 'It was an unfortunate accident!' cried Michelle. 'Poor, poor baby, do you want to see the doctor?' Michael waved everyone aside and, slowly regaining his breath, he told Michelle 'Not to worry, sweetheart, it was my fault, I wasn't looking at what you were doing.' *Too right it was your fault, sweetheart,* thought Michelle. *That'll teach you to have wandering eyes.* Michelle's jealousy knew no bounds and she would stop at nothing to ensure their future as the nation's golden couple and prospective American dream remained secure.

The rest of the morning passed without incident. The ship was a hive of activity. There were dancing classes in The Court Ballroom, Fencing for Beginners in the Mermaid Lounge, spa treatments in The Salon, a talk on the history of La Coruna in The Theatre, and a host of other activities throughout the ship.

Passengers who chose not to eat in the restaurants came and went from the The Lobster Pot, *Opulence's* 24 hour self-service restaurant/cafeteria, greedily stuffing themselves with a variety of breakfast fare still available until noon when the lunch fare would be laid out. A few children ran back and forward from the self-service ice-cream machines and some passengers just enjoyed sitting at the window looking out at the vast expanse of the ocean, people watching and drinking endless cups of tea, coffee, champagne and freshly squeezed fruit juices. Even on a vessel as luxurious as this, money didn't always have the need for formality.

The Oyster restaurant was busy at lunchtime with everyone not wanting to miss the delicious food provided by the best chefs in the world. The best thing about being an 'A' star passenger was that The Oyster boasted an al fresco dining area adjoining the restaurant and this was called The Sea Bed. The Sea Bed could seat approximately eighty passengers and was very very popular, especially on days at sea when the weather was glorious.

Mia, Cosmo, Louisa, the Teasdales, Chris, Denise and the Bensons all made their way to lunch early. They shared Lewis the butler and he had made them aware that if they wanted to secure a seat they must arrive early if they were to experience The Sea Bed for themselves.

They were seated by their white jacketed waiters at glass tables with white wrought iron decorative legs. The standard white, purple and silver parasols shaded the passengers from the searing sun and sweltering heat.

Baccarat crystal pitchers of iced lemon and mint water sat on the tables alongside white and purple floral arrangements, solid silver cruet sets and cutlery. White linen napkins finished the luncheon look. The waiters handed over the white leather-bound menu wallets as the passengers perused today's lunch menu.

The choice was phenomenal. A selection of lunch options included: club sandwich with marinara sauce and beetroot crisps, avocado and red grapefruit cocktail, sweet pepper soup, salads, cold cuts and pasta dishes. Today's excellent weather also added The Sea Bed barbeque to the menu. Four chefs, immaculately dressed in their chefs' whites, grilled a selection of ribs, steaks and vegetables on open barbeques. The delicious smell wafted throughout the deck and beyond and the mutterings of jealousy from The Sun Seeker deck rumbled like a Mexican wave at a football match. The Sun Seeker deck had its own barbeque area and was open for business but the smell of frying steak and onions wafting from another area always makes mouths water. For those who loved steak, the choice was endless. Filet, T-bone, New York strip, sirloin, rib-eye. Every steak imaginable was provided and cooked to perfection to the guests' own preference.

Rocky and Terry arrived for lunch a little later than the others. They were told that unfortunately there were no tables available, however if they would like to come back in an hour the maître d' was sure he would be able to seat them. Chris and Denise were watching the tale of woe unfold before their eyes and, with a calm exterior, Denise stood up and walked towards the maître d's station.

'We have two spare seats at our table which you would be welcome to if you don't mind sharing with us.' stammered Denise. She was now speaking directly to her idol, Rocky Fitzpatrick, rock god supreme, and he was staring directly into her blue eyes with a look of amusement spreading across his face. Rocky had never understood how females could become so tongue-tied when he looked or spoke to them. He was staring at this pretty blue-eyed girl with short choppy blonde hair, her cheeks as red as beetroot and not from the sun. Rocky immediately felt sorry for this lovely girl and, not wanting to appear an upstart, he grinned at Denise and in his light Irish lilt said, 'We'd be delighted to join you, wouldn't we Terry? Lead the way.' The maître d' grinned, knowing just how this small gesture will have made Miss Bailey and Miss Patterson's day.

Denise was beside herself. She couldn't stop blushing and beaming as she made her way back to her table where Chris was sitting open-mouthed, looking as though she was catching flies.

Oh shit, no way, thought Chris as she watched Denise scurry back to their table with two of the world's best-known rock stars in tow. Chris was speechless as Denise sat down grinning like a Cheshire cat. Rocky and Terry sat down opposite the girls and Terry extended his hand and formally introduced himself, his soft Irish lilt melting the heart of Chris.

'Wow, it's great to meet you,' spluttered Chris. 'When I got up this morning, I didn't think I'd be having lunch with The Jackdaws.'

Rocky also introduced himself and within minutes Rocky and Denise were laughing like hyenas, their eyes twinkling and their smiles getting bigger by the minute. Terry smiled warmly at the quieter pretty girl sat opposite him. He was used to this reaction but like Rocky he couldn't understand why. He was only plain old Terry O'Brien from Dublin who happened to play guitar in a rock band. Terry took in the sight before him. Chris was also a blonde but her hair was long compared to Denise's short choppy edgy style. Chris's soft layers framed her face and accentuated her hazel brown eyes. *Wow, she's a pretty girl for sure,* thought Terry as he poured ice cold water for the four of them.

The Sea Bed lived up to its reputation. The barbeque was

amazing and the restaurant food was sublime. Wine flowed, glasses chinked and the sun shone. A pianist played a selection of songs at the baby grand located on deck in The Sea Bed and laughter rang through the air as passengers loosened up and got to know each other. Strong sun and heat exacerbated alcohol intake and before long, even the stuffiest shirts were letting their hair down.

Michelle Benson, having already invited Mia to join them for lunch, sat with her husband, Mia and Cosmo, and gushed loudly for other passengers to hear about how worried she was that she'd killed her husband earlier when she dived in the pool. Michael played his part well and told the world that he forgave her.

'More wine, darling?' asked Michael.

'Oh go on then, another glass won't hurt,' a squiffy Michelle giggled.

Mia Manzo watched this playful couple so much in love and yearned for this type of relationship for herself. *Why can't I be this happy?* mused Mia, her thoughts abruptly cut off as Kurt appeared at her side and interrupted her.

'Hey, you're the Bensons, aren't you?' exclaimed Kurt. *No shit Sherlock*, thought an irritated Michelle. *Doesn't this guy have any manners?* Michael extended his hand to Kurt and said, 'Pleasure to meet you, Kurt, this is my beloved wife, Michelle.'

Michelle plastered on her best smile and extended her hand to Kurt. 'It's so lovely to meet you, Kurt,' enthused Michelle. 'We really must get you on *Coffee Morning* when you have time. The viewers will love it.'

'Cool,' replied Kurt who, with the same nonchalance as his entrance, departed just as quickly.

Mia, Michelle, Michael and Cosmo all looked at each other in amusement. 'Is he on drugs, do you think? asked Michelle.

'I do hope so,' chuckled Cosmo. 'I didn't bring enough with me.' The group laughed at Cosmo's comment and Mia then proceeded to tell them how she rescued the lovely Louisa Hudson from Kurt at dinner last night.

'I feel sorry for the poor girl travelling alone and she doesn't appear to know many people so I feel I need to keep a bit of a special eye on her. I can also make sure I give her all the tips she needs to survive Hollywood!' Michelle was hanging on Mia's every word. Desperate for a break in Hollywood, Michelle knew she had to make Mia her best friend.

'Anyone fancy an old fashioned?' asked Cosmo.

'I'm not sure mixing wine with cocktails in this heat is a good idea,' said Michael.

'Oh don't be such a stuffed shirt, Michael darling. We're on holiday.' Michael smiled at Michelle, looked at Cosmo and said 'Old fashioneds all-round, Cosmo, with Tito's chasers please.' The table erupted in laughter as Cosmo beckoned the waiter.

The Teasdales sat together by the replica Trevi Fountain on The Sea Bed. Jasper had switched off from Sarah's incessant chatter about shopping in the mall after lunch. 'I think I saw a Hermes Birkin on the shelf and I just got to have one Jas. Everyone who is anyone has one. Can you imagine what my mates will think when they see me with a Birkin?'

'What are you eating, Sarah?' snapped Jasper.

'I'll have a Caesar salad I think, babe.' Jasper ordered a Caesar salad and a New York strip, medium rare with a pepper sauce, dauphinoise potatoes and asparagus. Jasper's mind was elsewhere. In the six years he'd been married to Sarah, he'd become quite the expert at switching off. Jasper was taking in the other passengers with interest. Especially the good looking ones with plump tits and great legs. He was vaguely aware of Sarah's chattering in the background as he watched Michelle Benson and licked his lips as he did so. *Now there's another beauty who could keep me amused for a few hours,* thought Jasper.

An hour later, three bottles of wine, two further cocktails of choice and three Tito's shots each, Cosmo reminded a tipsy Mia that she had a hair appointment at 3pm and a Skype meeting with Burt Hayden, Hollywood producer extraordinaire, at 4.15. Burt was casting for a new drama series and wanted to speak to Mia about a possible part. 'You need to look your best for Burt, Mia, so I took the liberty of booking you in for a blow with Clancy.' Everyone laughed at Cosmo's intended innuendo. Gesticulating wildly to her dining companions and admiring public, she announced, 'Isn't he a darling? I don't know what I'd do without him. Everyone should have a Cosmo.'

Michael announced that he too had an appointment after lunch. He had signed up to a tour of the galley with the executive chef and asked Michelle what she intended to do with herself while he was tied up. 'Oh don't worry about me, darling. I'll go for a wander round the ship I expect,' replied Michelle. 'There's still so much of her that I haven't seen yet.'

The rest of the day passed by in a relaxed alcohol-fuelled haze. The ship's shopping mall was bustling with passengers eager to spend obscene sums of money on the best jewellery and designer wear money could buy.

Jasper and Sarah had gone to the mall. Sarah had remembered that there was a special event in the spa that afternoon on a new wonder filler. She was hooked on filler as it was, so it came as no surprise to Jasper when Sarah decided to go to the spa. 'I can always shop later, can't I babe?' trilled Sarah as she wiggled her way towards the spa. She left Jasper looking at a Greubel Forsey watch. A snip at a mere £750,000.

'Would sir care to try it on?' asked the young assistant. '

'Yes, I would,' replied Jasper. At the other counters, wives were whispering to their spouses, their eyes growing wide as salacious grins appeared on their faces while they thought of what 'treats' they would receive if they bought their spouse the desired piece of expensive jewellery.

Michelle Benson was looking at a gold, tanzanite and diamond pendant at the next display case. The price tag stated this AAAA grade tanzanite pendant would set her back a cool £350,000. Michelle was wealthy but not wealthy enough to justify a one-off piece of jewellery that expensive. *Damn,* thought Michelle as she frantically searched for an excuse to move away from this particular piece without embarrassing herself.

'Suits you,' Michelle said softly flashing her best TV smile. Jasper turned to acknowledge the unfamiliar female voice and smiled at the attractive red head who had just complimented him on his exquisite choice. The same red head who'd caught his attention at lunch. 'Thank you,' replied Jasper. 'I'm just browsing to be honest. Trying to kill some time while the wife has her spa appointment.' Michelle laughed and informed Jasper that her husband was also otherwise engaged and she too was acquainting herself with this majestic cruise liner.

Jasper was sure he recognised the woman but was at a loss as to where he knew her from so he engaged her in general chit-chat while scrutinising her body and trying to remember where he'd seen her. Jasper, although he watched TV, tended only to watch the news. His days were busy and he didn't have time for ordinary TV, so it wasn't surprising that he really didn't know who Michelle and Michael were.

He wasn't really listening as Michelle explained Michael's penchant for cooking and how he had jumped at the opportunity of touring the ship's galleys and having a private masterclass with Executive Chef Heinz Eriksson. Nor did he hear the bit about Michelle's TV career. Jasper's thoughts were elsewhere, like what would she look like with her legs wrapped round his head?

Jasper liked what he saw. A fortysomething red head with a full curvy bust, flat stomach and long shapely legs. Her green eyes spoke volumes and her lusciously glossed lips were crying out to be kissed. Jasper, never one to miss an opportunity, invited Michelle to join him for a drink while they waited for their respective spouses. Michelle, already tipsy from lunch, graciously accepted and Jasper told the assistant to 'Wrap the watch and have it delivered to my suite' as he placed his hand on the small of her back and guided her out of the Mother of Pearl jewellery shop towards the champagne bar.

Louisa skipped lunch in favour of a light salad and fruit platter from room service eaten on her balcony. *I am Britain's sweetheart and I have a front to keep up,* thought Louisa as she sat on her balcony, a lonely figure. *I just wish I could be me,* she thought. *I'm sick of portraying this sickly sweet, holier than thou person that I'm really not. Yes, I love my country home, yes I love my own company but I want to have fun now and then. I'm so glad I agreed to come on this voyage. I can't be myself publicly but I can have a bit of freedom for three weeks.* Louisa broke out in a huge grin as she checked her watch before hurrying into her shower to prepare herself for her appointment in an hour.

An hour later she was again enjoying her own company, taking a sauna in the ship's salon. She was sweating as the door opened and Kurt Robbins walked in. Louisa did not flinch at this intrusion and looked up at Kurt with her huge blue eyes, a seductive smile forming on her porcelain face. Neither spoke as Louisa shifted position slightly on the wooden bench, just enough to ensure the towel wrapped loosely around her chest slipped down an inch revealing part of her nipple.

Kurt was well aware of his good looks and chiselled jawline. His normally unruly hair was stuck to his head where he had built up a sweat working out in the well-equipped gym. His towel stuck to his buttocks and thighs exposing the bulge of his cock through the Egyptian cotton.

Louisa and Kurt merely looked at each other as he walked towards her. Dropping his towel, he grabbed her hair and kissed her hard, probing her mouth with his tongue. Louisa reached down and grabbed his cock. She started working it with expert strokes while Kurt snatched her towel away to reveal her breasts and hairless pussy. He fondled both breasts, nuzzling and biting at her nipples as she moaned softly. Within minutes, Kurt was sat on the bench and Louisa was kneeling before him sucking his massive cock with the expertise of a porn actress. Her moist mouth and warm tongue gently rimmed the tip before she ran her tongue from his balls to the head. Kurt moaned, his eyes closed as he twisted her hair behind her head and pushed her head down onto his stiff rod. Louisa stopped abruptly and stood over Kurt, her legs wide apart at either side of his head. Kurt gripped Louisa's buttocks and pulled her to him, immersing his tongue in her pink folds of moist flesh, lapping and sucking. Kurt could hear Louisa mewing softly. The harder Kurt sucked, the wetter she became. Kurt stopped suddenly and pulled her to the floor where he proceeded to fuck her with an intensity borne out only of animal instinct. Louisa writhed beneath him and bucked her hips as her orgasm ripped through her. This was all Kurt needed to see as he came and let loose his seed deep within her soul. Kurt rolled away from Louisa, lying on his back looking at the ceiling. His mouth and chin covered in Louisa's juices. Slowly his breathing returned to normal as he turned to face a spent Louisa then laughing he said, 'It's been too fucking long babe, too fucking long.'

Denise and Chris were getting ready for dinner, recalling every word spoken at lunch earlier and convincing each other that both guys fancied the pants off each of them. 'This just gets better and better,' said Denise. 'No one back home will believe us when we tell them we had lunch with the two hottest rock stars.' Chris rolled her eyes at her friend's exuberance. 'Only you would offer up two spare seats to the men of our dreams but I'm glad you did.'

Rocky and Terry were getting ready for dinner also and were having a similar conversation with each other. 'I'm really pleased we had lunch with Chris and Denise today, Rocky. They are really nice girls. Down to earth and not fazed by our celebrity status. I wouldn't mind spending more time with Chris, to be honest.'

Rocky grinned and agreed with his friend. 'Let's keep this between us for the time being, Terry, as I'm not sure what's going on with Todd and Ed at the moment and you know what Todd is like, I don't want him blowing it for us.'

Todd and Ed were having their own conversation in the bathroom. 'Look Ed, those two girls at the next table are fit and I'm going to crack on with the feisty one. Are you with me? Will you be my wing man and take her mate off her hands?'

'Course I will,' grinned Ed as he looked up, his top lip covered in white powder and his eyes glazing over.

Michael Benson watched his wife from the bedroom as she flitted around the living area of the suite searching for her camera. She was humming to herself and her mood since returning from the mall had been relaxed. She wasn't bitching at him like she usually did. Michael thought it a little strange and wondered if she was sickening for something but he couldn't really care less. As long as she left him alone, that would suit him nicely. Michael

Benson thought back to earlier in the day at the pool when he was admiring the beauty before him and felt a welcome stirring in his groin. *Soon, baby, soon,* he thought as he smiled to himself.

Michelle Benson was looking for her camera. She was sure she'd put it down on the glass table when she'd returned from her shopping trip but she couldn't find it anywhere. *I think I'm a little distracted,* mused Michelle. *A day fuelled with alcohol, heat and champagne with Jasper Teasdale is the best distraction anyone could wish for,* thought Michelle as she recalled her liaison with Jasper. They had made their way to the champagne bar where Jasper plied Michelle with a couple of glasses of the finest bubbles. He sat close to her and they chatted for ages. Michelle told Jasper all about her dreams while flirting outrageously with him. Jasper could see just what was on offer but wanted to play with Michelle as a cat plays and torments a poor mouse. When it was time to leave, Jasper drew Michelle into an embrace and nuzzled her ear as he told her how he had enjoyed her company. He then looked at Michelle straight in her eyes and brushed her lips gently but firmly. Michelle had fireworks going off in her head as she took this as a sign that Jasper truly fancied her and that something special could come of it. The champagne and touch of Jasper brought light and calmness to her so much so that she forgot how much she despised her husband.

Kurt was luxuriating in his whirlpool bath in his suite. A line of cocaine lined up on the marble top beside the sink. He was taking selfies on his mobile phone and posting them to Instagram and Twitter. His fans needed their daily dose of their idol and what better to stay in the headlines than to post a semi-nude picture of him in the bath. His blond fringe flopped forward as he scowled moodily into the camera. *Got to keep them on their toes,* thought Kurt as he reminisced about Louisa and their session in the spa's sauna an hour earlier. He felt an erection coming on as he relived every inch of her perfect body. *God that girl knows how to give head,* laughed Kurt as he masturbated himself back to reality.

Sarah Teasdale was taking a shower in their double marble shower cubicle and thinking about how Jasper Teasdale's days were numbered. Fed up with his aggressive attitude and bad moods,

Sarah knew only too well that he only wanted her to make himself feel better. *Well,* thought Sarah, *two can play at that game. I know I haven't got an education but I've been about and I always get what I want. You're no fun anymore Jasper. I want to be someone. I want to be famous. I want to be rich and I don't need you to have it. I have other options and I'm going to use them.*

CHAPTER 5

The 'A' star passengers from Deck 8's most sumptuous suites and penthouses gathered again in The Oyster for dinner. Beluga caviar was on the menu tonight and was being served chilled on ice in exquisite specially commissioned Michael Aram ocean coral caviar dishes.

Caviar was an acquired taste however all the 'A' star guests appeared to have acquired the taste as in the kitchen the waiters handed in the orders at the pass and sent the executive chef into culinary bliss to see that his speciality for this evening was appreciated.

The passengers were keeping the sommeliers busy tonight as they ordered bottles of Cristal, Dom Perignon and vodka shots to accompany the caviar.

The Jackdaws were unusually quiet. Ed and Todd were stoned to the point of comatose, leaving Rocky and Terry mortified to be in their company. Ed and Todd sat quietly eating whatever was placed in front of them, looking as though they required their mums to help them dress. Todd's bow tie sat at a jaunty angle while the sleeves of his dress shirt hung below his cuffs and dragged in his food. Ed hadn't fared much better. His cummerbund was back to front and he hadn't tucked his shirt in properly. Ed's mass of ginger curls had gone wild as he was too wasted to gel them. The maître d' had spoken to them as they entered the dining room and told Rocky in no uncertain terms that they would not be permitted to dine in The Oyster in that state again. Rocky apologised profusely and ushered the gruesome twosome to their seats. Rocky and Terry were both on edge as they kept a close eye on Todd and Ed. They were like coiled springs as they didn't know what the boys would do next or how soon they would snap out of their drug-induced state.

Rocky and Terry said hello to Denise and Chris and they tried to make polite conversation with them but they were too worried about Ed and Todd, so they decided to excuse themselves and take the lads back to the suite. Denise and Chris were devastated and thought that it had all been too good to be true as they watched their lunch companions depart. They were deflated. Having half expected to spend the evening with them in one of *Opulence's* many venues, they were being dumped with a pathetic excuse of having to babysit Ed and Todd. Denise was furious. Her anger rising to the surface was plain for Chris to see and when she was in one of these moods she wouldn't listen.

The girls ordered another bottle of wine and decided the only way to block out the embarrassment was to get blitzed.

Mia and Cosmo were making plans to spend the evening in the theatre watching the ship's company perform their version of *West Side Story*. Mia wasn't holding out much hope but they all had to start somewhere. Mia had played Maria on Broadway and in London's West End a multitude of times in her early days and she was interested to see what the ship's company could do. Cosmo had this afternoon returned his hair to his natural sandy blond and ditched his designer lensless spectacle frames. His trademark black lips now natural transformed Cosmo into an exceptionally attractive man. You'd have been hard pushed to believe that this was actually Cosmo. He had also dropped his campness in favour of a 007 look.

'Mia darling, you know how I go in phases,' Cosmo gushed, his slightly effeminate voice clashing with this handsome figure sat opposite Mia. 'I've got my eye on the male lead dancer. Marac is his name and he's hot to trot with me all the way to paradise and if things don't work out with him then I'm sure David the lovely purser will help me with a little irritation which has been bothering me since we sailed.' Mia laughed as Cosmo slipped back into his camp pout and raised eyebrows while describing his holiday fling. 'I intend to make my move after the show, darling, and I'm expecting to be twerking the night away on the high seas.'

Cosmo laughed as the sommelier approached to refill their glasses.

I am so lucky, thought Mia as Cosmo winked at her and downed his pinot grigio in one, urging her to hurry up as the show was due to start in 20 minutes.

Michelle and Michael enjoyed a reasonably pleasant dinner. There were no mutterings under Michelle's breath nor icy stares cast in his direction. 'I'm so looking forward to exploring La Coruna tomorrow,' Michelle enthused. 'I hear it's quite architecturally impressive which will suit you and there's always new shops to explore for me.' Michelle laughed at her comment while Michael enquired what she would like to do for the remainder of this evening. 'It's been a hot day, Michael, and I have the beginnings of one of my heads so I think I'll just go for a walk on deck then go back to the suite and have an early night.'

'Would you like me to come with you, darling?' Michael asked in his sweetest TV voice.

'I wouldn't dream of it, sweetheart. You go ahead and go to the casino if you wish. I know you love a game of blackjack now and then. I'll be fine, really.' The other diners looked on in total admiration for how the caring loving husband was looking after his wife. How they all secretly envied the Bensons. What a lovely couple they made,

The Bensons rose to leave the restaurant at the same time as Jasper and Sarah at the next table. 'Coming to the Calypso Club tonight, guys?' asked Sarah expectantly.

'Not me, I'm off to the casino but I may pop in later if you're still going to be around?' Michael announced. 'And dear Michelle is having an early night as she has one of her dreadful migraines coming on.'

'Oh you poor thing,' said Sarah. 'Do you have any painkillers? Do you want some? I always carry a stock with me, don't I Jasper?'

'Sarah's a regular walking pharmacy,' said Jasper, smiling at the loved-up TV couple. 'Seriously, if there's anything we can do, please don't hesitate to ask.'

'That's very kind of you, thank you,' gushed Michelle, 'but I'll be fine, really. You go and enjoy yourselves.'

'I'm going to take a stroll on deck to blow away the alcohol from earlier before getting hot and sweaty to Rum Punch,' giggled Sarah. Jasper just raised his eyebrows and grinned a salacious smile as he stared at Michelle.

The ship came alive again. The Jenkins boys running riot along the gallery deck followed by their bellowing dad, dodging well-heeled passengers en route to the theatre, casino, nightclub, shopping mall, planetarium and photographers studio. Tommy was stopping anyone who would listen to him to tell them that he saw the captain throwing someone overboard earlier in the day. Di Benson laughed and explained that her boys had vivid imaginations as she ushered them along the deck.

The younger passengers who had escaped the clutches of their parents were excitedly taking photos at every opportunity throughout the ship and deciding which cocktail they were going to have. Waiters going about their business, ships officers making their way from the dining room to their own quarters or their evening shifts.

A variety of music could be heard as you moved throughout the ship from fore to aft and deck to deck. The lively big band sound from the resident orchestra who were currently playing in the ballroom for the dancing, a classical pianist in the Dolphin Club, a harpist in the grand foyer entertaining transient passengers and those queuing to see the purser. A three-piece band in the pub and a Beach Boys tribute act in the Meridian Lounge, not forgetting the ever present Rum Punch in the Calypso Bar.

Opulence sailed onwards towards northern Spain, her very essence illuminating the night sky as she transported her passengers and their secrets on a voyage of discovery.

Chris and Denise made their way sulkily to Zone One. 'I suppose we may as well see what other talent there is on this ship since those two don't want to know us. I knew it was too good to be true,' said Denise. Dressed to the nines with killer heels, the girls' sequinned cocktail dresses clung to their lovely figures and hugged their curves in all the right places. They looked good and were looking forward to drowning their sorrows for what might have been.

Kurt returned from dinner to his suite with his manager Andy. Kurt's drug habit was spiralling out of control and Andy knew the signs well. He'd managed hundreds of popstars, actors and reality TV stars in his time and had seen it all before. The sudden rise to stardom by a cocky young kid with a big ego. Kurt had been in the business for five years and through luck more than his likeability he'd become the hottest new kid on the block, outselling the likes of Justin Bieber and Ed Sheeran.

Kurt was one-hundred per cent manufactured. His look, style and music were provided for him. He tried to dabble with writing his own songs but to be honest he could hardly string a sentence together let alone write a number one hit. His only saving grace was his voice. His vocal range was magnificent and he could take any tune and make it his own.

He'd grown from a cocky and arrogant fresh-faced youth into a cocky and arrogant man. Kurt had a great physique from his hours working out in the gym. He shaved when he felt like it and sported a short hairstyle with long floppy fringe. Kurt's blue eyes and sexy smile made him a fanny magnet and he was in his element.

Sex, drugs and cash make my world go round, grinned Kurt as he settled onto his bed to watch DVDs on the huge television. Kurt had met Todd and Ed earlier in the day and they found they had a few things in common, one of those being the white stuff, so Kurt shared his special powder with them and it had a similar effect on all three of them. Kurt was more used to the hard stuff and it didn't affect him quite as badly as it did the other boys but it was still enough to make Andy put him to bed with a stern warning that he needed to pull himself together if he didn't want his drug habit exposed. He was taking too many risks and would be found out if he wasn't careful. His career would be fucked, game over and he'd disappear into oblivion like many of him before.

'Stay here, Kurt, and don't leave this suite again, do you hear me?' Kurt nodded and sighed.

'You're becoming a fucking bore, Andy.'

Andy spun round and grabbed Kurt by the neck. 'Don't you

ever forget that I made you and I can break you, you trumped up little fucker. Do what you have to but do it in your own time, in the privacy of your own home. Got it?' spat Andy.

'OK, OK, I got it,' laughed Kurt, holding his hands up in mock surrender.

Andy turned and strode out of his suite, furious with the latest escapade with drugs on this ship of all places. *He's going to get his come uppance if he doesn't buck his ideas up,* thought Andy as he left the errant pop star to enjoy his evening.

Kurt picked up the phone and dialled the number. 'I'm all yours, babe, come on over,' said a confident Kurt. A few minutes later, Louisa Hudson slipped into Kurt Robbins suite to pick up where they left off in the spa earlier that day.

Purser David was sitting behind the desk in the foyer, desperately waiting for the clock to strike midnight. David had been on duty since 4pm and was looking forward to winding down with a few Peronis and a blow job. David smiled to himself as he thought about Cosmo. God he was handsome and he had the connections David so desperately craved. Cosmo had come to the desk earlier to report a loose towel holder in Mia's bathroom and David was instantly attracted to the gorgeous man before him. David's attention was not lost on Cosmo and despite his fascination for Marac, Cosmo was not averse to entertaining two at a time. David was tall and attractive and Cosmo allowed himself to flirt with David. '

I love your uniform, David. Very *Officer and a Gentleman* if you ask me. Have you whisked many paramours off their feet and taken them away to seduce them?'

David blushed at Cosmo's question but he was secretly delighted to have been noticed. 'I only ever whisk special people away, sir,' whispered David.

'Will you wear your hat?' asked Cosmo smiling.

'I will wear whatever sir requires, replied David. 'I finish at midnight tonight. I may take a stroll on the promenade deck then. It's been a long day. I like to sit on a lounger near the salon and relax watching the stars in the night sky.' The message was not lost on Cosmo who merely smiled and thanked David for taking his complaint about the loose towel rail.

'I may bump into you, David. Best make sure you have your hat with you.' With that, Cosmo winked, turned and walked away, leaving David with a semi-erection and thoughts of what he was going to do to Cosmo later.

It was 2.30am and the ship was slowly becoming silent as bleary eyed passengers made their weary way to their suites. Denise and Chris could hardly stand up they were so drunk. They'd decided to go through the top shelf with shots, chasing each drink. They'd danced themselves senseless, attracting lots of male suitors but not particularly taking interest in any. There were some very nice, wealthy young men on board but the girls were secretly still holding out hope for Rocky and Terry so the Harvard graduates were dismissed. The girls also spent a great deal of the evening bitching about the Hooray Henriettas who'd turned up in Zone One. Jessica and Olivia, also on the hunt for Todd and Ed, had decided they would go looking for them, and their hair flicking ways soon caught the attention of Denise.

'Look at the state of those two, Chris. God, could their dresses get any shorter? They're no more than a couple of good-time girls. Why do they keep looking at us?'

'Probably blinded by our beauty, Denise,' said Chris, at which both girls collapsed in hysterical laughter, much to the annoyance of Jess and Olivia.

They were now carrying their five-inch Jimmy Choos as they staggered back to their suite looking a little worse for wear. 'I really don't feel very well, Chris,' moaned Denise as Chris swiped her card into their door lock. Chris Bailey grinned at her friend and told her again that she loved her as Denise covered her mouth and ran into their bathroom to empty the contents of her stomach. Chris staggered giggling to the gorgeous white sofa and fell forward face first onto it. Denise collapsed in the bathroom, her flushed face resting against the cool marble floor and this is how the two girls would spend their second night of the cruise.

The decks were deserted with the exception of crew members

moving silently from one public area to another to clean up after the revellers. The ship was bathed in lights from the public areas, fairy lights on the decks and mood lights around the pools and the stars shone in the cloudless sky. *Opulence* made her way silently and smoothly towards northern Spain.

In the shadows of the overhang on Deck 6 aft, they looked like any other couple making out under the stars. Michael Benson was lost in a passionate embrace as he kissed with a ferocity and hunger he had not known for years. 'I love you and I want to be with you forever,' whispered Michael in a breathy voice. 'I'm going to leave Michelle and we can be together.' He drew a sharp intake of breath as he felt his cock being released from the constraints of his trousers and a warm wet tongue gently and expertly work his shaft.

'You don't have any idea how long I've waited for you either, babe.' Their eyes locked and tears dripped from Michael's eyes as he gave himself up to ecstasy, witnessed only by the stars in the blackness of the night sky.

Day three of the 24-day voyage broke with a gorgeous sunrise. *Opulence* docked at 6am as excited passengers woke early to make sure they had breakfast before the early morning tours left. The temperature was already 16 degrees at this early hour and The Lobster Pot was bustling. Many passengers chose the more relaxed breakfast option and were filling up on everything you could think of from the self-service stations offering eggs cooked every way you could imagine, sausages, steaks, bacon, beans, mushrooms, tomatoes, hash browns, fried potatoes, fish, cold meats, fresh fruit, continental cheeses, 40 different types of bread and rolls, hot and cold cereals and fresh fruit juices.

Di Jenkins was stuffing napkins full of breads, meats, cheese and fruit as Jenson and his siblings were filling empty plastic bottles with water and fruit juices. Sam Jenkins shook his head as he watched their antics. *Honest to god*, he thought. *I have plenty of money and the stupid cow still makes packed lunches. Well she can stuff her packed lunch, I'm eating out today. I'm sure there's a McDonald's in Spain.*

Crew were working like ants clearing tables and replenishing supplies of cutlery and crockery. The hot plates and cold fare was replenished continuously and they were very skilled at avoiding dawdling passengers and kept the public areas pristine. Even the most dedicated party animal couldn't tell when or how the housework and maintenance of the ship took place as the crew seemingly went about their duties under an invisible cloak.

The Pursers Office was inundated with passengers booking last minute shore excursions, changing currency and reporting lost passports and suite door key cards. David and Chloe flashed their Hollywood smiles at each passenger, no matter what the problem was. Chloe didn't mind working today. She'd visited La Coruna many times before and would much rather her eight hours off was taken during one of the beautiful Caribbean island destinations. *At least things will quieten down after 10am,* thought Chloe. *Most passengers will have gone ashore by then and I can sit down and have a coffee. My feet are killing me already.* David was surprisingly convivial this morning. He was beaming from ear to ear and overly cheerful. 'What's the matter with you today? Did you get your leg over last night or something?' said Chloe. David just laughed and said, 'Wouldn't you like to know!'

'Fuck me, who hit me?' groaned Ed as he tried to pull himself to a sitting position and, failing miserably, allowed himself to fall back onto the soft goose down duvet. Ed looked around carefully; his head felt as if it was about to explode. Even blinking sent a wave of pain crashing through his head and he felt nauseous.

He saw Todd sound asleep on the plush sofa a few feet away. What was he doing in my room? Todd was snoring gently, his mouth open and little trails of spittle glistening at the corners of his mouth.

Ed gingerly sat up and got out of bed and made his way through to the lounge. Rocky and Terry were eating breakfast in the dining room and waved at Ed as he made his way sheepishly towards them. 'Take a pew, Ed. Fancy some porridge?' Ed baulked at the very idea and slumped forward in his chair, holding his head in his hands.

'Guys, what the fuck happened last night? I feel like I've been hit with a sledgehammer.'

'Blame that on the mix of alcohol and cocaine, Ed,' shot Rocky in a disapproving tone. 'You and Todd really need to get a grip. We're playing our gig in Zone One in a few nights and we have rehearsals at 11am. Go and waken Todd and make sure you are both there on time. The crew have other things to do and we won't wait for you. Oh, and after rehearsals we're having a meeting so don't get any ideas about disappearing off. We'll meet back here directly after we clear up. We have things we need to talk about. We can have lunch in the suite, call it a working lunch.'

With that, Rocky stood up and drained his coffee. He looked at Terry who was chewing on a croissant and shook his head in resignation. *Something needs to change*, thought Rocky as he walked away from Ed in disgust. Ed looked at Terry and felt sick as he watched Terry bite into his golden croissant ladened with an inch of butter.

'You asked for that, Ed. Can't say you didn't, can you?

Ed just muttered and stood up and made his way back to his room which Todd had apparently decided to share last night. *Those two need to get a life*, thought Ed as he climbed back into bed and pulled his soft duvet back over his head.

Sarah Teasdale was admiring herself in the mirror. Buoyed by last night's little escapade on deck, she congratulated herself on how her plan was coming together. 'Not long now until I'm free of this bastard. Let's see how thick he thinks I am when I take him for half of his fortune.' Sarah smiled a smile that would have graced any toothpaste advert as she adjusted her ever-so-short hemline to cover her lace thong. *I'll never end up wanting for anything*, thought Sarah as she mentally mapped out her day's shopping with her arsehole of her soon-to-be ex-husband.

Cosmo was knocking on Louisa's door on Mia's orders. Louisa opened the door, looking as gorgeous as ever. She was wearing a lemon gypsy-style dress, embellished toe post sandals and a pair of Dior sunglasses perched on top of her blonde ponytail.

'Morning darling. Mia wants to know if you'd like to join us for lunch in the town? Mia just adores seafood and is so looking forward to indulging in goose barnacles and velvet crab, a speciality of this town. There's a darling rustic little restaurant on the outskirts of the city that she's visited many times before and she'd love it if you were her guest.'

'Why that's really thoughtful, thank you. Tell Mia I'd be delighted. I love seafood too.'

'We'll call for you in 15 minutes, darling. Don't keep us waiting.' With that, Cosmo turned on his size 11s and headed down the corridor to Mia's suite. *Well, that's taken care of what I was going to do today, I suppose, thought* Louisa as she applied some sunscreen to her nose.

Andy was breakfasting with Kurt in The Lobster Pot. Andy thought it would be good PR to mix with the 'B' star passengers and Kurt, always happy to be centre of attention, was revelling in the adoration shown by his fellow passengers. Andy had forgotten that as they were in port, most of the passengers would be going ashore but there were still a few who decided not to venture off the ship and were looking forward to having first pick of location on The Sun Seeker deck and an empty pool.

Life on board carried on as normal on port days with the exception of the mall. Duty and tax regulations did not permit the shops to stay open when in port, however when they'd cleared the Spanish water and headed back out into the Atlantic Ocean the shops would once again open an hour or so after sailing.

'Do you want to go ashore later, Kurt? We could go look at the architecture in the old city.'

Kurt laughed at Andy and insisted he'd rather poke his eyes out with hot needles. 'I'd rather just stay here and chill mate.' Andy was exasperated but secretly he was pleased that he wouldn't have to spend another day babysitting his ungrateful charge.

'I'll see you later then. I'm off for a bit of culture.' Andy walked off, just as two teenage girls excitedly spotted Kurt and screamed out for a selfie.

Michelle and Michael Benson were finishing up their breakfast in The Oyster. Eggs benedict was the perfect migraine cure.

Michelle was determined to keep up appearances no matter what. Michael was his usual congenial self and was looking forward to visiting the church of Las Capuchinas which displayed Baroque style from the 18th century. Prior to Michael's big break into presenting, he was studying architecture and archaeology before dropping out when he was chosen to present *Twiddly Diddlies.*

Michael's love of architecture had never left him and he was still interested in beautiful buildings with decorative facades. He hoped to also have time to see the churches of San Jorge and San Nicolas. Raised a Catholic but now lapsed, Michael enjoyed visiting churches and was comfortable in their presence. Michelle, on the other hand, could not have cared a fig for wandering around stuffy churches looking at the brickwork. She was more a beach babe but today was more than content to appease her husband for a short while and accompany him on his mission in the old city until she got bored, then she could make her way to town and to the shops. She may be physically seen on Michael's arm, but her mind was very much on Jasper Teasdale. Ever since their meeting yesterday, Michelle was captivated by this stunningly attractive if a little arrogant man. She felt a pang of jealousy when Jasper mentioned Sarah by name but was determined to enjoy whatever 'friendship' developed over the next couple of weeks. Jasper had plied her with champagne yesterday.

Michelle was drunk from lunch, and champagne on top of this loosened her up and made her brazen. She knew Jasper was attracted to her and she was happy to get to know this gorgeous guy better, as long as it didn't complicate things between her and Michael; after all, they had their career to think of. The British public would never forgive her if she and Michael split up. Their career would be over and this was something Michelle was not going to let happen at any cost. *I'll just have to be very careful,* giggled Michelle to herself as Justin sat close to her, his hand on her thigh. Michelle knew Justin wanted her. Her delusion made her think Justin wanted more than just a fuck! Justin was only interested in a new piece of ass for the length of the voyage. As soon as he was home, Michelle Benson would be just a name, a flash in the pan, dead to him. Justin piled on the charm and a drunk Michelle lapped it up. As he kissed her goodbye, she was aware of the look in his eyes and read into it exactly what she wanted to.

Michelle snapped back to the present as Michael was rising to leave the restaurant. This was a man on a mission. He had a date with history and she was conspiring about how to plan her next meeting with Jasper.

Denise and Chris walked slowly from the port into the old town. Both felt a little worse for wear after drowning their sorrows and collapsing in drunken stupors in their suite. They could both have easily stayed on board but thought a walk on dry land would do them good. There was nothing to beat a good dose of sea air to blow away a hangover.

They were bitterly disappointed. There was nothing to blow away their hangovers. By noon it was a sweltering 88 degrees Fahrenheit and the mercury was still rising. The sun beat down and there was no air to cool them. 'We'll just have a look at the shops and head back to the ship I think, I feel a siesta coming on later and it's probably what we need. A sleep and a large glass of Alka-Seltzer. We could go on deck and get a cabana where we can relax in the sun. Do you fancy that, Denise? The usually boisterous life and soul party girl Denise just nodded weakly to her best friend.

'Remind me never to drink Southern Comfort with vodka shots again.' As she said it, Denise baulked and turned to the quayside where she proceeded for the third time that morning to vomit last night's bar bill into the still Atlantic Ocean.

Back on board *Opulence*, Commodore Griffiths was enjoying a rest on his private balcony in a suite near the bridge reserved on a special quarter deck secure area for the senior officers. The Commodore had just had a Skype call with Joy, his wife of 23 years. Joy was bringing him up to date on how the family were doing as he'd been at sea for three months and wouldn't be home until the end of this voyage. All was well. Elizabeth had just started her job as an intern at a well-known fashion house in London and Jake was off to Ibiza with his friends for a two-week holiday.

The Commodore enjoyed this quiet time where he could be

himself and speak to his lifetime companion. *Only another three weeks and I'll be heading home to our beautiful manor house in Devon.*

In port, *Opulence* was quiet. Most of the 600 passengers had gone ashore to take in the delights of the lovely northern Spanish town. The only busy areas on *Opulence* were the galleys. Chefs sweltered in the melting heat preparing the most exquisite food for this evening's hungry passengers. From about 5pm the quay became busy with returning passengers. Crew stood on the quayside beside the gangway, assisting the passengers back on board with their purchases and souvenirs and dishing out cool towels and cold drinks. Coaches and private chauffer-driven cars pulled up and spewed out guests who were chattering about how enjoyable their trips had been. Door cards were scanned and passengers electronically counted on board.

It should be a reasonably quiet night tonight, thought Chloe as she greeted guests in the foyer. *The heat and the day on shore usually makes for a pretty quiet evening. They'll all go back to their suites now to relax before dinner.* Her smile faltered slightly as she heard the Jenkins brats shouting as they entered the security area in the foyer. Tommy was screaming again as his new water blaster had been taken by a crew member to be put through the X-ray machine and Tommy was throwing the mother of all tantrums that it had been taken from him. Jenson was shouting at the nervous Indian crew member to give his brother back his toy immediately or he'd be sorry, while Diana and Sam were having their own full-blown argument at the amount of souvenir shopping Diana had done and they had struggled to carry back to the ship.

'You really need to get a grip, Di. Those boys are little bastards and you give in to them every time. TOMMY shut the fuck up will you and wait. You'll get it back in a minute. JENSON come away and leave the man alone, you little shit.' Tommy and Jenson ignored Sam while Di struggled to carry some of her purchases, simulataneously trying to console Tommy and Jenson. Packages and bags were dropped to the floor as bellboys scurried to help. 'ENOUGH NOW!' bellowed Sam Jenkins. Everyone stopped and looked at this strange little man with a bald head and tattoos up his arms and on his legs. Sam was livid. The veins in his neck were about to burst, his face was puce and his temper had boiled over. Sam dealt with his unruly brood in the only way he knew how. He brought his arm back and sent a stinging blow to young Tommy's face. Tommy, completely shocked at the ferocity of the slap, was momentarily stunned into silence as he drew in a sharp breath and tried to take in the stinging blow. Within seconds, Tommy was again screaming, this time in pain as a red mark appeared on his cheek. At the same time, Jenson received a backhander to the head and Sam grabbed his hair and shoved him towards the foyer. 'I've had enough, do you hear me? Shut up, Tommy, or I'll give you another.'

Crew members stood by open-mouthed at the scene before them. They had come across unruly children before but the treatment of these children by Sam and Di Jenkins was tantamount to child cruelty. Di, because she had no boundaries, and Sam because he was physically abusive.

Sam grabbed Tommy and Jenson and frogmarched them towards the lifts. Three bellboys scurried after them with armfuls of parcels and shopping bags. Kyle clung to his mother's hand and didn't utter a word. Even he knew when Dad had enough and he didn't want his face to be on the end of Sam's hand either.

Di hurried after Sam, shouting at him to let the boys go and stop being an arse. Sam yelled at Di to 'Shut your fuckin' mouth as well or you'll get the same as Tommy when we got to our suite.' Di screamed back at Sam that he was a bullying bastard and that she wished she'd never married him and that when they got back she was going to divorce him and take him for everything.

Sam Jenkins had been lucky. He grew up in Newcastle in a family where screaming and shouting was normal. There were no boundaries. Dad never worked and spent all their benefits at the pub or on drugs. His wife had seven children by the time she was 24, having started at 12, and she was one of life's victims. Subjected to domestic abuse constantly, both physical and emotional, but wouldn't leave. Dora was more than happy to stand by day by day watching Ken beat the living crap out of the kids but when tackled all she'd say was she loved him. Dora was and always would be one of life's victims. Ken died ten years ago after taking a particularly bad beating when he tried to intimidate the new-kid-on-the-block drug dealer. Dora was living in supported accommodation as she had turned to alcohol and drugs and been evicted from her property. As usual, it was everyone else's fault but not Dora's. Blaming her kids for Ken's death and the fact that most of them were either in prison or knocked up and living in temporary accommodation by the time they were 14, Dora was quick enough to demand help from every support service going but would never take responsibility for her life. Dora enjoyed being the victim.

Sam watched the chaos he was dragged up in and decided that he would better himself. Sadly, although he made a fortune, Sam still couldn't buy a decent upbringing and had the same abusive mentality as his father. Buying and selling rundown old motors from the age of 13, he'd quickly become business savvy and built up a successful secondhand car dealership by the time he was 21. This gave him a lucrative income and by the age of 27 he'd expanded his empire to three dealerships all dealing in high-end vehicles. Despite his background, his wealth had grown but not his manners. He remained Sammy Jenkins, the local hard nut with a foul mouth and temper to match. A chip off the old block.

Sam met Di down the local pub when they were both 16. They knew of each other as they were from the same area but they hadn't got together until they were 16. Their relationship was off and on for years until eventually Di announced she was pregnant with Jenson and forced him to do the honourable thing and make an honest woman of her. Sam was reluctant to get married. He didn't particularly like children and he didn't want to get married either. His fortune was his and he didn't want to risk any money-grabbing whore getting her hands on it. Sam bought his own house in a nice little estate when he was 22 years old but you couldn't take the council estate out of either of them.

Their relationship was tempestuous and Di hated her posh neighbours who stuck their noses up at her when she sat on her front doorstep smoking and shouting at her kids who were running up and down the quiet cul de sac. Di was a force to be reckoned with. Di was loud and foul-mouthed and her neighbours despised her. She wouldn't think twice about having a slanging match in the middle of the street with one of the boys attached to her hip. All the boys were spoiled and while Mum indulged them, Dad steered clear. They irritated him and when he did have to spend time with them his patience was frayed within an hour.

Di decided they needed a family holiday and had booked the cruise a few months earlier. Di always liked to show off and her rationale was that now that they lived in a seven-bedroom detached mansion in Cheshire, she'd give these posh knobs something to talk about. She may not be married to a Premier League footballer but she could keep up with the Joneses and would be the talk of the town, so she spent a fortune on a cruise on *Opulence* having heard great things about this ship. It didn't matter that Di didn't have a clue about cruising; it was expensive and that was all she was interested in when bragging to her friends how much it had cost her. Although expensive, the Jenkins had the cheapest accommodation on board. It still set her back around a half a million pounds for the privilege and Sam was seething. He'd much rather have gone to Marbella with his shady male friends, no wife and definitely no kids. Now, he was going to be stuck on a ship with a load of posh gits and no way of getting away from his bitch of a wife and his demon kids. Sam tried desperately to cancel the booking and get his money back but to no avail. He was lumbered with the holiday.

Senior purser Alan Danvers and David were watching the scene unfold. David was upset at the way Sam had slapped the boys. They were little shits but they didn't deserve to be beaten by their thug of a father. Alan Danvers was also seriously concerned at what he, some crew members and other embarking passengers had just witnessed. 'Don't worry David, I'm going to have a word with the security officer. This can't be allowed to go on. We've already been approached 18 times by concerned passengers so we are duty bound to do something about it.'

Opulence was fairly quiet once she set sail at 6pm. The majority of passengers were washing away the sweat of a sizzling day while others relaxed on their balconies or their oversized stuffed sofas, having pre-dinner drinks and discussing their thoughts on their first day ashore.

Many passengers were tired, mainly as the heat had been pretty unbearable, and a few had forgotten to put on their sunscreen and they ended up with sunstroke. The combination of heat and spending hours ashore exploring the sights of La Coruna would make for a quiet night on board.

Rocky and Terry made their way to The Oyster alone. Todd and Ed decided to do their own thing this evening and it didn't involve getting dressed up and behaving themselves. Denise and Chris were happy to see the boys but were also wary about appearing too keen in light of what happened last night when they were seemingly ignored in favour of Todd and Ed.

'Hi girls, how are you today? Did you go ashore?' Terry was the first to break the slightly awkward silence.

'We had a great day thanks, what about you?' Chris kept up the polite banter while Denise tried to maintain a nonchalant attitude.

'Girls, I'm really sorry about last night. You may have noticed the other two were a bit worse for wear and we had to take them back to the suite and make sure they didn't cause any problems.'

'Hadn't even noticed,' retorted Denise a little too quickly. 'We had a fantastic night didn't we Chris? We had a tour of the bars on the ship and can't even remember where we ended up or who we ended up with, to be honest. All I can say is that it was a brilliant night from what I can remember!!' Denise watched Rocky intently, hoping to see a glimmer of disappointment at her innuendo but she was the one who was disappointed.

'Ah, that's great to hear, Denise, we felt a little guilty at the time, didn't we Terry? Having to rush off like that 'n' all. We thought you might have thought us rude but it looks like you had a craic last night so it's all good.'

Denise was a little taken aback at Rocky's seemingly nonplussed response. She had hoped there may be a vague glimmer of jealousy but there was nothing. Just a cordial comment about how he was glad they had a great time.

Denise was peeved. They may be the biggest rock stars on the globe but she really thought they had liked them. She watched Chris and Terry chatting away and her stubborn nature would not give way to forgiveness. Terry was tucking in to filet mignon and Chris was happily savouring her lobster and truffle ravioli while Denise picked at her rack of lamb.

Rocky joined in the conversation with Chris and Terry and the three of them laughed just like they did yesterday lunchtime. Chris didn't harbour any animosity and was again enjoying their company. Denise was quiet and quite sulky. She continued to glug back her Chateau Mouton-Rothschild 1945 like it was mineral water while thinking to herself that Chris was a traitor for acting as though nothing had happened. *Who cares if I have another hangover tomorrow*, thought Denise.

Andy, Kurt and Louisa were sat together again. Mia had asked Louisa to join her for dinner but Louisa declined siting; it would seem very rude if she were to abandon her table companions at such an early stage in the voyage. Kurt was a little more subdued this evening. His usual brashness replaced with what could only be classed as a sulky child attitude. Andy was entertaining Louisa with tales of his talent bank and they were both laughing hysterically at some of the antics which came to light. 'Lighten up Kurt, will you? What must Louisa think?' Louisa dressed in a goddess-style white Yves Saint Laurent silk was smiling at both men. She knew that Kurt was annoyed that she was getting on well with Andy and he suspected that Andy fancied her and this was his way of taking the first steps to getting to know her better but Louisa also knew Kurt was jealous and he was sulking like a child.

Kurt's childlike quality was what had attracted Louisa to Kurt the first time they met. Louisa was staying at the Four Seasons Hotel in Beverly Hills when Kurt booked in there on his way back from a whirlwind tour. Andy had arranged for Kurt to be interviewed by CBN and didn't realise that Louisa was also at the Four Seasons. They bumped into each other by accident in the lift and there was an instant chemistry which brought out Louisa's dark side. Kurt turned on the charm and flirted outrageously with Louisa, not phased at all by her Hollywood status as the hottest actress on the planet. Kurt invited Louisa to join him in his room for a drink and was dumbfounded when she agreed. Louisa eventually returned to her suite at 3am, smiling like a Cheshire cat. Kurt lay in his bed thinking how lucky he was to have pulled the hottest actress. Everyone wanted a piece of her and he got it. He got up and went to his bathroom where he fished a joint from his toilet bag and then fell back into bed reliving the last few hours spent with Louisa. After a few Jack Daniels, Kurt suggested they may be comfier on his bed. Louisa didn't need any encouragement. She led him by the hand and as soon as they were in his bedroom she ripped her blouse apart exposing her breasts. Kurt roughly grabbed hold of Louisa and proceeded to ravage her. Forcing her down onto the bed, he unzipped his fly and picked Louisa up, thrusting her none too gently on to his erect penis. Louisa yelped as Kurt pulled her hair back and kissed her upturned throat. He pounded into her hard and bit her nipples causing little marks to form. Louisa dug her nails into Kurt and drew blood as she gripped his shoulders. Kurt and Louisa both shuddered simultaneously as their orgasms ripped through them. It was over pretty quickly but it had an intensity that Kurt had never experienced before and one that he liked. A few more Jack Daniels later, and a couple of lines of cocaine for Kurt, and he and Louisa had certainly made each other's acquaintance.

Since then, Louisa and Kurt met when they could and enjoyed each other's bodies. No one but the two of them knew of their arrangement. It wasn't so much a relationship as a friends-with-benefits arrangement. They shagged when they could and they both enjoyed sex. It was good between them but it would do neither of their careers any good if word got out. They had to be so careful and had managed to continue to see each other for the past few months, stealing precious time with each other when their schedules allowed. Kurt and Louisa were both cut from the same cloth when it came to sex. They both liked it rough and edgy. They took chances and their sex life bordered on violent. Louisa would never live this down if word got out. She had an image to maintain and she was determined that no one could ever know.

For now, Louisa was happy to dine with Kurt and his agent knowing that they could get together when the notion took them. The fact that she acted like he was annoying her maintained her cover story. Yet again, Louisa played a blinder.

Kurt liked Louisa more than he let on and he'd like to have gone public about their relationship and maybe move it to a more romantic basis but he couldn't allow himself to be seen with a girlfriend. His fan base would not allow this and his career could be ruined. Louisa, on the other hand, was merely using Kurt for sex. She had no desire to get involved with him. He was a kid. Good in bed but a sulky little boy at heart and she wanted a man. *Andy's not too bad,* thought Louisa, smiling coquettishly at him while sipping her champagne and laughing at his tales of errant celebrities. Kurt was watching Andy intently as he regaled Louisa and was angry that his manager was trying to get into Louisa's pants. Kurt knew Andy well enough to know that Louisa was his type and Andy was making the most of the opportunity.

At the next table, The Bensons had joined Mia and Cosmo for dinner. Michelle had secured herself an invitation to dine with Mia this evening following their poolside liaison. Mia didn't really mind and for the time being she was happy to entertain Michelle who was regaling Mia and Cosmo with their tales of traipsing round ancient churches and her subsequent shopping trip where she picked up a lovely little Armani two-piece skirt suit.

'Darling, I don't do stuffy churches either,' drawled Mia. 'Cosmo and I had lunch with that delightful actress, Louisa Hudson. Do you know her?' she said, while nodding to the next table where Louisa was sat with Kurt and Andy. 'She has a complexion to die for and a figure even Gigi Hadid would be envious of.' Michelle knew very well who Louisa Hudson was but she and Michael had never been lucky enough to land the big interviews. This trip may just be the lever needed to bag the beauty for an exclusive interview. The newly appointed reality stars and long-standing journalists always got the big fish and despite being the faces of morning TV there were some celebrities who were still way out of their league. This rankled with Michelle as she always saw herself as the star of the show and she firmly believed that without her, Michael would be nothing. Michael Benson, tall, dark and handsome. Even for a man in his late 40s he turned heads. Michelle didn't particularly want him but she didn't want anyone else to have him either. Michelle was insanely jealous if Michael's eyes wandered or if another woman glanced at Michael, but he served a purpose and that was to keep them both firmly in the media. The nation's sweethearts. They needed this. She needed this. Michael was her passport to success.

'Ah yes, the delightful Miss Hudson,' Michelle said, grinning at Cosmo and Mia as she glanced over at the beautiful young actress and talked about how they were desperately hoping to land an exclusive interview with her one day. 'Who knows, we may even manage to seal the deal on this cruise,' giggled Michelle as she flirted with Cosmo and Mia. Michael noticed his wife's exuberance and merely thought it was because he'd bought her the Armani suit she'd admired. Little did Michael know that the real reason for Michelle's' gaiety was sitting at the table next to theirs.

Jasper Teasdale was once again looking his usual sour-faced self. *His bitch of a wife was holding court like she thought she was really something special,* thought Michelle. Sarah was dressed from head to toe in cherry-red Versace. Her raven hair was loose and straight and her eyes dark and smoky. She looked stunning. The sommelier and two waiters were attending to the Teasdales as Jasper tasted the Domaine de la Romanee-Conti 1990 which was glinting like rubies in the Baccarat crystal glasses. Once again, every eye was on Sarah, and Michelle was seething. She was jealous of anyone who took the attention from her and even more so of those who caught Michael's eye. Since her drinks with Jasper the previous afternoon, Michelle had become infatuated with this gorgeous wealthy man and she was determined to make him notice what he was missing with his airhead doll.

Jasper glanced over every so often and caught Michelle's

eye. Fuelled by champagne, heatstroke and ego, Michelle was determined to make sure she was the centre of attention this evening. 'Cosmo, sweetheart, you really must come and give me a makeover if you wouldn't mind? You make such a beautiful job of dressing Mia. I could definitely use some of your magic.'

'Leave the poor boy alone, Michelle. He's on holiday. I'm sure he has enough to do without giving you a makeover as well,' chastised Michael.

Cosmo laughed and said he'd be delighted to work with Michelle. He would transform her into even more of a beauty than she already was. 'It isn't difficult when I have such beautiful canvases to work from,' gushed Cosmo, smiling and toasting both Mia and Michelle.

Dinner passed in a haze of champagne, finest wines and ports. Rich sauces, truffles and the finest cuts of meat and fish. Baccarat clinked and sparkled, laughter rang out and the maître d' looked satisfied that all was as it should be.

CHAPTER 6

Day three of the voyage dawned with brilliant sunshine and a forecast in the high 80s. *Opulence* was now sailing quickly across the Atlantic Ocean to the Caribbean.

Passengers were milling around the shopping mall, taking dance, crafting and fencing classes, watching fruit carving demonstrations, wine tasting, sunbathing, having facials and other beauty treatments and playing bridge among other things.

The itinerary for the day was full of activities to suit all characters. Fitness training in the gym, a treasure hunt for the few children on board, tours of the bridge and other secure areas of the ship and a demonstration on non-surgical face lifts by a famous American doctor, the latest cosmetic craze to hit the states. All activities were well attended and there was an air of excitement and anticipation as they sailed towards their second port of call – the beautiful island of Antigua.

They would then be cruising to Tortola, St Maarten, St Kitts, Martinique, St Lucia and Ponta Delgada, before heading home to Southampton.

Chloe and David were having a well-earned coffee break from the Pursers Desk. They'd been attending to passenger whims all morning and advising on shore excursions in Antigua and some of the other ports of call. The bookings for the submarine reef tours were selling like hot cakes and the ships private helicopter was also fully booked for the Caribbean. David was telling Chloe all about his escapade with the lovely Cosmo. 'I'm sure he really likes me, Chloe, he said as much, said that he is looking to settle down but just needs to find Mr Right rather than Mr Right now. He's planning on leaving Mia Manzo at some stage and he's loaded!' David didn't stop to draw breath. He was ecstatic that Cosmo had stopped by to see him on deck after dropping not-so-subtle hints and he was determined that Cosmo could be his meal ticket out of Purple Cross.

'Don't be silly, David. You live in La La Land, mate,' slighted Chloe. 'As if Cosmo is going to give up his lifestyle with one of the world's most famous icons to shack up with you, a purser from Nottingham earning £23,000 a year. Oh yes, I can just see it.'

'Give it a rest, Chloe, you don't know what you're talking about. You weren't on deck with us and you didn't hear what he was saying to me. You're just jealous. You've got no one and no prospects, so stop trying to spoil it for me.'

Chloe drained her mug of coffee and left the room. *David was such a bitch, he should have been a woman,* thought Chloe.

The Jackdaws were in Zone One rehearsing for their upcoming gig. Todd and Ed were again in jubilant mood, assisted by the cocaine they'd snorted half an hour earlier. Rocky and Terry were more subdued and thankful that they'd turned up at all. Things were not good with The Jackdaws and it seemed that only Rocky and Terry could see it.

They were playing their number one hit 'Green Beans' when Olivia and Jessica appeared. Todd immediately recognised them from their first night and waved at them as he played a vibrating riff on his electric guitar, exaggerating the moves to show off to the girls. The two birds at the next table to them in The Oyster didn't seem to want to know, so these two would do the business and keep them entertained for the voyage.

Olivia and Jessica moved to the front of the club and sat themselves down facing the stage. The Jackdaws finished their track and Rocky asked the girls if they'd mind leaving them to practice in peace. There was a note on the door advising that Zone One was closed until 11am which the girls had completely disregarded.

Jessica flicked back her long black glossy hair and fluttered her false eyelashes at Todd. Todd turned to Rocky and told him to chill out. 'The girls aren't doing any harm Rocky, wind your neck in buddy.'

'We're trying to rehearse here, Todd; we don't need any

distractions.'

'Oh shut it, Rocky, you're like a whining old man these days. For feck's sake, just chill out. They're not doing any harm.' Olivia had joined Ed at the drums and was banging the high hat and giggling. Ed started a complicated fill-in as Olivia was crashing the cymbal and they were laughing hysterically, lost in the thunderous beat of the drums.

Jessica was standing next to Rocky with her arm around his shoulder. 'Oh come on darling, don't be such a spoilsport. We only want to watch you rehearse and then we'll let you take us for lunch.' The salacious smile didn't go unnoticed but Rocky merely thanked Jessica as he moved from her grasp and ignored her comment about lunch. He turned to Ed and shouted at him to stop messing around as they still had three tracks to cover. Jessica followed Rocky to the stage and grabbed his jacket as she again told him not to be such a spoilsport and loosen up. Terry watched all of this unfold and knew that Rocky's temper would soon get the better of him. He jumped off the stage and walked towards Jessica.

'It was lovely of you to come and see us but as you can see we're really tied up at the moment and still have some tracks to rehearse. It's probably best if you just sort yourselves out for lunch as we don't know when we'll be free exactly.' Ed was now exchanging mobile numbers with Olivia and put his arms round both girls as he escorted them to the door of Zone One.

Rocky looked at Todd who was now arguing with Terry and decided that this was the last straw. *As soon as we get home, The Jackdaws will be looking for a new drummer and bass guitarist,* thought Rocky. *I've had enough and I'm not the one leaving. Ed and Todd have changed and they're too big for their boots now.* Todd and Terry's voices were becoming louder as Todd grabbed Terry round the throat and shoved him up against the wall. 'Don't you feckin' speak to me like that again, do you hear? I've had enough of you two. We're the best rock band in the world and you two act like you're 70,' Todd spat as he nodded towards Rocky. 'You don't tell me what to do, OK?'

Terry, not wishing to inflame the situation, merely stayed quiet and put his hands up in a form of surrender. He could easily have punched Todd and knocked him flat out but he knew that they had to get through this cruise and wanted it to be as drama-free as possible. Rocky knew he'd need to make a call to their manager before the holiday was over.

Terry made his way back to his guitar as Ed took up his place at the drums. Rocky and Todd glared at each other as Ed counted them in to their next track… 3,2,1.

Jessica and Olivia were furious that Rocky had asked them to leave. Brought up in Chelsea and Kensington, both girls were gifted with silver spoons. Whatever they wanted, Daddy ensured they had. The things they both lacked were manners and respect. Their wealth had come with rudeness and thick skin.

The girls had attended Chateau de Rosey in Rolle, Switzerland. Their fathers, both successful international bankers, were happy for their darling daughters to have the very best that money could buy. If Rosey was good enough for royalty, then it was good enough for their beloved girls. Jessica was a stunner, long sleek black hair, brown eyes and an hourglass figure and Olivia's thick chestnut hair, blue eyes and slightly fuller figure made them both stand out in a crowd. They were immaculately turned out each day with false eyelashes and manicured nails, their designer handbags never off their wrists and their six-inch heels ever present. Jessica had an unfortunate attitude. A narcissist who treated others like dirt, she was not the most pleasant person to be around. Olivia was the ugly sister, so to speak, and she was not as confident as Jessica but looked up to her friend and emulated her whenever she could. She encouraged Jessica's attitude and they were a formidable duo to contend with. It was such a shame that something so enjoyable to look at had such a bad core.

'How fucking dare he, like, speak to me like that,' drawled Jessica. 'Who the fuck does he think he is? Just because he's like a celebrity doesn't give him the right to throw me out.'

'Don't worry, Jess, he's nothing but a pumped-up little singer. He's like not even that good looking when you compare him to like Ed and Todd! Anyway, we've got Ed's number now and I've to text him and let him, like, know where we'll be having lunch and they'll join us.'

'Ya, well let's like make sure we keep their interest this time, Liv. If we're going to secure our own TV show, we like have to have a celebrity profile and the only way we can do that is to like be seen with the biggest rock band on the planet.' Jessica decided that she needed to change for lunch and was now throwing a selection of outfits onto her bed with reckless abandon, not in the least concerned that the outfits were in the region of £3,000 a piece. 'Ralph can hang these back up later, Liv, now what the fuck am I going to wear to, like, trap my rock god?'

Olivia laughed her annoying high-pitched hiccup laugh as she roughly started manhandling the clothes thrown on the bed. 'How about this little Gucci sundress Jess? It, like, shows your boobs and legs off really well.'

'Perfect, Liv. Help me find my matching Jimmy Choos will you? I have a feeling, like, after lunch we'll need to be looking our very best at all times as the paparazzi will have new fodder.' Olivia picked up the phone in the suite and rang for their butler Ralph. 'Make us appointments to have our hair and make-up done at 5pm today and there's clothing needing to be hung up,' she said brusquely before ending the call without a by your leave.

Michael and Michelle were strolling on deck when they bumped into Jasper, Sarah, Mia and Cosmo, all with the same idea of a stroll around this gorgeous vessel before lunch. Jasper looked handsome in his white shorts, flip flops and lilac-coloured polo shirt. His gorgeous broody eyes obscured by Ray-Ban sunglasses. Sarah looked stunning in her turquoise blue bikini and matching cover-up, her hair swept back in a French plait and her face made up immaculately. Mia was wearing cream linen trousers and a silk camisole while Cosmo was dressed in blue shorts, a blue and white t-shirt, captain's hat and Armani sunglasses. They all looked stunning. Michelle immediately felt her heart race and her stomach flip when she saw Jasper and at the same time she was seething. She smiled and extended her arms while glancing at Michael who was smiling broadly as he greeted them all individually with handshakes for the men and kisses for the ladies, complimenting them on how beautiful they looked. Michelle's jealousy immediately surfaced and she was furious with her husband. If anyone was going to play away it would be her with that gorgeous man Jasper. Jasper was smiling and exchanging pleasantries with Michael and Cosmo while Sarah was asking Michelle if they'd like to join them all for pre- lunch drinks. Michelle turned it on and graciously accepted Sarah's invitation, knowing that, despite her jealousy, she would get to spend yet more time with Jasper. Michelle pushed forward and linked arms with Jasper as they all made their way to the Calypso Club.

Cosmo looked up at the ceiling as his orgasm came to an end. David smiled at Cosmo and asked how he felt. 'I feel great, darling. You certainly know how to keep a man happy.' David was elated. Here he was with the man of his dreams and his passport to a better life. Cosmo had come to the Pursers Desk half an hour earlier after a few cocktails and asked David to come and take a look at the pipework in his suite. Thirty minutes later, Cosmo was feeling relieved in more ways than one. He was aware that David fancied him and he'd made it clear that this was just a holiday fling and nothing more. David however, only heard what he wanted and was confident that once Cosmo had felt his mouth on his cock, he would soon change his mind and their relationship would become much deeper.

'I have to go, David. Mia will be wondering where I am. Anyway, it's nearly lunchtime and I'm sure they'll be missing you on the desk?'

'Don't worry about me Cosmo, I've been ensuring customer satisfaction so I won't be getting into any trouble.' David smiled salaciously as Cosmo zipped his flies and grabbed his sunglasses from the bedside cabinet.

'I'll see you later, David. Ciao, darling.' With a flourish, Cosmo swept from his suite and left a smitten David longing for more and a little upset that Cosmo hadn't even kissed him goodbye.

Kurt and Andy were having a relaxing morning in the spa. Andy had just had an Indian head massage while Kurt took advantage of the full body massage. His choice probably cemented by the gorgeous young Filipino girl attending to him.

'Are you having lunch today, Kurt?'

'I don't know yet, mate, probably just order room service or get something later in The Lobster Pot. I'll see how it goes.' Kurt was unusually subdued. Andy sensed a change in his mood over the last 24 hours and hoped he hadn't overindulged in his habit again.

'Well I fancy a griddled rib-eye steak so I'm going to go to the restaurant. I'll catch up with you at dinner. Be good.'

Kurt raised his hand to wave goodbye to Andy and let out a long sigh. *Thank fuck he's gone. I feel like I'm on holiday with my father. He won't let me breathe. He's my agent not my fucking babysitter.*

Kurt turned over and looked at his masseuse. Sareena was overawed at her famous celebrity and smiled at him with gleaming white teeth. Kurt stared at her pristine white zip-up tunic and raised his hand allowing his fingers to gently touch the zip fastener. Sareena put her hand on top of Kurt's as he slowly pulled the zip down, exposing her breasts which were encased in a white lace bra. Sareena backed away from Kurt and moved towards the door which she locked. Kurt lay on his back gazing at the light fitting and thinking how he was the luckiest boy in the world. He had dick and every female under the age of 40 wanted it.

Louisa had spent the morning sunbathing on deck alone. She had taken a plunge in the pool and was drying off on one of the cabanas in the baking sun. She looked beautiful as always. Louisa's thoughts drifted to her current situation. *I'm the world's hottest actress and everyone expects me to go to church on Sunday and act like Mother Teresa. I'm so annoyed with Tom. Why in hell did he package me as a sweet, god-fearing virgin? I'm going to have to burst his bubble as I can't go on like this. I'm on holiday and still acting the part he created for me. My alter persona Louisa Hudson. Well fuck him and fuck this bullshit. I'm going to ring him and have a chat. He's not going to control me any longer.*

Tom White was Louisa's manager and had decided the first time he saw her that she had to have a squeaky clean girl-next-door image. The British public were fed up with brats and wannabees with no talent. Louisa was different. She was a nice girl and had bags of talent. The fact that she was stunningly beautiful also helped and Tom knew that this find would secure both their futures but there was a price to pay. The British public wanted to see a nice wholesome girl. They would engage with her and support her. This was the way forward and Tom was determined that the young up-and-coming actress would do anything to crack the big screen so he pretty much laid out who she was to be from day one. Louisa was happy to play the part at first but a few years on and it was becoming boring. She couldn't be who she really was and was frustrated at being stifled by her goody-two-shoes image.

Louisa wasn't the girl-next-door she was portrayed as, she was a fantastic actress to have carried it off so well but as the old saying goes, all publicity is good publicity, so Louisa was intending to live her life the way she wanted and burst Tom and the public's bubble very soon. *I'm not going to hide my real self any longer*, she thought.

The rest of the day passed in luxurious nothingness. Drinking, eating, shopping and enjoying a calm sail across the ocean towards the Caribbean. Cruising was pretty much repetitive but on this vessel it was divine. If you wanted to order lobster at 2am and a cheese and tomato toastie at 4am you could. Your wish was the crew's command.

CHAPTER 7

The passengers awoke to blinding sunshine and searing temperatures once again. After a fairly unremarkable voyage, *Opulence* had arrived in the Caribbean at the beautiful island of Antigua. Views from the balconies were swaying palm trees, golden beaches and divine turquoise sea. The whirr of the ship's helicopter's rotors fading as it whisked away its first lucky passengers of the day.

Here passengers could choose from mere relaxation on some of Antigua's most beautiful beaches or retail therapy, depending on their mood. Antigua wasn't exactly the Milan or New York of the fashion world but it did boast some rather quaint artisan outlets which discerning tourists couldn't miss.

The disembarkation area was bustling with excited travellers, desperate to feel dry land under their feet after a few days at sea. *Opulence* was moored 600 feet from the port and tenders were being used to take excited passengers to shore. Chloe was responsible for managing the passengers who had booked *Diamond*, the ship's 25-seater submarine. Excited passengers on the first reef dive were gathering in the foyer to be led down to the hold where they would board *Diamond*. Mia, Cosmo, Michelle, Michael, Jasper and Sarah had arranged to go ashore together and spend their time viewing the island by private tour. The pursers had arranged a limousine and a guide to take them on a six-hour private sightseeing excursion.

They were all gathered in the foyer with the exception of Sarah, who was as usual late. Jasper was apologising to his friends. 'I'm so sorry, this is typical of Sarah to be honest. Timekeeping was never her strong point.'

Everyone smiled sympathetically with the exception of Mia. 'Sarah was well aware of our meeting time. The limo will be waiting for us and we have still to board the tender to get us to shore. What on earth is keeping her?' asked Mia with a hint of irritation in her voice. Jasper replied that he left her trying to decide which handbag and shoes she would wear. His embarrassment was not lost on the group.

Kurt, Andy and Louisa walked past. They exchanged pleasantries with the waiting group and Michelle asked what they intended to do. 'Oh, we're just off to Deep Bay Beach for some relaxation and water sports,' replied Louisa. 'The guys were talking about it last night and I asked if I could tag along.'

'Have a wonderful day, whatever you are doing. Catch up tonight, perhaps,' shouted a slightly giddy Michelle. With that, Louisa jumped excitedly and shoved Kurt and Andy in the back as they moved towards the stairs and the waiting tender.

Shouting broke the excited chatter of the disembarking passengers. The Jenkins had arrived. As usual, it was chaos, with Diana trying and failing to control the boys. The family looked a sight. Sam was wearing a grey vest-style top with knee-length garish multicoloured shorts and flip flops; the boys wore matching outfits. Diana was wearing a cerise pink crop top and black leggings with five-inch heeled sandals. Granted, they were all designer but looked like something from a pound store on the Jenkins. Unfortunately, Di's muffin top and thunder thighs drew more eyes than her tight leggings. The boys were running amok and screaming at their mother to hurry up as they wanted to go on the banana boat. Sam looked as though he was three sheets to the wind already and it wasn't even 9.30am. He shouted at them to be quiet or they'd be getting his foot up their arse.

'Oh my god,' groaned Mia, rolling her eyes. 'I do wish someone would have a word with them. This is ridiculous. We paid a fortune for this trip and look at what we end up with, present company excluded,' Mia added.

'Well said, Mia,' gushed Michelle. 'We should have a word with the pursers when we return from our tour later, that's if we ever get away.' Michelle smiled directly at Jasper who by this time was becoming angry with his errant wife. Michelle disliked Sarah and was happy to make digs and snide remarks where possible. Michelle thought her a trumped-up materialistic little tart which may have borne some fact but Michelle was just pure jealous. Not only was Sarah stunning but she had exactly what Michelle wanted – Jasper. *What on earth is Jasper doing with that slut?* fumed Michelle silently. *He is too good for her. He is so attracted to me. I want this man in my life one way or another and I'm sure we can have a liaison which will suit both our needs.* Michelle was so hung up on her fame that she would not allow anything to come between her and her career. She had a vision that she and Michael would be the nation's sweethearts for years to come and she loved the lifestyle their popularity afforded them. Jasper was rich and handsome and he fancied her without a doubt but if she allowed her and Michael's partnership to dissolve then she would disappear into oblivion with Jasper and this she was not prepared to do. Well, at least this was how she saw it in her own warped mind.

'I'm here!' shrieked Sarah as she came hurrying towards them, looking stunning as usual. 'Sorry to keep you but I just couldn't decide on these Jimmy Choos or a pair of Louboutins.'

'I would have thought a pair of flat sandals would be better suited to a sightseeing tour of the island, Sarah,' shot Michelle.

Sarah glared at Michelle and looking at Michelle's choice of sensible comfortable wedges said, 'I like to look good all the time, Michelle, and that includes fashionable. I wouldn't be seen dead wearing old woman's shoes.' With that, Sarah turned and flounced off towards security. Jasper was furious and smiled apologetically at Michelle who was left open-mouthed. Mia, Cosmo and Michael were all stifling smiles and Michael thought Michelle got exactly what she deserved.

Cosmo decided that in order to alleviate any atmosphere between Sarah and Michelle, the group should go for cocktails before heading out on their tour. Cosmo entertained the passengers on the tender as they headed to shore by singing a few sea shanties and doing a brilliant impersonation of Johnny Depp's Captain Jack Sparrow. When they finally disembarked the tender, Cosmo asked the chauffeur to take them to the best bar on the island. The limo was stocked with champagne and spirits and Cosmo poured a glass of bubbles for everyone to toast their great day in Antigua. Michelle sat sulkily furthest away from Sarah while Sarah held court with anyone who would listen. Sarah couldn't care less about Michelle. *She's nothing but a jealous ageing hag and I won't let her get away with speaking to me like that,* thought Sarah. Jasper was immersed in conversation with Mia and Michael and Cosmo were chatting while Sarah's voice bounced off the inside of the limousine, grating more and more on Michelle.

The group were taken a short journey to the clifftop above St John's to the luxury Cove Blue Waters Hotel. Cosmo arranged for the group to sit on the terrace overlooking the ocean and ordered rum punches all round. *If we've got to get through today with each other then we need to loosen up a bit,* thought Cosmo as he ordered a second round of the cocktail with a kick before the first had even been placed on the table. The atmosphere was great apart from Michelle's mood which caused a little awkwardness within the group. *She acts like a spoiled bitch at times,* thought Michael as he turned his attention back to Jasper. Michelle was silently fuming. Jasper hadn't bothered to even so much as glance at her today in the same way he had done the other afternoon when they spent some time together.

All was tranquil on Deep Bay Beach. The turquoise sea lapping over the white sands of the beach. Palm trees swaying gently in the warm breeze, beach bars open, Caribbean music playing and waiters delivering delicious cocktails and snacks to beachgoers. The occasional whirr of *Diamond's* rotor blades had everyone looking up at the ship's helicopter as it flew overhead, collecting and dropping off passengers all over the island. There was lots of guessing as to who was the lucky person to be in the helicopter at that very moment.

There was an abundance of water sports for those who didn't want to lie on the sands soaking up the baking sun. Water doughnuts, banana boat, pedalos, snorkelling, jet skis, parascending and much more.

The beach was busy and Kurt, Andy and Louisa found

themselves a spot at the back of the beach under some palm trees which offered a welcome bit of shade. Kurt was practically drooling as he watched Louisa shake out her blonde ponytail and remove her lace cover-up to reveal a scanty navy bikini encrusted with multicoloured stones. Her gorgeous figure was emphasised to its full potential and he quickly turned away under the pretext of looking for sunscreen in his holdall to avoid an embarrassing situation.

It appeared their dressed-down appearance and sunglasses and hats had offered the welcome anonymity they needed to enjoy their day. Hardly anyone took any notice of the hottest actress in Hollywood and the best pop star on the planet.

Andy took his towel and laid it out on the sand. His shorts highlighting his muscular thighs and his well-defined ripped torso wasn't what you would have expected under his relatively conservative dress. 'Who is up for a spin on the jet skis then?' said Kurt.

'I wouldn't mind a go,' said Louisa.

'Me too,' said Andy.

'I haven't been on one before though, so I'd prefer to double up if that's OK?' said Louisa. Kurt, ever the boy racer said, 'I'm sure Andy won't mind you doubling up with him, would you bud?' Andy smiled graciously and told Louisa she'd be welcome to ride with him.

The three of them made their way to the water's edge and ordered two jet skis. Kurt jumped on his and took off like a man possessed. 'I think we'll leave the kid to his tricks,' said Andy as he gently took his and Louisa's ski out onto open water.

A few hundred yards away there was a lot of shrieking and shouting. The Jenkins were there with all the mayhem that usually surrounded the family. Sam was drinking lager from a long glass while Diana was drinking sex on the beach. Her garish cocktail with its umbrella and sparkly twizzle stick somehow fitted into the family unit seamlessly. Tommy, Kyle and Jenson were all playing in the sea, splashing each other and dunking each other under the water. Kyle then decided it would be fun to soak their parents. The boys each filled a bucket with sea water and ran at their parents where they proceeded to empty the buckets of water all over them. As Sam and Diana were spluttering from shock, the boys were already refilling their buckets and squealing as they ran back towards their parents and threw more water over them. Mayhem ensued. Sam Jenkins shot up, his face purple with rage. Diana was screaming at the boys who were by then throwing water over anyone within a 12-feet radius of the Jenkins. Sam ran at them as fast as his overweight bulk would allow.

'You fucking little shitbags. Just wait till I get my fuckin' hands on you. I'll make you wish you'd never been born. Fuckin' get here, you bastards.'

Sun worshippers all around were appalled at Sam's language and the behaviour of their unruly children. Diana was screeching that she'd spilled her drink when she got drenched and was yelling at Sam to do something.

People all around, who were victims of the boy's behaviour, were standing up shouting at Sam and Diana. One man had grabbed Kyle's bucket and was refusing to give it back. Kyle was kicking the man while insulting him. Another man in his 30s grabbed Kyle to stop him kicking the older gentleman and Kyle started screaming at his father that he was being attacked. Sam immediately marched over to the fracas and with one punch he knocked the younger man to the ground. Sam grabbed Kyle's bucket from the older man and shoved him with such force that he stumbled back and fell over his wife.

'Don't you ever touch my kids or their stuff again, you bastard, do you hear me?' Sam was raging. He was stomping up and down the sand, his temper out of control. The people who had been around them were quickly gathering their belongings and moving away.

Within minutes, 20 feet of sand had been cleared of bodies and the Jenkins were alone. Diana was grabbing Sam's arm and trying to calm her husband with the promise of more alcohol.

'Come on Sam, forget those fuckers, they're nothing. Look at what we got? We got money and a nice house and we have good holidays. They're just jealous. Let's have another drink, eh? I fancy a blue lagoon this time. Do you want a lager?' Kyle, Jenson and Tommy were shouting for chips and coke.

'I wanna go on the banana boat!' shouted Jenson.

'Shut up you lot. Diana go get them their chips and get me a large Bacardi while you're at it. At least we got some space on the beach now that those boring old fuckers have gone. We'll have something to eat then we'll have some fun, eh kids?' Sam laughed so hard he had a coughing fit as Diana trundled up the beach with her brood.

Andy, Louisa and Kurt missed all the action on the beach as they were happily zipping about on their jet skis. Kurt was showing off to Louisa by riding really fast then turning on a sixpence, throwing up lots of spray and soaking them. Andy was enjoying the feel of Louisa's soft skin against his as she clung to him on the back of their ski. Kurt was already planning his evening with Louisa. The heat made him hornier than normal and he couldn't wait to get her into bed tonight.

The day passed relatively without incident. With the exception of Kyle Jenkins' face planting onto a shallow rock and splitting his lip open and cracking his front tooth, Sam's outburst on the beach and Sarah and Michelle's jibes at each other earlier that day, you could say that things had gone well in Antigua.

Tenders were running back and forth all day. By 6pm everyone was back on board *Opulence,* ready for a 9pm sail. Denise and Chris were sorting through the souvenirs from their shopping trip and Dr Alastair Wright-Porter was stitching up Kyle Jenkins' lip. *That boy would have a sore face for a few days,* thought the nurse as she watched Alastair Wright-Porter inject anaesthetic into Kyle's lip. Kyle screamed blue murder while Sam shouted at him not to be a wimp. Nurse Emma actually felt sorry for the boy.

Chris was feeling the divine fabrics of the scarves she bought as souvenirs. Denise had opened a bottle of the local liqueur and poured one for each of them. 'I wonder if The Jackdaws went ashore today?'

'Not sure Denise. They are playing in Zone One in a few days so they may have stayed on board to rehearse.'

'I can't wait to see them play, Chris. I'm so excited. We're their VIPs.' The girls laughed at the thought.

Todd and Ed had gone ashore in Antigua with Jessica and Olivia. They got as far as the first bar out of the port and that was their destination until they got ejected for lewd behaviour. The girls were over the moon that they were out with two of The Jackdaws and they were enjoying the attention from the boys, including the endless drinks and cocaine.

'I could get used to this life, Ed, if we didn't have to work,' laughed Todd. 'Did you hear Rocky lecturing us this morning about behaving and staying sober? When is he going to learn he's not my fucking boss?'

'I know what you mean, Todd, he's getting on my tits too. Mind you, there's a pair of tits I wouldn't mind getting on,' leered Ed as he lunged for Olivia's boobs. Olivia, Jessica and Todd laughed hysterically as Ed juggled Olivia's boobs in his hands while shoving his face between her cleavage. Olivia was wearing a thin chiffon top and crop jeans. Ed's frantic pawing released one breast from her bra and he then took it in his mouth. He sucked on her breast in full view of the other patrons and staff. Todd made a grab for Jessica's boobs and they were all still laughing and giggling when the manager came over and asked them to leave.

Todd was indignant and tried to use his fame to his advantage. 'Do you know who I am? You need to chill out man, we weren't doing any harm. You'll never fuckin' work again, you arsehole, I'll make sure of that.'

'I know exactly who you are and you're not welcome in my bar.'

With that, Todd upended his stool, swiped his arm across the bar and sent glasses and bottles crashing to the floor. The manager and two of his staff took Todd by the elbows and escorted him from the premises. Ed and the girls followed them out. Jess and Olivia were shouting to let Todd go and Ed was squaring up to the escorting party.

'Oh come on guys, let's go. This lot are a load of wankers. I don't want to drink in their poxy bar anyway.' Todd turned and gave the flip sign to the manager as he stormed off, followed by Ed and two wannabee WAGs teetering on their designer heels.

They jumped in a local taxi and were taken to another bar further inland where more or less anything goes and they continued their party until it was time to head back to the ship.

Dinner again was lively. Passengers were buoyed up by their time ashore and were excitedly swapping stories of their day. Jasper was his usual grumpy self. Sarah was her usual loud and bumptious self. Mia was exasperated by Sarah's behaviour and had held her tongue all day for the peace of the group, however poor Cosmo was getting it full barrels at dinner.

'What a bitch. I can't believe he puts up with that. I know he's miserable but she takes the biscuit. A trumped-up little tart with no manners. What on earth does he see in her, I wonder?'

'Who knows Mia? She must be good in bed', laughed Cosmo. Mia rolled her eyes and muttered for god to give her strength.

Michael Benson had enjoyed his day. Ogling at beauty and for once it wasn't him on the receiving end of Michelle's venom, he was upbeat. Michelle was still smarting at the way Sarah had dared to speak to her and Jasper's disinterest in her and Michael felt a sliver of satisfaction that the beautiful Sarah had put Michelle in her place. *She got what she deserved*, thought Michael.

Denise and Chris were chatting away excitedly, looking forward to the resident band Rum Punch in Zone One later that evening. Rocky had already told them that they wouldn't be at dinner tonight. As they were due to perform, they preferred to eat in their suite and gather themselves ready for the performance. Terry told Chris that they expected to see the girls right up front at the gig and that they'd be looking out for them. Terry invited them to join him and Rocky for drinks after the show.

Rocky and Terry were seething. Ed and Todd had turned up back on board just before *Opulence* was due to sail. They were very drunk and completely wasted. Rocky was worried that they were too wasted to perform. 'Ah, wind your feckin' neck in Rocky, will ya, we're fine. I'm going to bed for a couple of hours then I'll be right as rain. Stop panicking old man.' Todd turned and made his way to his bedroom, Ed following close behind towards his. Ed was so wasted he couldn't even speak.

'Something's got to change soon, Rocky. We can't go on like this.' Rocky just sighed and made his way onto the balcony.

'Do you want to order dinner now, Terry, or shall we wait for a bit?'

'Let's wait for an hour or so. I fancy a drink to say farewell to Antigua.' Terry picked up the phone and ordered two rum punches from room service. 'We'll sit out here and enjoy the sights, Rocky. It's beautifully balmy and we're not playing until 10pm tonight so we have plenty of time to chill. I'll check on the gruesome twosome in a couple of hours.' Rocky just smiled and settled down on a sunlounger. He closed his eyes and drifted off.

Olivia and Jessica were also wasted. They were at the Set Sail party in the Calypso Club. 'We need to like start tweeting photos of ourselves with Ed and Todd, Liv. That way it'll set the media ablaze and we'll like be famous soon.'

'By the time we get back, Jess, we'll be like stars, thanks to The Jackdaws.' They clinked their mojito glasses as they threw their heads back and laughed while gyrating to Rum Punch's calypso sounds.

Mia was looking forward to Tortola. 'I think tomorrow we should do our own thing, Cosmo. I don't want to be stuck in the middle of an atmosphere again.'

'Jasper has already asked me if we would like to team up with them tomorrow, Mia. I told him yes.' Mia rolled her eyes again. 'I don't suppose it will matter if it's just them and us I suppose. I really can't stand another day of Michelle Benson!'

'Sarah irritates the hell out of me,' drawled Mia 'but I can just about put up with her.'

'Did Jasper say what they were going to do?'

'He mentioned something about lunching at the Sugar Mill Hotel. Apparently, it's set into the hillside and runs down to the beach and is supposed to offer superb views.'

'OK that's fine. A quiet day is good for me.'

'I was rather hoping we could do something a bit more exciting than just sitting around, to be honest Mia. I'm not sure another day of peaceful relaxation will appease Sarah.'

'I'm sure there are other things to do on the island, Cosmo. You could always pop off for a couple of hours if you want?'

'Thanks Mia. I may just do that.'

'So Mia do you want to come to Zone One with us tonight? The Jackdaws are performing and I love them. Jasper doesn't think they are too bad either do you, Jas?' Jasper nodded and agreed that he quite liked The Jackdaws. He was into the bad boy image in a sadistic way but he did enjoy their music. 'Yes OK, we'll join you. Thank you. I love The Jackdaws too.'

'Hang on a minute guys. Don't you think we should invite Michael and Michelle?' said Cosmo.

'Oh do we have to?' huffed Sarah.

'I don't think it would look very nice if we were to completely ignore or ostracise them just because of your bad mouth, Sarah. I happen to like them so yes we should invite them to join us,' said Jasper.

'Whatever,' huffed Sarah as she rose from the table and headed towards the door. Jasper looked at Mia and Cosmo and shrugged his shoulders.

Once again the ship was coming alive. It was 9pm and there was a buzz of excitement throughout. Zone One was filling up quickly. It seemed that everyone on board wanted to see The Jackdaws in action and seats were quickly being filled.

Olivia and Jessica had rushed back to their suite after the Set Sail party and changed into their trashiest designer outfits. Crop tops and tight jeans, a fresh application of make-up, a line of cocaine and tequila shots completed the look. They were now firmly ensconced at the centre table at the front, with just the dance floor separating them from the stage. Their intention was to make their way to the front of the stage just before the boys came on. Looking round the club was a mish mash of characters. Practically every passenger was filling up the club. Super rich and moderately rich mingled with the disgustingly rich.

Jessica was sipping her cocktail and sussing out the competition around her. She was making mental notes of the other female passengers who may be in the correct age range for The Jackdaws. Jessica was not happy. There was an abundance of beauties on board and Jessica did not like competition. She was so spoiled she felt that she had first refusal on anything and anyone. Jessica had got in with Todd and Ed and as far as she was concerned that was it. They were off limits. Her celebrity life was not too far away in the future and she would do whatever it takes to get it. Jessica was spiteful and had a foul temper. Glancing back around the room, Jessica was thinking, *Watch out bitches, stay away or you'll have me to deal with!*

Mia, Cosmo, Jasper, Sarah, Michelle and Michael were sitting by the pool drinking champagne, waiting to make their way to Zone One. Sarah actually apologised to Michelle although she didn't really mean it, she just wanted Jasper to be in a good mood and it seemed to do the trick. Jasper was being very amenable. He was in a great mood and regaling the company with funny stories. He was quite the gentleman – charming and smouldering and Michelle was hanging on his every word. Sarah felt a pang of guilt as she watched her husband in full charm mode. This was the Jasper she fell in love with. Her guilt didn't last long though. Sarah had plans and they didn't include him.

Denise and Chris were merrily tipsy and had also made their way to Zone One early. They were seated in the front at the next table to Olivia and Jessica. Jess and Olivia were looking the girls up and down with disdain. They knew from Todd and Ed that Denise and Chris had caught the attention of Terry and Rocky and this wasn't lost on them. Jessica thought that just because she had money she should have the best of everything and that included the lead singer of The Jackdaws. She wasn't particularly pleased that they had ended up with Todd and Ed. Yes, they were Jackdaws but they weren't Rocky. What had those two bitches got that they didn't?

Denise and Chris were well aware of Jessica and Olivia. They didn't like their Hooray Henrietta attitudes. They thought they were rude and ignorant. Money can't buy manners!

Louisa, Kurt and Andy were enjoying post-dinner drinks in the atrium of the ship. They were watching the world go by and posing for photographs with other passengers. Louisa was dressed in head-to-toe leather and looking forward to watching The Jackdaws. Kurt was watching Louisa and looking forward to when they went to bed later. Andy was watching his bank balance and smiled to himself that his plan was unfolding nicely.

Sam and Diana Jenkins were in the middle of a full-blown argument on their balcony. The boys were running between rooms from the adjoining doors, chasing each other with pillows and towels. ‘Don’t be so bloody selfish, Sam. I want to see The Jackdaws as well. This is a once-in-a-lifetime opportunity.’

‘Look, you silly bitch. You have to be 18 to get into Zone One so you’ll need to stop here and look after the boys.’ ‘

Fuck off Sam, we can use the babysitting service. I’m not staying in.’

‘We’re not using the fucking babysitting service, you silly mare. You are their mother so you can have one night in with the little fuckers. I’m going out and if you don’t like it then you can book yourself and the brats on a flight back to the UK tomorrow when we dock. Now shut the fuck up, woman, and do as you’re told.’

Diana proceeded to throw the crystal lamp adorning the gorgeous table at Sam’s head. ‘You’re a selfish bastard, Sam Jenkins. I wish I’d never met you.’

‘That makes two of us, sweetheart now if I have to tell you to shut up again you’ll fuckin’ wish you’d never been born.’

Diana ran into the master bedroom and threw herself on the bed. She was crying her eyes out as her boys ran riot in the suite and her world crumbled around her.

Todd and Ed were drying themselves off from their power showers. Both had slept soundly for three hours and had been woken by Terry. Rocky had ordered them room service and an overflowing trolley of gourmet food had just been delivered. The boys knew that they had to have stamina to get through their set so Rocky ordered T-bone steaks, French fries, sides of broccoli, carrots, mash and runner beans. There was also an assortment of pasta dishes.

Rocky was pouring large tumblers of iced lemon water for them while Lewis was preparing to serve them. Todd and Ed were by no means completely sober but they were better than they had been earlier. Rocky had insisted they take a couple of painkillers and do what they needed to do to ensure they got through tonight without incident. Ed wanted a hair of the dog but Terry merely threw him a look which said 'don't even dare'.

The four Jackdaws came round the table together. The tension was palpable. Todd and Ed had missed the walkthrough and they knew they had pushed the boundaries. They knew they'd have to be a little humble as tonight was a very important night for them; there was a certain amount of tension between them still, however they were amenable knowing that tonight was important for them so they tucked into the platters of food before them with gusto. *Anything to keep Rocky quiet,* thought Todd.

Commodore Griffiths made an announcement on the ship's tanoy that The Jackdaws were making a special appearance in Zone One at 10pm and encouraged everyone to go and see the show.

The atmosphere in Zone One was electric as ninety-eight per cent of passengers packed into the club to see The Jackdaws. Crew in the other bars were relieved to have a well-deserved respite as their areas emptied in favour of Zone One.

The boys were always a little tense before a gig and this was no exception. They were going to play to some of the world's wealthiest with connections which could set them up for life. They changed into their own individual styled leathers and made their way at 9.45 to Zone One. They were taken round the back of the stage by an external entrance to the area adjacent to the lift. The sound checks had been done earlier and all was good. The lights were dimmed as the DJ announced that The Jackdaws would soon be on stage. There was a rush of hands in the air beckoning waiters as passengers ordered drinks prior to the start of the show. A waiter took a few jugs of iced water backstage for the boys as they ran through their final order of play.

A few of the younger element screamed as the lights dimmed

and a round of applause broke out as lots of passengers rushed onto the dance floor to the front of the stage. There was a barrier about three feet from the stage to stop over-excited passengers getting too close during the gig. Jess and Olivia were hot on the heels of Denise and Chris. Caught up in the melee, Jess found herself behind Denise and Chris and tried desperately to elbow her way forward. The lighting changed on the stage and a piece of drum music hailed the entrance of The Jackdaws. Rocky and the boys took their place on stage waving and smiling at the crowd before launching in to their first song, 'Real Houses and Butterflies'.

Zone One was heaving. Sweaty bodies cramped together on the dance floor as the boys rocked the roof off. Finally, after 80 minutes and many of their bestsellers like 'Concrete Credit Cards', 'The Wallflower', 'Ripped Hearts', 'Tomorrow's Destiny', 'Feel the Burn' and 'Playing Solo', they closed their gig with their latest and biggest hit, 'Green Beans'. Zone One erupted and the boys took their leave with air kisses, smiles and handshakes for the lucky passengers who barged their way to the front.

Rocky and the boys were sweating and elated at their performance. They toasted each other with fresh iced water and even Todd and Ed seemed to have sobered up completely and were more like the old Ed and Todd from Dublin.

The DJ was now hammering out the latest pop tunes and the club had started to thin out with many middle-aged passengers going to quieter areas for drinks. Denise and Chris went back and sat down while Jess and Olivia made a show of themselves on the dance floor. They had been drinking heavily all day and with the heat in the club their expensive make-up had decided to make a stand. Their mascara was running down their faces and there were big patches where foundation had melted away.

Todd came out from behind the stage and put his arms around the two girls. As he was leading them away to have some fun with him and Ed, Rocky came out and made his way to where Chris and Denise were sitting. A few of the passengers came forward for autographs and selfies as Terry joined him. The girls waited patiently for them to finish and then accepted their invitation to join them for the midnight buffet on deck. *It doesn't get any better than this*, thought Chris as they left Zone One and headed towards the lifts.

CHAPTER 8

Opulence docked in the British Virgin Island of Tortola at 6am. The weather looked set to be another glorious day.

The restaurants were quieter this morning in favour of in-suite dining. The crew put it down to too much of a good time at Zone One the previous night. Room service was kept busy as they delivered freshly squeezed fruit juices, eggs of all denominations and delicious freshly made breads and pastries. Fresh fruit was also a favourite and many exotic fruits were included in the breakfast.

A limousine arrived at the quayside to collect the Manzo party to take them to the Cove Blue Water Hotel. Michael and Michelle gave their apologies but decided to spend the day on board, making use of the spa facilities rather than visit Tortola as they had already spent time there on a previous holiday. The truth was that once again, Michelle had had too much to drink and was suffering a massive hangover and she didn't feel like going ashore. Michelle was selfish though and decided that Michael would not be going either. There was no way she was leaving him open to temptation when she wasn't there to keep an eye on his wandering eye.

The Manzo party made their way to the limousine and Sarah asked if they'd mind stopping off for some shopping first. Jasper groaned and told Sarah that the shopping in Tortola was not exactly Rodeo Drive. Cosmo interjected and said that he would also like to take some time looking around the town before heading to the hotel. Jasper, visibly miffed at Sarah's selfishness, turned to Mia for her reaction. Mia merely said that if Cosmo and Sarah wished to do some shopping and sightseeing they could meet up at the hotel later. Sarah grabbed Cosmo's hand and ushered him out of the limo. 'We'll eat at 1.30 so make sure you are there by then,' drawled Mia. The limousine started up as Jasper turned to Mia and said,

'Looks like it's just you and me then. I do hope you can put up with me for a few hours?'

Andy decided to take himself around Tortola alone. The day at the beach on Antigua was great but there's only so much of Kurt that he could take. Anyway, it looked like Kurt wouldn't be short of company today as he seemed to get on well with Louisa, if yesterday and last evening was anything to go by. Andy just hoped that Kurt wouldn't destroy Louisa but he acknowledged that she was an adult and needed to take care of herself. He wasn't her agent and he didn't intend to babysit both of them.

Todd and Ed had made their bleary way back to The Jackdaws' suite at 4am, after spending a few hours with Jess and Olivia. Rocky had arranged for the band to have a photo shoot in Tortola and when Todd found out that Denise and Chris had been invited to go along he insisted that Jess and Olivia should be invited. The eight of them jumped in the minibus and headed inland to the unspoilt beauty of Tortola to meet the photo shoot crew. Rocky was already irritated with the noise from Ed, Todd, Olivia and Jess. They were screeching and talking loudly as though it was Jess and Olivia who were the stars.

Rocky and Terry raised their eyebrows at Denise and Chris, as the four of them tried to stifle their giggles at the meaning of the boys' actions.

Michael Benson was in a foul mood. 'Look here Michelle, you are the one who can't handle your drink. Why should I be forced to stay behind with you while everyone else is off enjoying themselves?'

'Oh shut up Michael. I know exactly why you wanted to go with them, don't think for a minute that I'm stupid. I'm not having it and neither are you, if you excuse the pun. I don't trust you and I'm giving you no room to mess up my career so get used to it.' Michael stormed out of their suite slamming the door behind him and headed to the Calypso Club for a drink.

Jasper and Mia were sitting on the terrace of the Cove Blue Water, drinking margaritas. The view was spectacular and the air warm. Mia looked stunning with her long blonde hair hanging in loose curls and her Gucci sunglasses shading her sparkling blue eyes. Mia was dressed in a white Gucci lace summer dress with strappy sandals, her tanned legs flattered by the lace hem of her dress.

Jasper looked at his watch and wondered where Cosmo and Sarah had got to. 'We told them 1.30, didn't we? Where the hell could they be? I'll bet Sarah has found something and disregarded the time as usual,' exclaimed Jasper.

'Oh don't worry, darling. We will go ahead and order lunch for ourselves. If and when they deign to join us they can see to themselves.' Mia picked up the menu and asked Jasper what he wanted. 'I think I'll have the arugula and beet salad; I need to watch my weight.'

'You look great Mia, have some fries,' laughed Jasper. 'I think I'll have the lobster,' said Jasper, motioning to the waiter to come and take their order.

'Isn't this just beautiful, Jasper? I could stay here forever. Sometimes I wonder if the pressures of Hollywood are worth it. There are times I just want a normal existence.'

Suddenly their tranquillity was shattered as a loud 'Yoo-hoo!' pierced the air. Jasper groaned with embarrassment as Sarah bounded towards them, adorned in cheap trinkets bought from local sellers. Cosmo followed sedately behind, looking very handsome in his navy shorts, white t-shirt and navy deck shoes. Cosmo was au natural and his face was fresh and attractive without make-up. Cosmo kissed Mia on both cheeks and apologised for their tardiness.

'A truck carrying local fruit overturned on the main road leading to the cliff route and it's absolute chaos. At least we are here now. I'm starving.' Cosmo grabbed the menu and immersed himself in it. Sarah looked drunk. Her inane grin and slightly slurred speech was a dead giveaway.

'Have you been drinking, Sarah?' asked Jasper.

'Nothing like stating the obvious is there?' laughed Sarah.

'Yeah, I had a couple of drinks, so what? Have you got a problem with that?'

Jasper glanced towards Mia and Cosmo. His jawline taut and his eyes flashing with anger. Jasper ignored Sarah as she continued to show Mia her 'tat' bought in the town centre.

'Did you buy anything, Cosmo?'

'No, there was nothing to take my fancy. I just took myself off for a walk and strolled around while Sarah was shopping.' Cosmo seemed a little tense and not his usual unflappable self.

'You need something to eat, darling,' said Mia, thrusting the menu towards him. Cosmo didn't bother to look at the menu. He asked Sarah if she was ready to order and beckoned the waiter over.

'I'll have the Cove burger and a beer,' said Cosmo.

'And I'll have the linguine and a strawberry Dakari,' giggled Sarah. 'Hey Jas, did you see the gorgeous jewellery in the hotel's shop? There's a lovely diamond bracelet in the cabinet.'

'Well I'm sure it's quite happy in the cabinet, Sarah, as that's where it's staying.' Sarah's face dropped and she became petulant. The atmosphere for the second day running had changed for the worse due to Sarah's attitude. Cosmo looked from Mia to Jasper and shrugged his shoulders.

'Ah here's our drinks. Bottoms up, chaps,' said Cosmo in his best British accent.

At the southern end of the island in the hills, the photo shoot was well underway. The Jackdaws, dressed in their trademark leather rocker outfits leaning against palm trees, surrounded by stunning flora. Jess and Olivia milled around the photographer hoping to get asked to join in with a few photos of their own, while Chris and Denise went for a short walk, taking in the breathtaking scenery. Chris and Denise couldn't be happier. Rocky and Terry were real gentlemen and they knew that they genuinely liked them. Their relationships had moved forward quite quickly after the boys' outstanding gig last night. Rocky and Terry spent the whole night in the girls' suite. Nothing sexual took place but they snuggled up to each other, Rocky and Denise and Terry and Chris in their individual rooms. They kissed and spooned. All of them wanted to take it further but the girls wanted to wait until they were sure they could trust the boys and Rocky and Terry were well brought up and wouldn't push themselves on the girls until they were ready.

'Will you move away from the camera please?' An annoyed photographer swiped at Jessica with his hand as he tried to angle the camera for the last shots.

'Keep your wig on honey, I like only want to watch what you're doing. Honestly, anyone would, like, think you were Gilles Bensimon. I'll bet you've never had anyone like as famous as The Jackdaws to shoot before, have you?' Dan the photographer shot Jessica a filthy look and yelled at his assistant Marie to remove Jess and Olivia immediately. 'Get those irritating bitches out of here now!' Turning towards Todd, he curtly told him, 'I have a job to do. You are paying me good money to get these shots and I won't have it ruined by some jumped-up little tarts with no respect.' Todd started to argue with Dan. 'Hey man, you need to chill. They're not doing anything wrong.' Rocky shot Todd a glare and told him, 'Shut up. They're a pain in the arse now just bloody let's get this over with and then you can do what you want with them.'

Todd was furious and his dark gaze finally gave Dan what he was looking for. A sultry shot of three of the boys leaning against palm trees, with Terry crouching among the birds of paradise and holding his finger to his mouth in a 'shhhh' gesture.

Jessica could be heard in the background shouting. 'Get off me, you pleb. Like who the fuck do you think you are?'

'You are disrupting the shoot, so you need to leave. Go and wait in the minibus, they should be done soon.' Al, a hulking security guard from New Jersey, appeared by Marie's side. 'You got a problem here?'

'No, it's fine. The girls are going to sit in the bus until we've wrapped.' Al opened the door to the minibus and stood aside, gesturing with his hand for them to get in. Jessica was furious and shouted, 'Daddy will sue the arse off of all of you for, like, treating me this way. Just you wait and see.'

Dan called the wrap and everyone relaxed. Everyone that is except Todd who took exception to the way his girl had been treated. Denise and Chris returned from their walk just as the boys were packing their things up and loading the minibus. 'Let's get back to the town centre and Todd can do what he wants,' said Terry. Rocky nodded and told the girls to get on board and be prepared for a rough ride.

Kurt and Louisa were strolling through the town centre looking at souvenirs and being stopped occasionally by excited tourists who recognised them. 'Shall we just get back to the ship, Kurt? I think I've seen enough for today.'

'Yeah, come on babe, let's go. We can have a dip in the pool and get jiggy on the balcony.' Kurt laughed at his suggestion as he grabbed Louisa's hand and dragged her towards the port.

Michelle Benson was fuming. How dare Michael take off like that this morning! Where was he? Who was he with? Did he go ashore or is he still on the ship? Michelle's mind was working overtime and she was working herself into a frenzy. She'd tried calling his mobile 23 times since he'd stormed out but he wasn't responding. She'd sent 16 texts and they too had been ignored. Michelle walked the length and breadth of the ship looking for him but to no avail.

Michael was sitting alone in a wooden shack bar located on the outskirts of the town centre. The bar was called The Raggedy Man and Michael looked just that. If it wasn't for his expensive watch and sunglasses, you could easily mistake him for a hobo. He was drunk and very angry as he heard his mobile ring yet again. Looking at the digital display, Michael saw Michelle's name appear as the caller. Michael pressed the reject button and ordered another beer with a whisky chaser. *Why won't she just leave me alone and let me be? I'm sick of the woman. Our marriage is a sham; our lives are a sham. She's fame crazy and will do anything to stay in the spotlight including forcing me into staying in this farce of a marriage. I hate her. I wish she was dead.*

The sun shone, the alcohol flowed and the crew went about their business readying themselves for the evening ahead.

Opulence departed Tortola on a warm evening. Dinner was served as usual in the decadent splendour of designer gowns, diamonds and black tie. All was as it should be with the exception of the absence of Michael Benson at dinner. Michelle was fuming with her husband who had returned from shore a little the worse for wear. Michael had refused to go to dinner with the screaming shrew and told her to 'Fuck off' and do what she wanted. He would order room service and have his meal brought to their suite. Michelle was spitting feathers and threatening Michael that if their popularity waned and they lost their place on TV she would never forgive him and she would make him pay.

Michael laid on the bed, drifting into an alcohol-fuelled sleep. His memories taking him back to earlier in the day when he had managed to catch some special stolen moments with his love.

Michelle was sitting alone at their table explaining to Mia and Cosmo that Michael had caught too much sun and was suffering with heatstroke so he was resting in their suite. Mia cordially invited Michelle to join her and Cosmo and the waiters quickly arranged a place for Michelle at Mia's table.

Dinner passed without much event. Michelle excused herself saying she was going to have a walk on deck and blow away some cobwebs. Truth be told, she was still furious with Michael and wanted to stay as far away from him as possible. She was also hoping to bump into Jasper who she overheard telling Sarah that he was going to the Cigar Lounge after dinner. The Cigar Lounge was located starboard aft on Deck 6 and Michelle knew that it was likely that Jasper would notice her from the glass windows framing the deck as she strolled past.

Mia and Cosmo retired to their respective suites for an early night and left everyone to go about their nightly desires.

CHAPTER 9

St Maarten dawned balmy and calm with the promise of another scorching day ashore. The ship was wakening up with the usual bustle, excited for the adventure awaiting them on terra firma, with temperatures forecast for a balmy 93 degrees Fahrenheit.

Michael Benson awakened in his suite feeling a little worse for wear. His head throbbed and his mouth was dry. His bed was empty and he listened for Michelle in the bathroom. Rising slowly, he made his way through to the lounge area and called Lewis. 'Please can you bring some freshly squeezed apricot juice?' Michael made his way to the balcony where he would wait for his juice and Michelle to free up the bathroom.

Rob, Louisa, Kurt, Denise, Chris, The Jackdaws, Mia, Cosmo and the Teasdales had all previously agreed to meet and breakfast together in The Oyster.

The Porpoise Restaurant was fairly empty, with the majority of passengers opting for the relaxed Lobster Pot. The Jenkins were there as usual with their unruly brood. Sam Jenkins was a little subdued. He'd been asked to go and see the chief security officer the previous evening. Scott McDonald was an ex Royal Marine who joined the Purple Star Line as security advisor ten years before. Scott had received a plethora of complaints about the Jenkins family since they boarded at Southampton. Most of the complaints were in connection with the unruly behaviour of the boys and the foul language used by the whole family. However, Scott was more concerned with the abuse of the boys by their father and after discussion with Commodore Griffiths it was decided that Scott would speak to Sam Jenkins and put an end to this once and for all.

Sam Jenkins arrived at Scott's office situated on Deck 2 at 9pm the previous evening. He had no idea why he'd been asked to attend and was belligerent at having to lose precious drinking time to speak to the stuck-up officers.

Senior Officer Scott McDonald wasted no time in getting to the point. 'Ultimately, Mr Jenkins, if your abusive behaviour towards your children continues then I will have you removed from the ship and handed over to the police to face charges of child abuse. Do you understand me?'

Sam Jenkins was stunned. He thought it was a joke. 'I don't make jokes at the expense of children's welfare, Mr Jenkins. I trust I will not have to speak to you regarding this again? I have to inform you however that I intend to speak to Children's Services and the police when we arrive back in the UK. Our CCTV images and crew statements will support my complaint. Oh, and before you go, please be aware of your language in the public areas of the ship. Your language and that of your family is unacceptable and we will not allow it to continue. If necessary, we will have you removed from this vessel.'

Sam Jenkins did not know what to say. He knew he could be in real trouble and the last thing he wanted was to draw more attention to himself. He had things to think about and left the office with an apology and a promise that it wouldn't happen again.

Sam and his family were seated at a large round table in the corner of The Lobster Pot. The boys were noisy but seated. Sam and Di had talked the night before after Sam's talk with security. They both knew that they couldn't continue like this. They had to discipline their boys but it had to be done without beating them. Sam did not want to end up in some Caribbean jail.

Jenson was shouting to get his dad's attention. 'Dad, Dad I saw a man kill a woman last night.' Sam and Di were deep in conversation about how to proceed with disciplining their spoiled brood. 'DAD! I saw a man kill a woman last night!' screamed Jenson. Sam turned quickly to Jenson and told him through gritted teeth to be quiet.

'Listen Jenson, I won't tell you again. Stop shouting and stop making up these stupid stories. The other day you were running your mouth about the neighbours at number Thirty one and their drug dealing and look where that got us? It nearly got me arrested.

You're nearly ten years old and too old to be attention-seeking like this. Now shut up and stop shouting.' Something in Sam's unusually calm demeanour scared Jenson enough to clam up and eat his breakfast. Kyle and Tommy also stopped their boisterous banter and looked at their dad with surprise. They hadn't seen Sam like this before and were wary of the situation. They sensed an underlying calmness which to them spelled danger. They weren't used to Sam being subdued and not raising his voice. Di suggested a new game for the family to play. Everyone had to talk and not shout and the first one to shout would have to go to bed at 7pm. Now if there was one thing the Jenkins boys hated it was bedtime. They liked to do as they pleased and their parents were lax on bedtime rules. They went to bed when they fell asleep. The boys grinned and thought this new game sounded good fun. Each one eager to see which of their siblings – or mum and dad for that matter – would end up with a 7pm bedtime.

Mia and Cosmo strolled around the promenade deck soaking up the sunshine. *Opulence* had docked in St Maarten but Mia had decided that she would rather spend the day on board. Sarah and Michelle's niggling had become tiresome and Mia would be quite happy sitting by the pool sipping cocktails. *It's not as if I've never been to St Maarten before,* thought Mia. *Who knows, I may even find something else to keep me occupied?* Mia smiled to herself as she linked arms with Cosmo and giggled as the breeze wafted through her hair.

The Jackdaws were again at loggerheads. Todd and Ed had spent the night with Olivia and Jessica and barely grunted at Rocky and Terry when they returned to the suite to shower and change. Todd and Ed intended to spend the day with the girls in St Maarten. They were sure they would find a decent bar not far from the port.

Rocky and Terry had spoken with their agent via a Skype call and between them decided that when they returned to the UK, they would leave the band and look at setting up as a duo. This decision was huge and both boys had doubts, but these were outweighed by the tension and atmosphere as it was. Ed and Todd were beyond redemption. They had let the fame and trappings that went with it go to their heads. They took so many drugs they were constantly wired and incapable of common sense. Rocky and Terry were unsure about whether to tell Ed and Todd about their decision before the end of the cruise but until then they were going to come to terms with the fact that The Jackdaws were breaking up. A day with Chris and Denise just relaxing would do them good. The boys grabbed their sunglasses and high-fived each other as they went to collect the girls.

Sarah waved goodbye to Jasper from the bottom of the gangway. Sarah was intending to put her plan into action and grasped the opportunity when Jasper was complaining that he needed time to Skype his CEO regarding a deal opportunity which presented itself last night following a conversation in the Cigar Lounge with a business executive from Japan.

'I don't mind if you want to stay on board, Jas. I am happy to go ashore on my own. I'm sure I'll bump into someone to keep me company anyway. I think Louisa is intending on going so I may tag along with her.'

'OK, that'll suit me. This deal could take the company to the stratosphere so you go ahead and enjoy yourself. I'll see you when you get back later this afternoon.'

Sarah pulled up her cream lace shorts which accentuated her gorgeous long tanned legs and said a silent prayer which thanked god that the Japanese businessman had made Jasper's acquaintance the night before. *That was easier than I thought, now for some real spending.*

'Thank fuck that stupid bitch has given me some space. I'll spend an hour Skyping with Jarvis and move this deal forward then I may have time for some fun.' Jasper fired up his laptop and sent a text to a willing partner. 'She's up for it as much as I am so let the Teasdale do some teasing.' Jasper started laughing hysterically at his own joke while fantasising about what would transpire later.

'Your fresh apricot juice, Mr Benson.'

'Thank you, Lewis, just leave it here if you will?'

'How are you and Mrs Benson this morning, sir?'

'A little under the weather if I'm honest Lewis. I had too much to drink yesterday and don't think I'll be going far today. I'm trying to clear my head with sea air but I think I may be forced to take some painkillers.' Lewis smiled and produced a packet of headache tablets from his pocket.

'I always come prepared, sir. Perhaps a couple of these will help?' Michael thanked Lewis and advised him, 'Mrs Benson is having a shower. I'll stay here until she's finished. You know what these women are like.'

'Will there be anything else, sir?'

'No thank you Lewis. I'll take these tablets and have an easy day I think. My body won't allow me to do much else.' Michael smiled weakly as Lewis left.

He picked up two tablets and popped them in his mouth. He washed them down with the fresh apricot juice and grimaced at its chilled sweet taste. He laid back on the sunlounger and closed his eyes. 'Just a few minutes resting my eyes until Michelle's finished in the bathroom.'

Opulence was once again quiet, with the majority of passengers taking advantage of the beautiful island of St Maarten.

Mia was taking a leisurely swim in the infinity pool. Kurt was also in the pool. He seemed fairly normal today. He hadn't taken any cocaine for a few hours and he was as sober as he could be. Kurt was chatting with Mia and telling her some colourful tales of a young popstar. Mia merely laughed and remembered herself 25 years ago.

'Would you like another drink, Mia?'

'Yes Kurt, that would be lovely, thank you.'

Kurt helped Mia out of the pool and handed her a towel while he beckoned a waiter over. 'What would you like Mia?'

'I'll have a Grey Goose with fresh lime and lots of ice,' said Mia.

'Sounds cool; I'll have the same, mate.'

Kurt looked Mia up and down. She was a beauty, there was no getting away from that and despite being old enough to be his mum she was fit. 'I wonder if I'm in with a chance here?' thought Kurt, as they settled onto the plush sunloungers to dry off and await their drinks.

The day flew by in another heat haze filled with champagne, cocktails and hangover cures.

By 4pm, *Opulence* was starting to come to life again. Afternoon tea was being served. Waiters served the guests with the most delicious finger sandwiches, pastries and scones with cream and jam. Those on the deck rushed their afternoon tea to stop the bread curling up and the cream melting. It was fun to take it on deck but in searing heat such as this even the best cuisine became casualties.

Andy had returned from his trip ashore with a few souvenirs for his nieces. He needed to speak to Kurt as he'd met up with Manny Dubrow the previous night and they had discussed Kurt breaking in to the world of film and TV. This was the meeting that Andy had set his sights on and it had finally happened. He'd arranged to meet Kurt at 5pm in his suite and was happy to leave Kurt to his own devices for the day, fully aware that Louisa had been seen with Sarah as they disembarked earlier.

Michael opened his eyes slowly. The sun was blinding and he was squinting as he tried to sit himself up. 'Oh dear god, what has happened?' Michael sat up and blinked in quick succession. He finally found his bearings. He was sitting on the sunlounger with a jug of curdled apricot juice on the table next to him. Slowly he started to remember. He woke with a hangover this morning and Lewis gave him some painkillers for his head. *I must have drifted off again while waiting for Michelle to finish her shower,* thought Michael. He looked down at himself and saw that his arms and legs were bright red. He'd been lying in full sunshine for hours and was burned to a crisp. *Oh my god, look at me! If I'm like this now, what will I be like in a few hours? Why didn't Michelle waken me or at least cover me up? I know she's pissed off with me, but surely she wouldn't be this cruel to let me burn and get sunstroke?* Michael got up gingerly, wincing from the stiffness caused by his sleeping posture and the sunburn. He made his way from the balcony to the lounge and shouted for Michelle. There was no response so he made his way through the suite, room by room looking for her. Michelle was nowhere to be seen. *Lairy bitch*, thought Michael. *She could have at least woken me up before she went out.*

Michael gasped as he caught sight of himself in the full-length mirrors in the dressing area of the suite. 'Dear god, look at the state of me!'

Michael was the colour of a ripe tomato. His face and neck, three-quarters of his arms and from the bottom of his shorts to his toes were glowing. *I'm going to hurt like hell unless I can get some help here*, thought Michael. He went to the telephone and called Lewis. 'Can you deliver me a few buckets of ice, please? I want to take an ice bath.'

Michael ran the large jacuzzi tub with cold water. He switched the air conditioning to full and prepared some body cream to help with damage limitation when he had finished his bath. Lewis and three stewards arrived carrying large domestic rubber buckets of ice. They proceeded to fill the bath with the ice while Lewis asked Michael if he would like him to call the doctor.

Michael declined the offer of the doctor, satisfied that he would be fine after his bath but he asked Lewis to procure some aftersun to help sooth his burn. Michael waited for the crew to leave then gingerly stripped off his t-shirt, shorts and underpants. He stepped into the tub, wincing at the freezing temperature as he did so. Slowly he lowered his body into the water until it covered his shoulders. He used a flannel to place across his forehead and he splashed iced water over his face. Michael lay back and hoped that the damage wouldn't be too great but he wasn't holding out much hope. *Where the hell is my wife?* he thought.

Sarah returned to her suite looking tanned and relaxed. Jasper was there, looking equally tanned and relaxed. He was in the jacuzzi on the balcony enjoying a Chivas Regal on the rocks.

'Did you have a nice time in St Maarten?' asked Jasper.

'It was lush, Jas. You should see some of them houses on the island.'

'Houses? You went sightseeing rather than shopping?'

Sarah laughed as she flicked her sleek hair back over her shoulders, 'Yer, I went for a cultural day, Jas.'

'Did you meet Louisa?'

'Yer, I saw Louisa as we were getting off this morning and we hooked up. What have you been doing? Did your business call go well?'

Jasper was stunned. Sarah never took an interest in his business dealings unless it was to ask how many millions he'd made from a deal. 'There's a long way to go with this deal yet. It's in its infancy but I'm hopeful it'll go well.'

'Oh good, now what am I going to wear tonight?' Sarah was already making her way to the bedroom through the patio doors which separated it from the balcony. Jasper shook his head in resignation. Nothing would ever change with Sarah. She was a bimbo and would amount to nothing.

Sarah disappeared into the bedroom and went straight to the bathroom to run a bath. As it was filling, she went to her dressing room. She removed a slip of paper from her Louis Vuitton and hid it in a secret compartment of her matching jewellery box which was located in the large safe. Not long now, not long now.

Cosmo was in his suite talking on the phone with David. 'Listen David, I can't see you tonight, OK? I'm busy with Mia. She wants me to take her to the casino later and then there's the midnight buffet so I won't have time to slip away. Let's leave it for another night. You're beginning to act like a wife.' Cosmo laughed lightly but David was seething on the other end of the phone. He'd been on duty most of the day and was due off at 6pm. He rang Cosmo to arrange a liaison but Cosmo was decidedly cool today.

'Listen Cosmo, I've been at your beck and call since we sailed and you know I like you but I want more time with you. I thought I could come to your suite later and we could hang out in your outside tub?'

'Not tonight, David. I really am busy. Don't' forget Mia is my employer and I'm working. Another time, eh? I'll contact you.' Cosmo put the phone down. Boy was that guy getting in deep. It was only a bit of fun after all.

David slammed the phone down in the office which led off from the Pursers Desk. 'Fuckin bastard,' he fumed. 'I'm sure Mia Manzo won't be up all fucking night. He could make time for me. What the fuck is wrong with him?'

Amanda, his on-duty colleague, heard the phone slam and knew that her last hour on duty was likely to be bumpy. When David was in a mood it was best to ignore him. *Roll on 6pm,* Amanda thought as a thunderous looking David emerged from the office and took his place at the front desk.

Michael stayed in his ice bath for an hour. He could feel the water beginning to turn warm and the ice had melted. He rose from the tub and stepped onto the cool marble floor. His skin was beginning to sting and despite the towels being soft and fluffy he wasn't going to chance drying himself off. *I'll go on to the balcony and drip dry I think,* thought Michael. He stopped to pour himself a large glass of iced water from the bar before going onto the balcony. The heat hit him like a slap to the face. His sunburn started stinging within minutes and he felt the beginnings of another headache; he thought that this may be sunstroke and it was unlikely he would venture far again this evening. He would order from The Oyster and have it delivered. *I wonder how Michelle will be when she sees this? She's in a foul mood as it is and has been avoiding me since last night. No doubt this will tip her over the edge. I know her well enough to realise that she'll think I'm an embarrassment to her. I really don't want to hear her whinging voice right now.*

Michael returned to the suite and donned his fluffy white robe emblazoned with the Purple Cross Crest. It was slightly uncomfortable on his shoulders but as long as he sat still and didn't let it rub he'd cope. Michael was hungry but he also felt nauseous. *Perhaps something light will calm my stomach,* thought Michael as he picked up the menu to decide what he wanted to eat while he waited for Michelle to show her nasty face.

The Jenkins family had passed a reasonably nice day in St Maarten. The boys were fairly well behaved for a change and were all desperately trying to win the game which they'd been set that morning. Sam was still loud but he was more aware of his aggressive manner and swearing and he did try to tone it down. Di was also doing her best to be a pillar of society. She kept the boys in line and reminded them of their manners. Sam was quite impressed with them and bought them each a toy of their choice. When they returned to the ship, they even voluntarily handed over their new toys to the security staff while they were being checked back on board. Jenson approached Senior Security Officer Scott McDonald and proceeded to tell him that he saw a man kill a woman last night. Scott bent down and told him he must have had a bad dream as murders don't happen on *Opulence*. Jenson shook his head and told Scott that he did see it happen and that the man had his hands round the lady's neck and strangled her. Scott just smiled at Jenson as Di again pulled her protesting son away and explained that he had such a wild imagination. Scott McDonald was pleased to see a new calmness had settled on the Jenkins family but how long would it last? He was keeping a very close eye on them.

Andy, Louisa and Kurt joined Cosmo, Mia, Sarah and Jasper for drinks in the Champagne Flute before going to the casino. 'Has anyone seen Michael and Michelle today?' asked Mia. The shaking of heads and 'No' coming from the group instigated discussion as to where the Bensons could have got to.

'Did they go ashore?' asked Sarah.

'They weren't with me,' responded Andy.

'Mia and I didn't go ashore and we haven't seen either of them all day,' said Cosmo.

'I haven't seen them either,' said Louisa.

'Neither did I,' said Jasper.

'I hope they are OK? Perhaps someone should go and see if everything is alright?' said Cosmo.

'I agree, Cosmo. Off you go and tell them they are welcome to join us if they wish,' ordered Mia. Cosmo took his leave and made his way to the Benson's suite.

When the door to the suite opened, Cosmo could barely contain his laughter. Stood before him looking like a belisha beacon was Michael Benson. He was wrapped in the customary Purple Cross White Robe but his face and legs were scarlet. He looked hysterical.

'OMG!' exclaimed Cosmo. 'What on earth has happened, darling?'

Michael led the way to the lounge, hobbling and hunched, and sat down slowly. His skin had started to tighten up with the burns and he was in lots of pain. Cosmo followed him concerned for his welfare.

'I fell asleep on the balcony this morning and only woke around 4ish. I'd been in the sun with no shade all day and as you see I'm badly burnt.'

Cosmo gasped at the severity of the situation as realisation of what happened dawned on him. 'Why didn't Michelle waken you? Why did she let you sleep that long without intervening? Talking of Michelle, where is she?'

'I don't know. I haven't seen her since yesterday morning. We had a bit of an argument and I stormed off. I got rather drunk and I passed out when I got back to the ship yesterday. I don't really remember much until I woke this morning. She was in the shower when I got up and I fell asleep on the balcony. I thought she may have gone to the spa or somewhere when I woke earlier but I haven't seen her since. I think she's really pissed off with me.' Michael gave a small smile but winced at the pain.

'She wasn't at dinner tonight but as you know the ship is huge and she could be anywhere. My guess is that she's still avoiding you and wants to worry you. She'll no doubt flounce in later,' said Cosmo. He then realised that Michael was in a bad way and said he needed to see the doctor. Michael protested but Cosmo insisted and made his way to the phone. He called Lewis and asked him to arrange for the doctor to visit immediately. Cosmo then set about making Michael comfortable. Cosmo had taken a course in first aid and this was his chance to show what he could do.

He lifted Michael's legs up onto the soft leather sofa and plumped up some cushions behind his back. He filled the empty glass with iced water and made Michael take copious sips. He went to the bathroom and brought back a cold flannel which he placed on Michael's forehead. Michael's eyelids were already swelling and he looked very uncomfortable. Cosmo fussed around Michael, refilling his glass as soon as it was empty and waited until Doctor Hans Liebherr arrived with Nurse Caroline. Hans Leibherr was 37 years old and had worked for the Purple Cross Line for four years. He was an excellent physician and adored by all his patients and the crew.

'Now then Mr Benson, what have you been doing with yourself?' Michael weakly explained that his wife was taking a shower and he had stupidly fallen asleep on the balcony. Hans examined Michael thoroughly and announced the obvious. Michael was suffering from severe sunstroke and sunburn. He praised Cosmo for making Michael drink and for the cold flannel to try and reduce his temperature.

'I think it would be better for you to spend the night in the infirmary where we can keep an eye on you, Mr Benson. Your temperature is raised, you are severely dehydrated and I want to put in an IV line. We can also give you gel packs and cream to ease the pain of the burning.'

Michael started to protest but Cosmo jumped in and insisted he go. 'I will find Michelle and let her know what has happened, Michael. You need to get yourself well again and it's probably only going to be for one night, isn't it doctor?' Doctor Hans agreed that if he responded well and his temperature returned to normal he could come back to his suite tomorrow.

Michael was feeling so poorly by now that he agreed. Nurse Caroline rang for a stretcher chair to be brought to the suite and Michael was duly carted off to the Medical Centre.

Cosmo returned to the Champagne Flute where the others were waiting. An hour had passed and Mia was visibly annoyed. 'Where have you been, Cosmo? I asked you to call on the Bensons, not gallivant around the ship. We are waiting to go to the casino.'

Cosmo quickly explained what had happened. He left out the details about the argument but explained in his own inimitable style about how poor Michael had been carted off to the Medical Centre for the night as his body temperature was so high it could kill him. Audible gasps erupted from the group. Everyone was visibly shaken. 'Poor Michael. I do hope he's going to be alright?' said Jasper. 'Should we go and see him do you think?' asked Louisa.

'I don't think he's to have any visitors tonight guys. It's 10.30pm and they're stabilising him now. He'll be fine I'm sure but I expect he'll just want to sleep as soon as they get his pain under control. I do however think we need to find Michelle. None of us have seen her tonight so maybe we should go looking for her and let her know about Michael.'

'Good idea Cosmo, we should split up and take different areas of the ship and meet back here in an hour. Does everyone agree? Are you all happy to do that? The casino doesn't close until 5am anyway.' Andy remarked.

The group quickly split themselves into search teams, agreed to meet back at the Champagne Flute at 23.45 and dispersed on the hunt for Michelle.

An hour later the group started returning to the bar in dribs and drabs. 'Any luck?' asked Andy. Everyone shook their heads. There was no sign of Michelle anywhere.

'Did anyone go to their suite to see if she had gone back there?' asked Mia.

'She's not there, Mia. I checked there before coming back here,' said Cosmo.

'This is very strange don't you think?' said Jasper. 'No one has seen her all day.'

'Michael said she was in the shower when he woke this morning,' announced Cosmo.

'Perhaps she went in to St Maarten, got pissed and missed the boat,' laughed Sarah.

Jasper shot her a filthy look as he tore into her. 'Shut up, Sarah. Michelle hasn't been seen for some time. This is cause for concern not for your pathetic and unfunny jokes.'

Sarah, glared at Jasper and spat back, 'Funny how you're always concerned about everyone else Jasper. If it was me, you wouldn't bat an eye, would you? But Mrs Goody Two Shoes Benson goes missing and suddenly you're full of concern.'

Jasper stood quickly and excused himself. 'If you don't mind, I'm off to the casino now. I'll catch up with you later.' Jasper turned and walked away his eyes burning into his wife.

The group were embarrassed at what just happened between the Teasdales. They decided to join Jasper in the casino but no one's heart was really in it any longer. The fact that Michelle hadn't been seen for some time and her husband was in the Medical Centre had somehow put a dampener on the night. Sarah told the group she wasn't joining them and flounced off on her own. No one seemed very sorry to see her go.

CHAPTER 10

Opulence sailed gracefully through the night from St Maarten to St Kitts. Jasper won £200,000 on roulette and Cosmo won £83,000 on blackjack. Both were jovial and invited the group to the Commodore Club for a nightcap. A great cheer went up and Kurt shouted that it was Cristal all round as they could afford it. Everyone laughed as they made their way to the Commodore Club.

The club was fairly quiet. It was 2.30am and most of the passengers had gone to bed. The group sat themselves at the rear of the club on a plush semi- circular banquette in purple and white velvet. The waiter took their order for two bottles of Cristal and duly served the happy group without delay.

'I wonder if Michelle's shown up yet? I left a note in her suite about Michael and told her we were going to the casino but I'm worried that she hasn't turned up.'

'Don't worry, Cosmo,' said Louisa. 'I'm sure she'll be fine. I must admit, though, that I too am beginning to wonder where she could be.'

'I'm going to speak to the purser,' announced Cosmo. 'Michelle hasn't been seen for hours and I think we need to report it, especially with her husband lying in the Medical Centre.'

'Listen Cosmo, why don't we finish our drinks then we'll both go and check if she's back in her suite? She may have got wasted and not seen the note. If she's not there, then I'll go with you and we'll report her missing.' Everyone agreed this was the best way forward and they finished the two bottles of champagne.

Andy and Cosmo made their way to the Bensons' suite. Andy decided it would be best if Louisa went to her suite and settled for the night and reassured her that he and Cosmo would take care of finding Michelle. The corridors were quiet and the lighting dimmed. Andy rang the bell and knocked on the door. They waited but there was no reply. Just then, Kam the assistant butler popped his head out of the crew pantry which was situated about 30 feet away. Cosmo beckoned to Kam who quickly joined them. He explained what had happened but Kam was already aware. Lewis had brought him up to date earlier. Andy asked Kam to open the door to the Bensons' suite as they hadn't been able to find Mrs Benson for a few hours. Kam refused. It was more than his job was worth to give passengers access to someone else's suite. Andy and Cosmo begged Kam to let them in but Kam would not be persuaded. Instead he suggested he call a security officer to attend and then he may be allowed to let them in. Andy and Cosmo agreed. A few minutes later, Tony Pritchard arrived. Tony was a junior security officer and was currently on the graveyard shift. The boys explained the situation and Tony allowed Kam to open the door. Tony escorted Andy, Cosmo and Kam into the Bensons' suite where they checked every room and the balcony but there was no sign of Michelle. Tony suggested that Andy and Cosmo accompany him to the security office to discuss this further. Kam locked the suite and, exchanging worried glances, they followed Tony.

It was 4.14am. Andy and Cosmo had been with Tony and Scott for an hour and a quarter. Tony had called Scott as he was concerned that a passenger was missing and followed protocol to ensure the senior officer was aware.

'Thank you for your help tonight. I realise it's very late. You must be shattered. If you don't mind, I may need to speak to you again tomorrow or rather, later today.' Andy and Cosmo were bleary eyed. They'd been offered numerous cups of coffee but it had been a long day. They left the security office and made their way to their respective suites.

'Do you really fear the worst, Andy?' asked Cosmo.

'It's not looking good is it mate? Anyway, let's see what tomorrow brings. Get some sleep, Cosmo. You did well today. I know you work for Mia but you seem to have got lumbered with sorting this out as well. Goodnight mate.'

'Goodnight Andy,' Andy walked on to his suite while Cosmo let himself into his.

Michael Benson woke in the Medical Centre after a fitful night. Despite the painkillers, he was in lots of pain. His skin was tight and he was still glowing. His temperature had been checked regularly throughout the night and had stabilised. Nurse Emma was on duty first thing and told Michael that after breakfast Doctor Hans would be in to check on him. Michael asked what time he could go back to his suite. Emma advised that it depended on Doctor Hans. Emma suggested that Michael eat some breakfast and, despite his pain, he was ravenous as he hadn't eaten for over 24 hours. Emma suggested scrambled eggs, muffins and tomatoes with fresh fruit and toast. Michael agreed and the order was brought to him within ten minutes.

Scott McDonald was perturbed. He'd give the order for a full passenger search to be undertaken quietly and without arousing suspicion with the other passengers. Scott had spoken to Commodore Griffiths earlier and made him aware of the situation. The Commodore sighed and prayed that he hadn't lost a passenger on his watch. 'Do what you have to, Scott, and keep me fully informed.'

Mia, Cosmo, Sarah, Jasper, Louisa, Kurt and Andy all went to breakfast in The Oyster. Despite having berthed at the beautiful island of St Kitts, everyone was distracted by yesterday's events.

'Any news?' asked Andy as he took his seat within the area of the other tables.

'I haven't heard anything, what about you Jasper?' asked Mia.

'Nothing here either, Mia. It really is a bit worrying now. Has anyone heard how Michael is?' said Jasper.

'Not yet but I'll send Cosmo to find out after breakfast.' Cosmo listened quietly to the chatter. He was tired but also worried. If Michelle really was missing, then this was a terrible thing to happen. Her husband was currently in the ship's Medical Centre quite unwell and unaware of his wife's disappearance. The poor guy. Who was going to tell him? Cosmo hoped it would be a member of the crew. Officer McDonald or Doctor Hans perhaps? Cosmo didn't mind visiting Michael but he wished Mia would have a little more thought about the situation. She could have waited until Michael knew before sending him off on an errand of concern. Cosmo was worried about what to say if Michael hadn't yet been told and asked about Michelle.

Luckily, most passengers, including the group, had gone ashore. Michael was still in the Medical Centre and had been visited by Officer McDonald who had told him that they were now treating his wife as missing. Michael was dumbstruck. Sure, he didn't love her but he had been married to her for 30 years. Scott McDonald had taken Michael's silence as trauma and suggested Doctor Hans may be able to give him a sedative if he wanted one.

'I'm fine, thank you Mr McDonald. I just don't know what to say. I thought she was in the shower when I got up yesterday. I didn't realise.'

'Now don't worry, Mr Benson. We are doing everything we can to find your wife. I will need to speak with you and anyone else who was with her when she was last seen but that can wait until you are feeling a little better. You look rather sore but Dr Hans tells me you are hydrated and can go back to your suite shortly.' Michael thanked Mr McDonald distractedly and closed his eyes as the tears rolled down his face. Scott McDonald walked out quietly to return to his office and see if there was any news.

'It's a complete mystery, sir' said Tony. 'We've checked the ship from top to toe and the police haven't found anything ashore. My guess is that she fell overboard.'

Commodore Griffiths and Scott McDonald both looked at each other with downcast eyes. Commodore Griffiths groaned. This couldn't be happening. 'I know these things are common at sea but in all my career I've never ever lost a passenger like this. Yes, I've had deaths by natural causes but never any suicides or unexplained disappearances. This is all I need. I have checked with the local police in St Maarten but they have had no sightings of her. Listen up everyone, we don't want to upset the rest of the passengers so I want a lid kept on this as best you can. Quash any rumours and advise we are investigating. Tell all crew to remain vigilant and not discuss this with passengers.'

'Yes sir' came the chorus from the gathered officers. Commodore Griffiths sighed to himself. His last cruise and this happens. Talk about your last voyage being one to remember.

Despite most passengers being ashore, rumours had quickly spread among the passengers. Most of the talk was around the British TV presenter who had disappeared. Rumour control was rife and word also spread quickly to the world press. Any nugget of celebrity news or scandal was sought after by hungry journalists and reporters. Social media was going mad with the news that Michelle Benson was missing and TV stations, newspapers and magazines were bombarding the ship and their contacts on board for the exclusive.

'But I did see the lady getting killed,' replied Jenson.

'Shut up Jenson and stop this nonsense. Your mum and I have had enough of your storytelling. You're nearly ten years old and you're acting like Kyle. Act your age, boy, and stop behaving like a little kid.'

'But, Dad I promise I saw it!' whined Jenson.

Diana decided it was time to distract the boys before Sam lost his rag again and suggested they all go to The Lobster Pot and get ice creams and when they had eaten them they could go in the pool. Sam reminded Di that the children's entertainment included a pirate-themed treasure hunt later which the boys would enjoy. The boys jumped around excitedly remembering the treasure hunt and the chance to run riot in the children's area with the Kids Club entertainers.

Mia, Cosmo, Sarah, Jasper, Louisa, Kurt and Andy were all eating lunch in The Sea Bed. They'd decided that it wouldn't be appropriate to go ashore with the mystery surrounding Michelle's disappearance, so they agreed to stay on board and support Michael. Andy and Cosmo had collected Michael from the Medical Centre and taken him back to his suite. Michael was subdued, which was only to be expected.

'We're all meeting for lunch in The Sea Bed at 1pm, Michael. We'd like you to join us. You need to eat.'

'Andy's right, Michael, we're here for you but you do need to keep your strength up. We'll pick you up at 13.15 buddy, no arguments and we will seat you in the shade, completely out of the sun.'

Michael sighed and thanked them for their kindness. 'I look forward to joining you for lunch.'

'That's settled then,' Cosmo said. 'We'll come back here for Michael at 13.15 and escort him to lunch.' The boys said their goodbyes to Michael and left him to rest until it was time for lunch. He'd been assured by Officer McDonald that they were doing everything they could to find Michelle and he should try not to worry.

Michael moved slowly towards the bar, his sunburned legs stiff and painful. He poured himself a large brandy and let out an almighty sigh as he downed it in one. He poured another and made his way gingerly to the sumptuous sofa where he laid down with his feet up. He closed his eyes and silent tears moistened the corner of his eyes.

Sarah was on her way to the Calypso Club when her mobile rang. She checked the digital display and nipped through a set of doors onto the deck. 'Hi babe, I'm on my way to the Calypso Club for a cocktail. Jasper is taking a shower before lunch. I'm glad you got my message. Jasper will pick up the tab for the rest of it.' Sarah laughed hysterically as she excitedly talked about the end of her marriage. 'I can't wait for us to be together babe. It's exciting innit?' Sarah listened to the caller then, obviously mimicking her caller's words, chuckled as she said, 'I love it when a plan comes together too. Gotta go now but I can't wait to see you. You have no idea what you do to me babe. I'm gonna give you something to remember. Bye babe, see you soon. Bye.'

Denise and Chris were enjoying time alone with Rocky and Terry. They had grown close over the last few days and it looked like the way the boys were talking that they may be in this for the long haul. Ed and Todd on the other hand were once again wasted. Their wannabee girlfriends and the boys were in the hot tub on the girls' balcony, drinking champagne and snorting cocaine.

'Stick with us girls, we're at the top of our game and no one can stop us. We're the best rock band around. We can have whatever we want.' Todd was slurring his words as Jess and Olivia laughed.

'Oh Todd, you're so funny darling. Will you give me an exclusive when I like land my first presenting job? Imagine the headlines. "Newcomer Jessica Harper-Levinson lands like the biggest names in rock for an exclusive interview."'

'I'll give you whatever you want, darling,' replied Todd as he lunged forward and thrust his hand down into Jess's bikini bottoms.

'Todd!' gasped Jess, her eyes darting towards Olivia and Ed.

'Ah don't worry about them, my little harleen. I think they're busy themselves.

Olivia was straddling Ed as the bubbles popped at the surface of the water. Ed's face was buried in Olivia's breasts, her bikini top lying over the edge of the tub. Olivia was bouncing up and down, her head thrown back and a glass of champagne in one hand. Jess laughed. *If you can't beat them, you may as well join them,* thought Jess as she ripped off her bikini top and grabbed Todd's cock under the water. *Life can't get any better than this,* thought Todd as he closed his eyes and snorted hard through his nose.

The Sea Bed was again proving to be very popular. The sun was beating down and despite the majority of passengers being ashore, the remainers who stayed on board all seemed to be drawn to the al fresco lunch venue.

Mia had requested a large table to accommodate the group. The maître d' immediately had the waiters move some tables together in front of the mini Trevi Fountain and placed the sunshades over the area to keep it cool. Andy and Cosmo collected Michael and escorted him to The Sea Bed where Louisa, Kurt, Jasper, Sarah and Mia were waiting.

'Ah here they are' said Mia as Andy, Cosmo and Michael walked into The Sea Bed.

Sarah jumped up, scraping her chair back as she rushed toward them. 'Oh Michael, I'm so sorry for what's happened,' gushed Sarah as she rushed forward and hugged Michael. Michael winced with the pain and pulled back slightly as she lunged at him.

'Thank you Sarah, I'm still in shock myself.'

'Sarah, come and sit down. Let the poor bloke get to the table will you?' shouted Jasper. Everyone around the table stood as they murmured soothing words. The women kissed and hugged Michael and the men embraced him in gentle manly hugs, aware of his very tender body. Michael was overwhelmed with their kindness. He was still suffering badly with his sunburn and he sighed with relief as he sank into his chair, well shaded by the white and purple sunshade. Even the walk from the restaurant to the table on deck killed him with pain. The searing heat was no friend to Michael.

'What would everyone like to drink?' asked Cosmo as the waiter approached the table to take their drinks order.

'Blue lagoon for me,' replied Louisa.

'Make that two,' said Mia.

'I'll have a spritzer,' said Sarah, and the boys all agreed that cold lagers would go down well in the melting heat of the Caribbean sunshine.

Everyone was rather subdued as they perused the menu. Finally, Michael spoke up.

'I know this is a shock for all of you, as much as it is for me. My beloved wife is missing and I am beside myself. I cannot imagine what has happened to her or where she is. I just want her back with me.' Michael's eyes glazed over as he spoke but he was secretly ecstatic at the thought that he'd just been held by the person he loved. The group felt his pain and told him they would do what they could to support him.

The waiter brought the drinks to the table and Cosmo stood up and invited everyone to join him in a toast to 'Michelle's safe return'.

Officer McDonald was meeting with the Commodore. 'We really have no idea what has happened, sir. It appears that Mrs Benson has literally just vanished. We can only suggest that she is missing presumed dead. Perhaps she fell overboard? We really are not sure. I've still to interview Mr Benson and the guests that he has befriended who have spent time in Mrs Benson's company but it's not looking positive that we'll find out what happened. I'm hoping to interview Mr Benson this afternoon. I heard he was lunching with his friends so I'll wait until he's back in his suite before taking his statement.'

'Very good, Scott. Keep me informed, won't you?' replied Commodore Griffiths. Scott McDonald left the Commodore's private quarters, baffled at the mysterious disappearance of a famous celebrity. There was something niggling at the back of his mind but he couldn't put his finger on it. *Ah well, let's see what Michael Benson has to say later,* thought Scott as he made his way to his suite to change his shirt.

CHAPTER 11

Michael Benson was lying on his bed resting. After lunch, Andy, Cosmo and Jasper all took turns to sit with him to keep an eye on him. The doorbell to the suite rang at 16.50 hours. Jasper answered the door and invited Officer McDonald into the suite. 'Michael is resting at the moment but I will go and let him know you are here. Please take a seat.'

Michael came through to the lounge and sat down on the electric leather reclining chair. 'You'll have to excuse me. I need to keep my legs elevated as much as possible to stop any fluid build-up in my ankles,' explained Michael.

'I really won't take up much of your time, Mr Benson. I just want to talk to you about the last time you saw your wife.'

'Perhaps I should go? You'll want your privacy,' said Jasper.

'No, please stay. I have nothing to hide and I'd like you here. A little moral support never hurt anybody,' replied Michael.

Jasper asked Officer McDonald and Michael if they would like a drink. Officer McDonald declined, citing he was on duty but Michael told Jasper he would join him and that Jasper should choose. Jasper poured both of them a large whisky with ice and settled on the sofa opposite Officer McDonald.

'Can you start by telling me when was the last time you saw your wife?' For the next hour Michael answered every question put to him. He answered them all honestly but omitted to tell him about the argument and the fact that he had stormed out of their suite in a bad mood. Despite what had happened, Michael could not allow their cover of a happily married couple to slip. Scott McDonald made notes throughout and at the end of the interview he thanked Michael for his time and apologised for having put him through this.

On his way back to his office, Scott McDonald was unlucky enough to come across the Kids Club on their treasure hunt. There were only five children taking advantage of the afternoon's activities and the Jenkins tribe made up three of them. Jenson spotted Scott and ran up to him asking if he'd found the murderer yet. Scott laughed and told Jenson that there is no murderer loose on the ship and that he's not to worry. Scott also suggested Jenson should not talk about this anymore as it may upset the other children. Jenson became agitated and told Scott that he was just like the rest of them. 'No one believes me. I can show you where it happened. I saw it, I tell you.'

Scott walked away, Jenson's words still ringing in his ears. Could this kid have seen something? Scott dismissed it as an attention-seeking child's ramblings and overactive imagination.

The day passed by much like the others. Most of the passengers were ashore and the remainder were indulging in luxurious spa treatments, lazing by the pools and drinking alcohol by the bucket load.

Scott McDonald had been holed up in his office all day putting together his notes from everyone he'd spoken to in relation to Michelle Benson's disappearance. Everyone said the same thing. Michael and Michelle Benson were the world's most loved-up couple. They were happy both on and off screen. Michael Benson was devastated about his wife's disappearance and it seemed that this was a very tragic accident. Scott could only conclude that Michelle had gone for a walk on deck and fallen overboard.

Something didn't seem quite right though. He couldn't put his finger on it but the fact that Michelle didn't appear drunk and it was very calm at sea made him question his conclusion. Jenson Jenkins' words kept popping into his head. 'I can show you where it happened.' Scott decided it would be worth speaking to him before he closed his investigation. He made his way to the Jenkins suite to speak to Jenson.

Sam and Di were happy to have Scott take Jenson off for ice cream. They were seated in Scott's office with a huge tub of chocolate ice cream which Jenson was demolishing with gusto.

'Mum doesn't let me have too much ice cream but I love it. She says it will rot our teeth but my teeth are good. It depends on her mood. Some days she's in a good mood and lets us have what we want then other days she's in a bad mood and just shouts all day.'

Scott reminded Jenson why he was there and asked him to talk him through what happened the evening Michelle disappeared.

'Well, me and my brothers was all in bed. It was quite late and Mum and Dad was out at the bars. Dad said I could play on my tablet if I looked after Tommy and Kyle. Anyway, they fell asleep and I got bored so I decided to go for a walk round the ship.

I left the room and I was frightened that I'd bump into Mum and Dad so I kept away from the inside of the ship and went on the decks. I walked around for a while. I was looking at the other boats and lights on the sea. I was hungry so I went into The Lobster Pot and got some pizza and a drink but I sat in the corner where the tea-making area is so no one could see me.

'Then I went on deck again and when I was on Deck 6 it was really quiet and dark at that part.'

'What part of the deck was that, Jenson?' Scott asked.

'The bit that goes in when you come round the back of the ship. There's no light there. I heard strange noises and when I walked round I put my head round the dark bit and saw them.'

'What and who did you see, Jenson? Think carefully.'

'There was a lady and she was making funny noises like she couldn't breathe proper. And there was another person but I couldn't see them proper cos they was wearing a hoodie and they had their back to me.'

'What was happening, Jenson, can you remember?'

'The other person had their hands round the lady's neck and she couldn't breathe. I saw her legs go soft and she started to fall down. I didn't know what to do so I went back round the back of the deck and waited. Then I heard another noise and looked round the corner. I saw the hooded person dragging the lady to the railings. Then they heaved the lady up and threw her over the side into the sea.'

'Are you absolutely sure about this, Jenson? Are you telling the truth? A lady has gone missing and it is very important that we find out what happened. We don't want any tales which are not true as that wouldn't be very nice for the lady's family.'

'I promise, cross my heart that I'm telling the truth. I'm not lying,' replied an indignant Jenson. 'Can I have more ice cream?'

'It's nearly dinner time, Jenson, and your mum and dad will have my guts for garters if you don't eat your dinner. Tell you what. You've been a great help to me so how about I arrange a special treat for you to say thank you?'

'Yer what's the treat?'

'Would you like a private tour of the bridge and engine room?'

'Will I get to drive the ship?' cried an excited Jenson.

'Yes, we'll let you drive the ship,' smiled Scott.

An ear-piercing shriek came from Jenson as he got up from his chair and ran round Scott's office shouting at the top of his lungs. Scott took the boy's hand and escorted him back to his suite, past the Pursers Office where David and Chloe looked at each other with raised eyebrows.

'It looks like we may have a murder case on our hands, sir. Jenson Jenkins was pretty convincing. He promised he wasn't lying and I believe him. I've always thought something was missing in this case, especially as Michelle wasn't drunk and the sea was calm that night. I'm pretty sure now this is a murder enquiry. The problem is that there is no body for DNA testing and, apart from young Jenson who can't identify the murderer or their gender, there are no witnesses. I've called it in to the British police but I'm afraid that we may be on a hiding to nothing.'

Commodore Griffiths sighed. 'This is a total nightmare, Scott. Are you sure that there's nothing you've missed?'

'Nothing sir. I've interviewed everyone, checked the area which Jenson identified and questioned anyone who was connected with Mrs Benson. We've even checked all the CCTV but there's nothing. Whoever did this is very clever and had obviously checked out the areas of vision beforehand. I'm beginning to think this was premeditated rather than accidental. I really am at a loss. The British police have told us that it is unlikely that anyone will be caught for this so we should put out an official statement that Mrs Benson's disappearance was a tragic loss at sea. We are to keep the suspicion of murder quiet. The police hope that if we throw the murderer off the scent they may slip up at some stage.'

'Fine, best do as they say then, Scott. Notify Mr Benson that it was a tragic accident and again let's play this down. Keep it as quiet as we can until this cruise is over. I'm sure there'll be enough press and questions to be answered when we arrive back in the UK.'

The group were sitting in the ballroom that evening commiserating with Michael about the news that Michelle had tragically lost her life by falling overboard.

Michael was subdued and still smarting from his burns. The group in general was subdued out of respect for Michael and his feelings but he asked them to carry on as normal as, although he was in shock, he was fine and didn't want this to ruin everyone's holiday.

The 12-piece band were playing some upbeat quickstep and the dance floor was filling up quickly. Strictly Opulent nights were very popular. An amateur take on a popular British TV programme where professional Latin American and ballroom dancers paired up with celebrities who were taught to dance. *Opulence's* version was the professional dancers pairing up with desperate passengers! The show was due to start in a few minutes and the group had decided to watch the show as they all felt they needed cheering up and they were sure some of the participants would make them laugh.

Mia asked everyone to raise their glasses to Michelle. 'Such a tragedy. She was a lovely lady. May her soul rest in peace.' The toast was completed as the band started playing the well-known theme tune and the spotlight rested on the entertainment officer who was hosting the competition.

Opulence continued on her way, silently through the calm Caribbean waters towards her next port of call.

Three days later saw *Opulence* set sail from her final Caribbean destination homewards to Southampton. Stopping at different ports of call was great but the real pleasure for most cruisers were the days at sea taking advantage of everything the ship has to offer or relaxing quietly and enjoying the peace away from real life. The last three days had been marred with sadness and disbelief from the group who had quickly become friends over the past couple of weeks. The final journey for some would be celebrated in quiet reflection around Michael.

Louisa was relaxing in Kurt's hot tub on the balcony. Kurt was lying on a sunlounger. 'So what happens with us when we get back, Louisa? Andy's secured me a casting with Manny Dubrow so I'll probably end up in Hollywood.'

'It's not a problem, Kurt. We've had fun on this holiday but it's not a given that we're a couple or that we'll be going public with a relationship is it?' laughed Louisa.

'What do you mean, it's just fun? Don't you want to go out with me? It's not impossible to make it work, you know. You spend most of your time in Hollywood anyway and I'm pretty sure I'll be moving into the world of movies so it could work out well for us.' Kurt was silently shocked at Louisa's statement. It's true he was a young single guy who could more or less do what he wanted and he was used to treating girls like shit, but Louisa was different. Spending a couple of weeks in her close company had shown him what it was really like to have feelings for someone and he was surprised at his reaction. Usually it was Kurt who loved and left them and now the tables were turned.

'Hey, don't be so serious Kurt. You've got your career and I have mine. It's been fun. Deep down you're a good guy but it'd never work. You'll get bored and move on. Come to think of it, I'll probably do the same.' Louisa laughed as she stretched her arm towards Kurt, beckoning him to join her. 'Come on, forget about getting all serious. They don't call this the hot tub for nothing.' Kurt's cock soon made him move towards her, his concerns of Louisa turning him down soon forgotten.

Sarah Teasdale could be found in her favourite place. The shopping mall. She'd visited the on-board shops on a daily basis but today she was determined to spend. She'd already bought a couple of Chanel handbags but today she had set her sights on making the Hermes Birkin hers. While she was at it, Sarah also threw in an Urban Satchel Vuitton. Sarah had attracted a bellboy to accompany her while she moved from one shop to another. Joining the handbags were some gorgeous Chanel silk scarves, Cartier bracelet and a Cashmere skirt suit. A mere £150,000 later and Sarah still wasn't finished. 'Take those to my suite, Danny, and meet me in the jewellers in one hour.' Sarah watched Danny the bellboy gather her packages and make his way from the mall to the lift.

Just time for quick champers before I hit the jewellers, I think, thought Sarah. 'Oh look there's Andy and Cosmo. Yoo-hoo guys. I'm going to the Champagne Flute. Wanna join me? I need to loosen up before I spend Jasper's money.' Sarah was laughing as she linked her arms through theirs. 'Let's crack a couple of bottles of Cristal, then you can help me choose some bling, eh?'

'Lead the way,' said Cosmo and Andy just laughed as they escorted the goddess that was Sarah Teasdale to the bar.

'You look stunning, Sarah,' gushed Cosmo.

'Thanks babe. Just a little number to keep Jasper on his toes, if you know what I mean.' Sarah flicked her long loose straight hair over her shoulder as Cosmo and Andy enjoyed the vision before them. Although gay, Cosmo could appreciate the female form and beauty. Sarah was wearing her obligatory heels with a tiny mini skirt and cropped top which outlined her breasts beautifully. Her long tanned legs set off the skirt and heels and her perfectly applied make-up enhanced her natural beauty.

'So, what are you looking for in the jewellers then, Sarah?' asked Andy.

'I've got my eye on a few things, Andy, but there's a diamond necklace that I love. It's 24-carat gold with 18 carats of diamonds. I thought Jasper could treat me as it's my birthday a couple of weeks after we get back. Call it an early birthday pressie.'

Andy raised his eyebrows and told her she was a lucky girl. Cosmo told her she was a girl after his own heart.

The champagne arrived and they toasted to 'Diamonds. Sarah's best friend.'

Mia was lounging with Michael on his balcony. Michael had invited the group for a barbeque that evening and Mia was taking her turn looking after Michael.

Mia sipped Pimm's while Michael stuck to tonic water with lime.

'I can't believe we'll be home in a few days. It doesn't seem possible that we've already been away for nearly three weeks. Have you spoken with your TV company yet, Michael? Are you intending to take time off when you get back?'

'I haven't quite decided what I'm going to do yet, Mia, to be honest. I don't know that I can face going back to the flat though. I just can't face the flat without my darling wife and I'll be rattling around there on my own so I've been thinking I might take a holiday or a bit of a break for a while until I've come to terms with Michelle's death. I really don't know how I'm going to go on without her,' Michael said as he broke down. Mia got up and put her arms around him, uttering soothing noises as if he were a fractious baby.

Michelle and Michael had bought a penthouse flat in Canary Wharf and had lived there for 12 years. It was handy for work and the views over London were amazing. The flat was modern and Michelle loved it. Michael had never really liked living there and couldn't see the point in staying there when he got back. Michael hated Michelle and was glad she was gone but he knew he had to keep up this act, probably for the rest of his life.

He had previously thought about what would happen now. He didn't want to go back to TV just yet and wanted to get away from it all. A cottage in the country would do as a bolthole. Somewhere far enough away from London to allow him the anonymity that he craved to begin his new life with his new love. They had discussed it and decided on Cornwall. There were some beautiful properties around the Cornish coast. Some so secluded that not even the postman knew where to deliver the mail. Michael's lover was a little less enamoured by the country location. They needed the bright lights, clubs, shops and designer lifestyle. Michael had laughed to himself as he wondered how they would take to country life for a while. 'It won't be forever, my darling. Just until it's safe for me to surface again. We'll be free then. Free to do what we want, go where we want to go and do what we want to do. Neither of us will ever have to answer to anyone else again and we can be free to love each other openly. My stumbling block is out of my life forever and you will soon be free.'

The lovers had toasted each other and their future with champagne before slowly undressing and making love with such passion that left them both sated in ecstasy. Lovemaking had never been like this before. Wrapped in each other's arms and stroking the tanned skin and luscious thighs, Michael could not be happier. That was the night a year ago they planned Michelle's demise. There was no going back.

Michael's thoughts were sharply jolted back to the present by Mia's voice. 'I'll ring Cosmo now. He can ask Andy to come up. Or is it Sarah's turn to sit with you? I can't remember. Anyway, no matter. Cosmo will know.'

'Don't bother, Mia. It's not necessary. Really. I'll be fine. I'm just relaxing and I need to Skype with my agent anyway. Then I'll be having a shower and getting ready for my barbeque tonight, so don't bother with any more babysitters. I really am fine. Thank you all for your concern and for looking after me this last few days. I truly appreciate it.'

'Are you sure, darling? It's no trouble.'

'No really, Mia. Don't worry. I have things to do later and I could use a little time to myself. I've not been alone since Michelle disappeared and I need to get used to it. Anyway, I'll be tied up creaming my sunburn and that's likely to take me an hour,' Michael attempted a laugh as he guided Mia through the suite to the door. He kissed her gently on both cheeks and told her he would see her at 8pm.

Denise and Chris were once again in the company of Rocky and Terry. They were in the girls' suite talking about when they get back to the UK. 'We have a big tour coming up in a couple of months but in the meantime we'll be working on a new album. Will you come up to London and spend some time with us?' Terry asked them.

'Course we will, we'd love to, wouldn't we Denise?' Denise nodded enthusiastically as Rocky took her hand and suggested they all go for a walk on deck before getting ready for dinner. Chris couldn't believe how their luck had changed in the last two weeks. They joined the ship a fortnight ago, single and happy and it looked as though they'd be leaving it with famous boyfriends and completely ecstatic.

Ed and Todd were in Olivia and Jess's suite. It was a complete mess. The girls coming from a privileged background had had servants to do everything for them all their lives and holidays were no exception. They couldn't even pick up their dirty underwear from the floor where they dropped them. Ed was in the bathroom cutting some cocaine on the marble top. Olivia was naked in the jacuzzi bath and urging Ed to hurry up and join her and Jess and Todd were fucking in Jess's bedroom. They were intending to get wasted and spend the night on a bar crawl. Ed had bet Todd that he would be the last one standing tonight and Todd's competitive side had reared its ugly head. They'd started drinking Jack Daniels an hour before and between the bottle they'd nearly finished and the cocaine they'd snorted, they were well on their way.

Jess was straddled across Todd. She was leaning forward, her large breasts covering his face as he searched for her nipple with his mouth. She was riding him hard and had gripped his cock with her right hand. She massaged his balls as she pumped him and Todd's eyes' rolled in his head. 'Jesus Christ Almighty, what the fuck are you doing to me, woman?' Todd bucked violently under Jess as she rolled off him, his cum running down her thighs.

Jess was laughing. 'There's plenty more of that when we get back to London if you want it, Todd? You can even move in with me if you want? I've got a five-bed property and every night is party night.'

'Sounds good baby, sounds good.' Todd slapped Jess hard on her backside and she yelped and leapt up as he told her to go get him another drink. 'Have you finished those lines yet, Ed?'

'Yes mate,' Ed replied.

Todd jumped up and made his way unsteadily into the

bathroom. He spotted the coke lined up on the marble top by the sink and glanced to the left where he saw Ed and Olivia fucking in the jacuzzi. Olivia had her eyes closed and her head was resting on the side of the tub. There were bubbles in the tub which shifted with the motion of the water jets and Ed's thrusting. Todd stood for a moment taking in the scene before him. He turned back to the sink and snorted two lines as Jess walked into the bathroom. She hadn't bothered to cover her nakedness either.

Jess made her way to the sink and snorted a line of coke. She grabbed Todd's cock roughly and started masturbating him as she kissed him viciously. Todd pulled his head away and asked if she wanted a bit more fun?

'Always up for fun, honey. You should know that by now.'

Todd grabbed Jess's hand and led her through the washroom into the jacuzzi area. They stood watching Olivia and Ed who were lost in their coke-induced sex act. Jess climbed into the tub and Todd followed. Jess started rubbing her hands sensuously up and down Ed's back while he still pumped into Olivia. Todd forced his way in between Ed and Olivia and lifted Olivia towards him. He helped her to her knees as he stood up in the tub. Ed's vacant eyes watched him with interest as Jess's hands worked their way from his back down over his buttocks and round the front to his cock. She was now masturbating Ed as she moved round to face him. Ed's hands found Jess's breasts and he played with her tits as he took one in his mouth. Todd pulled Olivia's head towards his crotch. Her mouth found his cock and she started running her tongue up and down his shaft. She rimmed the tip with her tongue and took his shaft deep into her mouth. Todd groaned as Olivia expertly gave him the best blow job he'd ever experienced. Bodies slithered round in the large tub. Bubbles foamed over the edge onto the marble floor and four young people indulged in a drug- and alcohol-induced orgy.

Jasper Teasdale knew Sarah was shopping and had taken the opportunity to fire up his laptop and indulge in his secret pastime, watching online porn. Jasper was in his suite, relaxing on the leather sofa watching *Fuck me, I'm a Lady.* It was an amateur production which had been uploaded to the XXX site but it suited Jasper to a tee. It was filthy and debauched and kept him happy while his bint of a wife was no doubt buying more designer wear she didn't need.

His Skype with his lawyer earlier had gone well. The divorce papers were being drawn up and she would be served as soon as they got back to the UK. Jasper's lawyer was currently working out the finer details of the divorce. Sarah could have the London house and he would buy another London pad, but for the meantime he would move out of London to his family home.

Tetherington Manor was the family home of the Teasdales which Jasper inherited from his parents when they were killed in a car crash when he was 24. It was located in leafy Surrey and boasted an impressive 15 acres of well-manicured grounds with an electronic security gate. The Manor had nine bedrooms, seven bathrooms, and the usual rooms associated with aristocracy and wealth. Jasper loved Tetherington Manor and was determined that Sarah would not get it in the divorce. His lawyer was instructed to let Sarah have the North London house, the Aston Martin and a generous financial settlement. He hoped that this would be enough to keep her happy and he could walk away from this marriage with the bulk of his bank account intact. Jasper had new fish to fry and was in no doubt that his new love would require a certain lifestyle.

Sarah and Cosmo were in the jewellery shop. Sarah had just tried on the 24-carat diamond necklace that she coveted. It was stunning and Cosmo drew a sharp intake of breath when he saw it on her. The diamonds glistened and sparkled like ice crystals against her tanned skin. The light radiated from the gems, showering her neck with rainbow colours. The clarity and cut of the diamonds was second to none.

'What do you think, Cos? Does It suit me?'

'It's just stunning, Sarah, I absolutely love it.'

'In that case, I'll take it!' shouted Sarah, her confidence enhanced by the two bottles of Cristal she had shared with Andy and Cosmo.

The sales assistant beamed at the thought of making this sale. He would do well on commission with this one.

'Very well, madam, shall I box it and have it delivered to your suite?' asked Dillon.

'Hang on, Sarah,' said Cosmo, I don't want to interfere but don't you think you should speak to Jasper first? This necklace is an absolute fortune and he might want to know about it first.'

'Fuck Jasper,' laughed Sarah. 'He won't mind. He loves me. Anyway, a happy wife is a happy life innit?' Sarah howled at her own joke. The other passengers and staff merely stared at the beautiful drunken woman making a complete twat of herself.

Cosmo was worried that Sarah may have overstepped the mark and having witnessed Jasper's short fuse when it came to his wife, decided that he would excuse himself so as not to be drawn in to any unpleasantness which was sure to ensue when Jasper found out about the necklace.

'Oh, is that the time? I must dash, Sarah darling. We have Michael's barbeque tonight and I want to have a little rest before getting ready. I'll see you later darling.'

Cosmo kissed Sarah and turned and fled.

Sarah turned towards Dillon who was holding the leather-bound receipt holder and grabbed the pen from the holder. She swiftly signed the receipt and completed her purchase. 'Make sure you bring my necklace quickly won't you? I'll probably be back tomorrow for the matching earrings!' shouted Sarah as she wobbled out of the shop.

CHAPTER 12

Michael, dressed in cream linen trousers and an open-necked duck-egg blue shirt, was sitting on the sofa with a glass of iced water watching the hustle and bustle of the preparations for his barbeque. Lewis had brought a delicious platter of canapes to the suite and was in the process of setting up the outside bar with a bar steward from the Commodore Club.

Pedro Vasquez, a first-class chef from Venezuela, was in charge of the barbeque. He was setting up quietly with his assistant.

It was 7.45pm and the sky was just starting to darken. It was streaked with gorgeous reds and oranges, a message to those at sea that tomorrow would be a beautiful day. Lewis had switched on the outside balcony lights and it looked incredible. The hot tub gently bubbled away with the steam rising and the fairy lights twinkling as the evening turned to dusk. *The guests would be here soon and everything has to be perfect,* thought Michael as his attention was drawn to a loud shushing sizzle. Pedro had thrown some langoustine onto the grill and they had sizzled as they landed.

Andy and Louisa were first to arrive. Lewis welcomed them with a tray full of glasses of champagne. Both took a glass and made their way out onto the balcony where Michael was waiting. They both gasped when they saw how beautiful the balcony looked all dressed for the night.

They made small talk as the others arrived. Mia and Cosmo looked amazing, with Mia dressed in a lavender silk beaded cocktail dress and silver strappy heels. Cosmo was dashing with his light brown hair styled exquisitely, a black silk shirt and black trousers. The atmosphere was light and jovial and although everyone was sensitive to Michael's loss, they allowed themselves to laugh.

'Where do you think Sarah and Jasper have got to?' asked

Louisa.

'I have no idea,' answered Andy. 'Cosmo and I saw Sarah at the shopping mall this afternoon and she said they were coming tonight.'

'Perhaps she can't decide which of her 120 pairs of shoes to wear tonight!' Louisa shot sarcastically. Andy smiled and agreed that it was probably a wardrobe malfunction that was holding them up.

'HOW MUCH? You spent HOW MUCH, you stupid fucking cow?' raged Jasper. 'Why the fuck didn't you come and speak to me about this Sarah? £1.25. million on a fucking necklace? For Christ's sake, what on earth possessed you?'

Sarah was a little taken aback. She had seen Jasper in a temper before but this was not normal. He was raging. His face was taut and his mood thunderous. Spit flew from his mouth as he tore into her. 'I always knew you were a liability, Sarah, but this takes the fucking biscuit. You spent £1.25 million pounds of my money on a fucking necklace and didn't even have the decency to speak to me about it.'

'I didn't think you'd mind, Jas. You always get me what I want anyway and you know I've been looking at it for the last couple of weeks. Why are you acting like I've committed a fucking crime?'

'Are you fucking stupid, Sarah? £1.25 million is obscene. I could buy a new company for that amount! You seem to forget that I work and earn the money in this relationship while you do fuck all except spend it and I'm sick of it Sarah. In fact, I'm sick of you! If it wasn't for the fact that I said we'd support Michael, I'd throw you out of here right now. Do me a favour. Don't fucking speak to me. I don't want to hear your tramp voice, do you understand?'

Sarah nodded, completely taken aback by Jasper's outburst. She'd seen him in some moods but never one as fierce as this. He'd punched the wall behind her head as he spat his vitriol at her and she had to admit she was a little scared of him.

Perhaps it's best if I just stay quiet for now. He'll soon get over it, she thought as she pulled out a tangerine Chanel dress. *Anyway, Jasper darling, I'm taking exactly what I'm entitled to before I leave you. I deserve it for putting up with you and your moods for so long,* she thought. *Now, where did I put that tit tape?*

Jasper had stormed off. He made his way from the suite to the pub. This was one bar on the ship he'd never deigned to frequent. It wasn't his style. Jasper enjoyed the trappings of wealth and the social circles that it attracted. To be fair, the majority of passengers on *Opulence* were wealthy beyond belief but there were still a few who enjoyed the lively and more relaxed atmosphere of a British pub.

Jasper went straight to the bar without sitting and waiting to be served. 'A large Chivas Regal on the rocks,' he barked at the bartender. Jasper gulped back the amber liquid in one swallow and banged the glass down on the bar. 'Another,' he said as he thrust his glass towards the bemused bartender. 'In fact, when you've poured that one, just keep them coming until I tell you to stop. Got it?'

'Yes sir,' replied Ewan as he handed another glass to Jasper. *I just hope this guy calms down quickly and gets over whatever it is that's upset him,* thought Ewan. *I don't want to have to call security to remove him. The mood he's in, I wouldn't fancy their chances.*

Sarah was blissfully unaware of Jasper's drinking binge as she fluttered around their suite matching her Chanel dress with accessories and hairstyles. She decided to wear her hair long and straight this evening with a gold chain as a forehead decoration. Her short floaty Grecian-style one-shouldered cocktail gown was completed with gold strappy sandals adorned with crystals. The platform sole alone was encrusted with enough Swarovski crystals to buy an average family a people carrier including road tax and fuel for a year.

Sarah knew Jasper was in a mood but her own agenda to dump him when they got home gave her an inner strength to continue with the farce for another few days. She would turn on the tears and say she was sorry and beg for his forgiveness. That way she was sure she would get to keep the diamond necklace especially after she gave him one of her famed blow jobs. The thought of it made Sarah dry heave but she took comfort knowing that in less than a week she would finally be free of him and she would be a very rich young lady in her own right. Jasper Teasdale was worth hundreds of millions and she would make sure that she got her fair share of it!

Jasper had drunk five double whiskies and was now sitting at a table by the window. He was feeling calmer. A combination of the alcohol and the tranquil sea and dusky sky, he supposed. The pub was quiet. Most passengers were at dinner in one of the three restaurants. Jasper was aware that he'd agreed to go to Michael's this evening. If it wasn't for the tragic circumstances which had occurred, he would have stayed away from Sarah for the rest of the night but he knew he couldn't do that. Despite feeling calmer, Jasper's jaw was set tight. He hadn't shaved since yesterday and had designer stubble. His hair, having recently been washed, was lying naturally on his head. His usual slicked back fringe had flopped forward without the constraints of product to hold it in place and his eyes smoldered. Jasper was unaware of just how hot he looked in that moment, although the female bartender hadn't taken her eyes off him since he'd come in.

'I suppose the only consolation is that I spoke with Clive today and he's stitched the bitch up a treat. If she thinks she's going to come out of this marriage with half of my fortune she's got another thing coming. Despite the prenup, I know her and I know what she'll do if she gets the chance. I'm so glad I hired Duke Investigators two years ago. The photos and reports of her infidelity will be enough to seal her fate forever. I can forgo a house, a decent pay-off and a car but she will not take my family home or my wealth.' Jasper smiled to himself as he beckoned for another drink, knowing that he would soon have to go back to his suite and collect his bitch of a wife to go to Michael's. They were already late and Sarah had just texted him to ask if he still intended for them to go. He texted back saying he'd be back in ten minutes and to make sure she didn't keep him waiting.

Kurt had decided to join Andy and Louisa in the Bensons' suite. He'd not been as close to Michael and Michelle throughout the voyage but he felt sorry for the poor bloke and decided to go along and show his support. It wasn't just the fact that he was showing support though. Deep down Kurt was still reeling from the discussion he'd had with Louisa earlier that day. Kurt was the one who loved them and left them and now here was this hot actress telling him that he was only a bit of fun and they were going their separate ways. Kurt had been thinking about this all day and realised that he actually had feelings for Louisa. Yes, the sex was awesome but it was more than that. He missed her when she wasn't there and he had also realised he enjoyed being with her. *I'm going to have to go all out here to make her see that we're meant to be together*, thought Kurt as he dressed himself for Michael's barbeque.

The group were chatting amicably to one another, glasses chinking and the smells from the grill mouthwatering. 'Anyone seen Jas and Sarah?' asked Mia.

'Not since this afternoon,' piped Cosmo and Andy in unison.

'They're very late. I do hope everything is OK,' said Michael. 'Do you think we should ring and see if they are coming?'

Just then the doorbell rang and Lewis went to answer it. Jasper and Sarah walked out to the balcony looking every inch the George and Amal Clooney of *Opulence*, although even George and Amal couldn't hold a candle to the beauty of this couple.

'Sorry we're late,' shrieked Sarah as she took a glass of champagne from Lewis' tray. 'Jasper had some business to attend to, didn't you babe?'

'Yes, sorry guys, it was a rescheduled conference call which couldn't wait. I should have let you know earlier that we'd be late. Forgive me.'

'No need for apologies, I'm just glad you made it,' said Michael. 'Sarah, you look absolutely stunning. That colour really suits you.' Michael's eyes lingered on Sarah just a fraction of a second longer than necessary and it didn't go unnoticed by Jasper. Sarah, ever the centre of attention, threw her arms wide and twirled around on the spot. Her chiffon layer lifting in the warm gentle breeze to reveal her gorgeous thighs. Sarah was also braless and her pert and shapely breasts wobbled delightfully as she swirled round. Sarah giggled. 'Aw thanks, Michael. It's just a little number I threw on.' She winked at Michael as their eyes locked.

Mia had also caught the knowing look between Michael and Sarah and glanced at Jasper as she saw his jaw twitch. *Oh dear, it looks like Jasper is about to explode*, thought Mia. She linked her arm through Jasper's and guided him away from the group.

'Jasper, you must come and look at these lobsters. I've never seen any as big in my life. Do you like lobster, Jasper?' Mia's voice faded as she skillfully moved Jasper away from his wife. Despite Jasper telling Sarah to behave herself and not make a show of herself, she just had. Yet again she'd defied him and he wasn't happy. Jasper had returned to their suite to collect Sarah. She was quiet to begin with and told him that she was eternally sorry that she'd bought the necklace without telling him. She begged for forgiveness and dabbed at the non-existent tears in her eyes. *Well, I'm not ruining my false eyelashes with real tears on this prick*, thought Sarah as she acted the prodigal wife. They'd agreed to go to Michael's soiree and say no more about the earlier events in front of company.

Everyone could feel the tension between the Teasdales. It hadn't gone unnoticed. Champagne and cocktails flowed as the grill sprang into live, giving birth to the most succulent steaks, chicken and fish that anyone had ever tasted. Platters of salad, breads and pasta adorned the serving tables as everyone helped themselves to what they wanted. The seating was informal. The guests could sit at whatever tables they wished on the balcony. The warm breeze fanned the guests as the ship sailed on. The sky turned black and the balcony came alive with the beautiful lighting and twinkling fairy lights which adorned the setting. The alcohol flowed and moods chilled.

Sarah sat with Louisa, Kurt and Andy while Jasper joined Cosmo, Michael and Mia. Jasper was fairly quiet. He was enjoying sitting with Cosmo, Michael and Mia. He joined in the adult conversation about the benefits of cruising compared to world travel by other means of transport, while at the other table, it was a much lighter hearted and noisy affair.

Sarah was flirting shamelessly with Kurt and Andy while Louisa was getting very loose on cocktails and the help of the little white pill she'd taken a couple of hours before. Sarah and Kurt were loud, brash and very drunk. Andy excused himself and went to join the other table. 'Room for a little one by any chance?'

'If you mean, is there room on the adults' table, then please join us,' Mia said.

'I don't know how they put so much alcohol away, really I don't! We can drink but the days of it going straight to my head are over.' Mia didn't realise she too was slightly tipsy and it amused the others on her table. Mia was gorgeous and still very hot for an older woman. Her lavender dress which stopped just on the knee accentuated her long tanned shapely legs and her ankles were highlighted with the glistening jewels on her Swarovski heels. Lewis had put on the music system earlier and soft background music played throughout the meal. In the last few minutes, someone had obviously gone into the lounge and ramped the volume up. They'd sync'd their phone to some dance music and before you knew it, Mia had joined Sarah, Louisa and Kurt throwing some shapely moves as they danced under the stars.

The men, now on brandy, smiled at the ladies, then Andy, Cosmo and Michael got up and joined in. They were all dancing to 'Let's Marvin Gaye and Get It On'. Sarah grabbed Andy, Michael grabbed Louisa and Mia grabbed Kurt as they sashayed and swayed around the deck, grinding and getting down and dirty in the process.

Jasper looked on. Thank god Sarah was occupied. His cock was hard and it was becoming uncomfortable trying to restrain his erection in his trousers. *There's some fit bodies here alright,* thought Jasper. Even though he hated his wife, he still admired her beauty and her body. It had given him many hours of pleasure and would continue to do so until he served her with her papers. *Perhaps, I'll fuck her then present her with the divorce papers tied up in tissue paper and a ribbon,* Jasper laughed at the vision he imagined of Sarah's face when she opened it.

The party went on until the wee small hours. Everyone made their way back to their respective suites on wobbly legs, some worse than others as *Opulence* cut through the ocean, carving up nautical miles towards the UK.

Olivia, Jess, Todd and Ed awoke the following morning still in the girls' suite. They couldn't remember a thing about last night. The last thing Todd remembered was getting sucked off by Olivia in the bathtub. From then on it was a bit of a daze.

The four of them were intertwined on the huge bed in Jess's bedroom. Three empty bottles of Cristal and two of Jack Daniels were strewn across the floor along with half of Jess's wardrobe and dirty underwear. A large bag of cocaine sat open on the bedside table with white powder residue on the surface. A credit card and rolled up £50 note lay next to the bag.

Todd lifted the duvet to find Jess on her side, her hair covering her face and spittle dripping from the corner of her mouth. Ed was next to Jess, his hand cupping her boob as he snored gently. Olivia was scrunched up in between Todd and Jess.

'What the fuck happened here?' Todd exclaimed. His outburst woke the others.

'Oh fuck what happened? Where am I? Oh god I feel sick,' came the cries from the girls as they slowly sat upright to take in their surroundings.

Jess's false eyelashes had come loose and were sitting on her cheekbones like giant black spiders. Her mascara had run and her eyes were swollen. Olivia didn't fare much better. Her face looked like it had melted. Ed stuck his tongue out and was scraping his finger along its surface, balking at the white fur which stuck to his fingernail.

'What the hell happened last night guys?' asked a bewildered Jessica.

'God only knows but it was fucking awesome anyway,' laughed Ed.

Todd was trying to rack his brains about what happened. He had no recollection of anything. Three bottles of champagne and two bottles of Jack Daniels and a shed load of cocaine soon saw to that.

Jess had got up unsteadily and picked up the telephone. 'We need iced water, fresh orange juice, fresh fruit and eggs immediately. Oh and better bring enough for four people,' Jess barked as she terminated the call to room service.

On hearing the word eggs, Olivia threw her hand to her mouth and shuffled as fast as she could to the adjoining bathroom where she proceeded to expel the contents of last night's partying. Todd laughed as he heard Olivia's retching. '

Get it all up girl. You'll be fine.'

'Where the fuck is the paracetamol?' shouted Jessica to no one in particular as she emptied drawers and handbags onto the floor in a desperate effort to find them. 'Ah got them, now who wants some?'

All three of them took two paracetamols straight away. Ed and Todd dry swallowed theirs while Jess washed hers down with bottled water from the fridge.

Olivia was still in the bathroom.

'Like, where the fuck is that juice? It should be here by now. They are so fucking slow. If they worked for Daddy, he'd like sack them.' Barely four minutes had passed since Jess had made the call, but she was hungover and in a foul mood.

Olivia appeared from the bathroom clutching her head and moving very slowly. Every blink or slight movement felt like her head would burst. Jess and the boys were now in the lounge, lying on the furniture and wishing that they had the energy to just go back to their own suite. The girls wore robes while the boys had put their underpants from the night before back on.

The doorbell rang a few minutes later. Lewis entered and wheeled in a tray of steaming tea, coffee and scrambled eggs. Two jugs of freshly squeezed orange juice and iced water also sat atop the trolley. Lewis was not surprised to see Todd and Ed in the girls' suite. He saw it all the time in this job. He was, however, the epitome of discretion. He started to lay the dining table with the breakfast items but Jess stopped him.

'Just leave the trolley and go. We'll sort ourselves out.'

'Very well, madam,' Lewis said as he made his way back to the pantry. 'Jumped up little tart. I hope she catches some nasty STD.'

Jess quickly poured herself a glass of iced water. The others could get their own as far as she was concerned. She wasn't waiting on them. She drank the water greedily then poured herself another. Ed joined her at the trolley and picked up the jug of orange juice. He proceeded to drink straight from the jug which brought a protest from Olivia.

'Ed, for fuck's sake, like don't do that. It's disgusting. I want some juice too, you know and like I don't want your slobber in it.'

Todd turned and laughed. 'Chill out babe, you had his cock in your gob last night and I don't remember you protesting about that.'

Ed and Jess laughed as Olivia turned and fled back towards the bedroom.

'I think you've upset her, Todd.'

'Ah she'll get over it. Now who's for eggs and coke?' Jess and Ed grinned as they held out their hands with their plates.

The other two Jackdaws, Rocky and Terry, were on the private deck by the infinity pool. Denise and Chris were enjoying a dip as the boys chatted.

'I have no idea where the other two got to last night. I expect they're holed up with those two posh girls from London,' said Terry.

'Just another few days and it won't be our problem anymore mate,' exclaimed Rocky. 'I contacted Bernie yesterday and told him the score. I told him either he sacks them or we're leaving.'

'Let's hope he takes us seriously, then. Bernie's a decent agent but I hope he doesn't try and talk us out of it as we're currently his biggest income generator.'

'No chance of that, Terry. I told him in no uncertain terms and I also said that if he doesn't follow through, then I'll go to the press myself and reveal the truth.'

Just at that, the girls emerged from the pool. They grabbed the luxurious towels from the sunlounger and wrapped themselves in them.

'Brr, it's colder today isn't it?'

'It is colder, Chris, but it's still in the 70s. We're getting further towards home now and the weather is bound to change. We've been really luck so far,' said Rocky.

'It just seems much colder as it's about a 20 degree drop in temperature,' said Denise.

'What do you fancy for lunch, girls?' asked Terry. 'Do you fancy going to The Oyster and we'll see what's on the menu?' The girls both nodded eagerly and started drying themselves off as the boys packed up. They would need to go back to their suites to change into more suitable clothing for the restaurant.

'Let's hope Ed and Todd stay out of our sight today,' said Rocky, as he guided Denise towards the elevator.

Andy was in the Calypso Club listening to Rum Punch and drinking coffee. He had his laptop with him and was checking in with his office. 'Typical,' thought Andy as he looked at the emails from his PA Melinda.

Bonnie Roberts, Wow Factor Winner 2016, was caught coming out of The Skylark Club two days ago on the arm of a well-known married actor. Subsequent photos have emerged all over social media of the two of them inside the club coupled up, kissing and groping in the VIP area. The press has been after you for a statement since then and are getting impatient. I told them you would give them a statement by noon tomorrow.

Damn, thought Andy. *Typical youngsters who have a few drinks and get carried away. I'll sort the statement later and hope that it blows over.*

Andy emailed Melinda back saying that he would attend to it and asked Melinda to speak to Bonnie and read her the riot act. He would see her himself when he returned. Right at this minute, Andy was more concerned with a love-struck Kurt. Gone was the cocky, arrogant, self-important kid from a few days ago. Andy had watched Kurt carefully last night and noticed that he was hanging on to Louisa's every word which was unlike him. When they had all bedded down for the night after Michael's party, Kurt had turned up at Andy's suite and spilled his guts on how he felt about Louisa and her unrequited love. Andy took the fatherly figure approach and reminded Kurt that his career was about to take a new direction and it would be silly of him to tie himself down so quickly, especially as he would have a whole new fan base when he moved into movies. Kurt broke down and Andy felt sorry for him. He really was just a kid. A spoiled kid at that but he could see the vulnerable little boy crying out for normality. The good life had taken its toll and Kurt was now a victim. Andy had talked to Kurt for hours and eventually convinced him that he was still young and his new career would bring him into contact with many more Hollywood beauties who would no doubt fall for his charms. Kurt had cheered up and eventually made his way back to his own suite. Andy had his own affairs of the heart to protect after all and it had been so difficult trying to keep the secret.

Mia was lunching alone in The Oyster. Cosmo was arranging her hair appointment, manicure and massage for later that afternoon and keeping on top of her emails and admin. Mia ordered the apricot, fig and walnut French toast with ricotta cheese and a bottle of Chateau d'Yquem. The sommelier returned a few minutes later and poured Mia's wine. She tasted it and savoured the flavour of one of the most expensive white wines in the world. *I've been waiting for this moment*, thought Mia as she took another sip of the delicious wine. *It's time to celebrate and I'm going to enjoy every minute of it.* The waiter hurried over with Mia's lunch, beautifully arranged on the china plate. Mia smiled as she tucked in to her French toast and her new future which had now been secured.

Michael Benson was walking on deck taking in the sea air. He'd spent a couple of hours Skyping with his TV production colleagues and family members. Michael felt a little stronger now and ready to face the pitying faces of fellow passengers. A few who knew what happened had approached him on his walk and offered their condolences. Michael, ever the professional, thanked them for their good wishes and lapped up the outpouring of sympathy for his tragic loss. This wasn't the only reason for his buoyant mood.

His guests had left around 2am that morning after the barbeque and he decided he could now have a drink. He'd been taking it easy in front of his guests, worried that his mask would slip, but now it was different. They were all gone and he was finally alone. He'd poured himself a Tito's on the rocks. Michael then went into the bathroom and splashed his face with cold water. He then added some Straight to Heaven by Kilian. It was Michelle's favourite scent. Michael laughed to himself. 'I doubt if I'll be going straight to heaven.' Just as he was emerging from the bathroom, his doorbell rang. Michael opened the door and they fell into each other's arms. 'God how I've missed you,' he said as he kissed his guest passionately. 'I've missed you too, Michael, but it's done. We can be together now. No more secrets, no more hiding. I'll never treat you like she did. I've been waiting for this day for ages and I've planned things carefully. You'll never be unhappy again babe.'

Michael poured another Tito's and handed it to his lover.

'To us. I love you,' he toasted.

'To us, I think we got away with murder,' his lover responded with a grin. They took a drink and Michael scooped his lover up and carried them to the bedroom. It was only then behind closed doors that their full passion was unleashed. A sensual and erotic experience like neither had ever dreamed of unfolded. There were tears of joy and ecstasy like they'd never known. Michael's body shuddered as his orgasm ripped through him and afterwards he kissed his love and held them tight as they both drifted off to sleep, dreaming of their new future together.

Jasper Teasdale was also nursing a headache. He'd consumed a pretty hefty amount of alcohol last night. Luckily Jasper had a high tolerance to alcohol and he could drink quite a bit without it making him too ill. A couple of painkillers and he'd be as right as rain. Jasper was in the ship's library reviewing the daily newspaper. He was enjoying the peace and quiet of the library thinking about last night's events. He and Sarah returned to their suite after Michael's party. Sarah was extremely drunk and the alcohol had made her brave to the point of obnoxious. She'd started banging on about the diamond necklace again. Thinking that Jasper would have forgiven her by now, she placed her hand on his crotch and started rubbing his cock. Jasper pushed her away and told her he wasn't interested.

'Don't be silly Jas, you know you want it. Stop being so moody and make your wife happy.'

This was the catalyst for Jasper. 'Make my wife happy? How

fucking dare you, you little tramp. I've given you everything you wanted and you still take me for a mug by spending nearly £1.25 million of mine without discussing it with me. I'll tell you what will make me happy, shall I Sarah? It'll make me very happy if you just fuck off and get out of here. I don't want to see you or hear from you again tonight. Just go.'

Jasper was raging and Sarah was belligerent. 'You're a fucking idiot, Jas. You can afford it. It's no big deal. I can't see why you're acting like a fucking moron. You know you want me, don't you?' With this, Sarah pulled her left breast from the confines of her dress and held it towards Jasper. 'Come on babe, let me feel your tongue. Look how my nipple is hardening.' Sarah was massaging her nipple between her fingers and licking her lips like some Z-rated porn actress.

Jasper glared at his wife with disgust. 'You make me sick. Why don't you give it to someone else cos I sure as fuck don't want it?' With that Jasper left the suite slamming the door behind him.

Sarah, too drunk to be affronted, grinned as she thought how that left the door open for her. 'Well, he's just told me to fuck off and give it to someone else, so I better do as my dear husband wants.' Sarah tucked her boob back inside her dress and left the suite.

Louisa was in the health spa enjoying a relaxing full body massage. The events of last night had surprised her to say the least. Had she done the right thing? Would she regret it? Louisa cast her mind back a few hours. She'd left the party with Andy and Kurt who'd escorted her to her suite. They'd said goodnight and gone their separate ways. Louisa was mellow and undressed quickly. She couldn't wait to get into her huge bed and snuggle down under the goose down duvet. Just as she had got into bed, her doorbell rang. *What the hell? It's nearly 3am*, thought Louisa as she rushed to the door.

'What are you doing here, it's nearly 3am. You shouldn't be here. Perhaps you should go?' Louisa started to close the door, but the look on her visitor's face told her not to mess with them. Louisa stepped back.

'You'd better come in,' she said as those angry eyes looked her up and down. A few calming words with a promise of a talk at a later date and Kurt relaxed enough to be humoured into returning to his own suite.

Louisa was brought back to the present when her masseuse found a tender spot beneath her shoulder blade. 'Ow, that hurts!'

'Sorry madam. You are very tense today.'

I sure am, thought Louisa. *I just want to move on with everything.* The masseuse turned Louisa over and Louisa moved her thoughts to her new movie. *I must check my emails to see if the script has come through yet.*

Cosmo was unusually flustered. He'd been managing all Mia's admin since 9am and hadn't had time to have a proper breakfast. He was buried deep in making arrangements with a large well-known department store in Palm Springs for Mia to do a personal appearance to sign her new book *Secrets of a Starlet*. The store was being difficult and told Cosmo that Mia would not be able to bring a large entourage. Cosmo told the store that Mia always had a high level of security when she made appearances and the store guaranteed Cosmo that their own security officers would take charge and handle any situation. They assured Cosmo that Mia would be perfectly safe with them.

There was a gentle knock at the door. 'Fuck,' said Cosmo, 'I can't be doing with being disturbed.' Cosmo answered the door and much to his annoyance pursers clerk David was stood in front of him.

'Can I come in, Cosmo?'

'I'm really busy, David, what do you want?' Cosmo was in no mood for pleasantries. He was beginning to tire of David and found his constant need for attention off putting. David pushed past Cosmo and made his way to the sofa. 'What do you want David? I'm very busy and don't have time for this.'

'You know exactly what I want, Cosmo. I want what you've been giving me for the last two weeks. I want your cock. I want you. I'm in love with you, Cosmo, and I want to be with you.'

Cosmo's mouth hung open as he listened to David declaring

his undying love for him. It would be funny if it wasn't so pathetic. 'Listen David, we've had some fun but that's it. That's as far as it goes. I don't feel anything for you. I just wanted some fun on holiday.'

'You don't mean that, Cosmo, I've heard everything you said to me. You told me that there was more to this life for me than running after ungrateful passengers. You said I was special.'

'Yes, David but I told the same things to Marac. You're a great guy, buddy, but you're only my holiday fling. I'm not interested in him either. You need to understand that our lives are very different and that I don't love you.'

David looked crestfallen as he listened to Cosmo tell him he'd been barking up the wrong tree. 'So you were happy to use and abuse me, were you? You're a bastard, Cosmo Geller. A first-class bastard.' David stood up, his eyes filled with tears.

'Look David, I am sorry that I gave you the wrong impression, but I have to be honest with you. You were only a fling. Nothing more.' David flounced out of the suite, his shoulders heaving and Cosmo heard the sobs as the door slammed shut. *Where the fuck did that come from? Boy these Europeans need to lighten up,* thought Cosmo as he settled back down to his admin duties.

Sarah was sitting on her balcony wondering when her husband would be back. She felt ill. She'd had far too much to drink last night and her row with Jasper had taken its toll. She'd ordered lunch from room service and had finished half a bottle of wine with her club sandwich. A hair of the dog couldn't do any harm, could it? Sarah wasn't bothered about Jasper anymore. She was just hoping he'd calmed down enough to reassure her that he hadn't done anything stupid for the rest of the trip like cancel her credit cards. Sarah applied more lipstick then turned her attention to applying more sunscreen to her bare breasts. She'd make sure she had an all-over tan before this holiday was over. She closed her eyes and thought back to the events of last night. After Jasper stormed off, Sarah had followed but she knew exactly where she was going.

Sarah was in love and had been for some time. It had taken careful planning to get this far but for the first time in her life Sarah felt loved. Really loved. She was told she was loved too. Together they would emerge as the new power couple. She'd be an equal rather than second best. Her longed-for TV career was practically guaranteed and her careful financial planning would ensure they had a great lifestyle.

She'd gone to her lover. He'd taken her in his arms and they'd made love. They hadn't fucked, they'd made love. She brought him to the brink of losing consciousness, so great was his orgasm, and when she too was sated, they lay entwined in each other's arms and slept peacefully. She'd seen tears in his eyes and she cried because she was so happy. 'He told me he loved me'. Sarah smiled as she remembered every delicious detail of last night. Sarah snapped herself out of her thoughts. *No doubt Jasper will be back soon. If he asks, I'll tell him I walked on deck for a while then went to the bars to drown my sorrows. He won't know any different.*

Jasper was fuming. He couldn't remember being so angry in a long time. He'd stormed out of the suite and strode down the gold-carpeted corridor. 'I've given her everything she's wanted and she takes me for a mug. Well no more. I've had it. I don't care about her feelings anymore.' Jasper headed for the Seahorse Bar. Located between the library and the card room, the Seahorse was a quiet little bolthole for those who preferred peace and quiet. He ordered his usual Chivas Regal and took out his mobile. He quickly punched out a short text. A couple of minutes later his phone beeped. He looked at the text, and finished his drink in one gulp. Jasper made his way back to the lifts and didn't have long to wait, considering the early hour and lack of passengers. Once alighted, he made his way along the corridor and rang the doorbell of a suite similar to his. The door opened and Jasper allowed his smoldering anger to become a grin as he was pulled into a tight embrace.

'How long have we got, Jasper?'

'The rest our lives, my love.' Jasper kicked the door closed with one foot and their bodies blended together into the remainder of the night.

Opulence was now speeding across the Atlantic Ocean having left the warmth and calmness of the Pacific Ocean behind. For the first time during the voyage, the weather had let them down. Dull, overcast and cool, *Opulence* pitched and tossed her way towards the UK in a storm force 10.

Commodore Griffiths had notified the passengers in their morning tannoy briefing that a weather front had changed direction right into the path of *Opulence*. 'It is expected to last for 24 hours but I will keep you updated on any changes to the forecast.' The smooth, calm voice of Commodore Griffiths eased the worry of many of the passengers who found the pitch and toss of the vessel a little too frightening. Access to the decks had been stopped and doors locked. 'This is for passengers' own safety,' said Commodore Griffiths.

The ship was unusually quiet. The usual hustle and bustle of activities was non-existent as at least half of the passengers were down with sea sickness. The Medical Centre was queued to the hilt with green faces awaiting anti-sickness injections and the shop had sold out of anti-sickness wristbands.

The Lobster Pot was practically empty, as were the restaurants. The few hardy passengers not affected by the roll of the ship and the crashing 20-foot waves expected their day to go on as usual and this meant great food and entertainment.

A few people were dotted around tables in The Lobster Pot, eating as though they were still back in the Caribbean. Kurt and Andy were sitting at a table in the middle of the self-service restaurant having just arrived. Their attention was turned to a large man struggling to carry his tray to a table. His wife, a lady in her 60s, was holding on to the counter by the fresh fruit as she was finding it difficult to walk due to the sudden deterioration in the weather. The gentleman was thrown forward and ran for about ten feet as the ship lurched downwards on the back of a large wave. Then just as he came to a stop, he leaned forward and struggled to walk forward as the ship rode up a wave as she ploughed through the stormy Atlantic. Just as she was reaching the crest, *Opulence* tossed starboard and the struggling gentleman was sent flying to his right. His arms held upwards and out in front of him as he fought to keep his balance. The plate containing a carvery-style roast slid precariously to the edge of the tray as gravy slopped over the side burning his hand. A yelp escaped the gentleman as the hot liquid hit his hand and he drew it back, letting go of the tray. The roast came crashing to the floor as he lurched violently to the left and thumped full force into the edge of another countertop. He crumpled slightly as though winded. His wife shrieked from 15 feet away as she still clung to the counter. 'Thomas, are you OK? Thomas?' Thomas was struggling to speak but he lifted his thumb towards her in a gesture of 'I'm OK'.

Kurt and Andy both leaped from their seats. Andy going to the aid of Thomas and Kurt to his wife Alice. Andy held on to Thomas as he caught his breath and Kurt held Alice tightly to him as he helped her towards her husband.

'Oh my, I wasn't expecting this today,' whimpered Alice as she held tightly to Kurt's arm. 'Thank you, young man. I don't know what I'd have done without you. Tom has mobility issues and I have arthritis and I'm not sure how we are going to manage to have our lunch now.'

'Would you like to join us?' asked Andy.

'Why that would be lovely, if you're sure you don't mind?'

'Nah, it's fine darlin',' said Kurt. 'Come with me and we'll get you seated then you tell me what you want for lunch and I'll get it for you.'

Andy raised his eyebrow as a slight smile escaped his lips. 'Is Kurt feeling well?' Andy wondered.

They helped the couple to their table and Andy and Kurt battled their way back to the carvery counter where they loaded plates with delicious roast rib of beef, goose fat roasted potatoes, broccoli, cabbage, roast parsnips, carrots, French beans and cauliflower. It took the boys a couple of trips to safely return with the steaming food and drinks, assisted by two waiters who brought their cutlery and linen napkins. It was difficult to keep their footing but the general consensus was that if they were going to be ill then they may as well have their stomachs full.

For once, Kurt was getting his high from adrenaline due to the bad weather rather than from the buzz of illegal substances. Sitting at the table by the window, Kurt couldn't help looking out into the vast bubbling ocean. As the ship lurched to the side, their plates slid away from them towards the window. It looked to Kurt that the ship was going to roll over as the window leaned towards the water as the wave dipped. Glancing over to the portside of the ship, Kurt was amazed as the water and the horizon disappeared and the window flew up to the grey sky.

Tom, Alice and Andy chatted lightheartedly as the ship tossed and pitched. Kurt was quieter than Andy had ever seen him and suspected correctly that Kurt was frightened at the way in which the ship was rolling in the storm force gale. Tom and Alice were seasoned cruisers and nothing was going to spoil their enjoyment of a beautiful roast dinner.

'Help me, I'm dying!' cried Sarah.

'Oh shut up, Sarah, you're not dying, you're just sea sick. How about a nice greasy bacon sandwich and a cup of builder's tea? That'll make you feel better.'

'Fuck off, Jasper!' shouted Sarah as she retched and ran towards their master bathroom with her hand over her mouth. Jasper laughed to himself. *Serves the bitch right. I hope she stays sick until we get back to Southampton.* Jasper could hear Sarah retching and heaving as he settled onto the comfortable leather chair with his ever-present Chivas Regal. 'Hurry up Sarah, I've ordered lunch. It'll be here soon and it'd be a shame to waste it,' laughed Jasper as his wife continued to empty her stomach.

Mia had invited Michael and Louisa to join her for lunch in The Oyster. They all weathered the storm well and weren't feeling at all ill so they met in the restaurant and enjoyed each other's company while treating their taste buds and senses to a delicious culinary experience. Today was a theme day in The Oyster and it was to be a taste of the world. Numerous taster dishes which would be served to allow the guests to enjoy the flavours they may never have experienced before.

The selection brought to Mia's table included chilled pineapple with coconut rum, seared tuna with white radish, salmon soufflé, Chilean seabass with hazelnut and rosemary rosti, striploin of beef with Yorkshire cups, tortillas with mixed fungi, guacamole and asparagus and beetroot salad.

Cosmo groaned with delight when he saw the feast before his eyes. The vivid colours looked as though the dishes were pictures taken for a *New York Times* bestsellers cookbook.

'Wow, that looks amazing,' said Louisa as the waiters walked away. The group were clinging to the table as *Opulence* rolled. When she rolled left, they leaned to the right and vice versa. She continued to roll and pitch as they gripped the arms of their chairs as a reaction to stop themselves being thrown from their seats.

'It's amazing that none of us have been too badly affected by the weather really, isn't it?' said Michael.

'I'm not sure how Jasper and Sarah are as I haven't seen them today,' said Cosmo. 'I expect they are fine but maybe we should check on them after lunch?'

'Good idea, Cosmo. Shall we all go? That way we can go for a drink somewhere and spend the afternoon getting drunk. At least when I'm staggering around the ship, I'll have an excuse. Anyway, Commodore Griffiths' latest update just before lunch was that the storm is expected to rise to force 11. Hurricane force, I think? Perhaps we should make the most of today as it may be a case of heading back to our suites to entertain ourselves when the level 11 hits?' laughed Mia.

Everyone agreed that it sounded like a great idea and tucked into their taster dishes with relish.

'Keep the noise down will you, Liv?' snapped Jessica as Olivia hurled up in the toilet. 'You're like making me want to be sick as well with that noise. Like, do it quietly, can't you?'

'Sorry Jess but I feel awful.'

'We're supposed to be like having drinks with the boys in the Mermaid Lounge this afternoon, Liv. Have a glass of water and a couple of paracetamol. That should, like, make you feel better. Also it wouldn't hurt for you to like eat something either. No wonder you're retching. You like, need food. I'll order you an egg sandwich. That should line your stomach.'

Olivia continued to heave, her stomach lurching violently at the very mention of an egg sandwich but she didn't say anything. Jessica didn't take kindly to being disagreed with and Olivia wanted to keep the peace. If truth be told, she was slightly frightened of Jess. Jess had always been the strong, opinionated one to Olivia's slightly timid character. Truth be told, Liv was getting a little fed up with Jess's constant berating and opinions. Jess's use of the word *like* peppering every sentence was also grating on Olivia's nerves, along with Jess's infected drawl which she had started to speak with. *She's getting more like Kim Kardashian every day*, thought Olivia.

Jess was a wealthy young lady in her own right. Daddy spoiled her from the day she was born but Jess was so desperate for fame that she thought of herself as the UK's answer to Kim K, even affecting her voice to sound like her. The only similarity between Kim K and Jess were that both wanted to be in the public eye and would do anything to get there.

Olivia emerged from the bathroom and threw herself on their cappuccino-coloured sofa. 'You'll have to go without me, Jess. I don't think I'm up to it. I don't like the way the ship is rolling. I think it's better if I just go to bed.'

'Balderdash, Liv. You'll be fine. I've ordered sandwiches and once you've had that you'll be like, right as rain. We're meeting the boys at like 2.30 in the Mermaid so go and like spruce your face up. We'll have fun.'

Olivia didn't dare argue with Jess. When she was full of cocaine and alcohol she was a different girl but completely sober, she was Jessica's shadow. She did as she was told as she staggered towards the bathroom to splash her face and reapply her make-up. Nausea welling up with every step, Olivia thought she was in hell rather than on board the world's most luxurious liner.

'I'm fed up with your crap, man. You think you own this band, don't you? Well I've got news for you, Rocky Fallon, you don't own it and I'll do what I feckin' want, got it?'

Todd was screaming at Rocky. He'd woken early in the girls' suite and crawled back to their suite around 9am. Rocky and Terry were working on some new songs when Todd and Ed rolled in worse for wear and started taking the piss out of them.

'Pack it in and go get some sleep, why don't you?' shouted Terry. 'We've just about had it up to here with you two. You never bother to turn up for anything on time and when you do you're stoned out of your minds. You have no respect for yourselves let alone the band.'

Todd squared up to Terry, his fists clenched ready to strike. Rocky grabbed Todd's arms and stood nose to nose with Todd. 'I was going to wait until we were back in the UK, Todd, but enough is enough. You've taken the piss for too long and Terry is right. You have no respect for anyone let alone yourselves. When we get back to the UK, your contracts will be terminated. I've spoken to Bernie and told him the score. Both of you were brought in to our band.' Rocky's eyes looked towards Ed as he said it. 'And we welcomed you but you're out of control and I'm not having our gigs ruined because of your behaviour. Make the most of the last couple of days, guys, because when we disembark back in Southampton you're on your own. If you want transport back to London, then you'll have to organise it as you're not travelling back with me and Terry.'

The room was silent. You could feel the tension in the air. Todd glared at Rocky as he listened to his bandmate. Ed spoke first.

'You can't do this to us Rocky. We're part of this band and as such we have rights.'

'Any rights you had have gone,' answered Rocky. 'We're sorry it's come to this, aren't we Terry? But it's done. The Jackdaws will continue as you will be replaced but for now I suggest you pack your things and go to the Pursers Office. They have another suite reserved for you to move to but you'll be paying for it out of your own money, not the bands.'

On hearing this, Todd exploded. He brought his arms up quickly and drew his fist back. Releasing it with as much force as his drunken drug-fueled body would allow, he hit Rocky on the chin. The blow merely glanced off Rocky's jaw as Terry ran forward and grabbed Todd from behind, pinning his arms behind his back. Ed made to move forward but Rocky pushed him back. Ed was startled and hungover so he put his hands up in a gesture of surrender as he slumped onto the nearest chair.

'You think you're such a fuckin' god, don't you Fallon? Well let me tell you, you're nothing, do you hear me? You're fucking nothing. You can't sack us, we'll fucking sue you, you bastard.' Todd was screaming at Rocky as he shook his arms free from Terry's grasp. Todd stomped towards his room and slammed the door, screaming obscenities all the way. Terry moved towards where Ed was seated and told him to go and pack his things. We're going to eat now and we expect you two gone when we get back.' Ed got up slowly and looked at Rocky. He opened his mouth as if he was about to say something then closed it again as he dropped his eyes to the floor and walked towards his room to pack.

Rocky and Terry left the suite and headed to pick Denise and Chris up for lunch. 'I think that went quite well,' laughed Terry, grabbing the handrails to steady themselves as they made their way along the corridor.

The Jenkins family were all in their suite suffering from sea sickness. Added to that, young Kyle was terrified the ship was going to capsize with the angles of the tilt and he was crying and whining to this effect.

Sam Jenkins was in bed with his three sons cuddled in to him. Di was in the lounge area of their suite trying to concentrate on reading but feeling so awful that she just couldn't be distracted. She was waiting for a visit from the duty doctor to give the family anti-sickness injections. Di got up as she heard a knock on the door. Dr Fields was on duty today and apologised for the delay in getting to them.

'We've been inundated with sick passengers at the Medical Centre all morning, Mrs Jenkins. Even our off-duty doctors have come on duty to help out. Now, where are the invalids?' Di led Dr Fields to their bedroom where he witnessed the normally bumptious and loud Sam Jenkins and his unruly brood, lying white-faced and dribbling on the huge bed.

Dr Fields immediately gave Sam an injection and told him that he should start to feel better within 20 minutes but that he may be drowsy and sleep for a few hours. Sam couldn't care less. As long as he didn't feel so ill he'd be happy to sleep. Dr Fields asked the boys if they would like an injection or a tablet to make them feel better and in unison three little weak voices said, 'tablet.' Di got some glasses and water and each boy swallowed the little white pill which the doctor offered them. Finally, Dr Fields gave Di an injection and told her that all of them would probably sleep for a few hours but would feel much better later.

Di climbed into bed with Sam. The boys sandwiched between them. She pulled the goose down duvet over her chin as the rolling of the ship which caused them all to feel so ill now rocked them to sleep.

Opulence remained quiet that afternoon. Rain lashed the windows as winds of 85mph battered the ship. Only a few hardy passengers remained up. Most of the passengers were in their suites sleeping off the effects of the anti-sickness jab. The sky was dark grey and stormy. Michael, Mia, Cosmo, Andy, Jasper, Louisa and Kurt all found themselves in the Mermaid Lounge. Situated high on the ship at the bow, they had a bird's-eye view of the ocean and the storm which was causing so much misery to most of the passengers.

Sex on the beach, screaming orgasms and harvey wallbangers were the order of the day. Spirits were reasonably high and the group were enjoying being entertained by Mia and Cosmo who were loose lipped about some of the biggest names in Hollywood. The stories were more risqué, the more cocktails were consumed. Laughter rang out in the lounge which sounded odd to Herman the Portuguese bartender. Herman was feeling a little green around the gills himself but had another two hours before he could go and lie down. It was strange to be serving such a small group of guests in such high spirits in a storm force 11.

'I do hope poor Sarah feels better soon,' said Mia. 'I feel for her, even though I don't suffer from sea sickness. It must be awful. Is there anything she needs, Jasper? Cosmo would be happy to get it for her, wouldn't you darling?'

'Of course I will, Jasper. Is there anything?'

'Thank you, but Sarah will be fine. You all saw how she was

when you came to collect us. She's had the injection now and she'll sleep for hours so let's just leave her to recover.'

'Well if there's anything we can do, just let us know won't you?' said Mia. Jasper smiled his gorgeous smile and thanked her and the group for their concern, assuring them that they would be the first he would turn to if he needed anything.

'Is everyone looking forward to going home?' asked Louisa.

'I am,' said Michael, his voice low and sad. 'I've loved this holiday and meeting all of you but it holds too many bad memories for me. Poor Michelle. I wish I knew what happened that horrid night.' Michael's voice cracked and tears brushed his cheeks. Louisa moved over and put her arms around Michael.

'Yes, it's been truly awful for you, Michael. I don't know how you've coped. You've been so brave. I don't know why you didn't fly back from the Caribbean,' said Mia.

'I was hoping she'd be found on the ship. I suppose I was living in hope that it was all a bad dream and that she'd reappear,' Michael said softly.

'I think I'll start my packing tonight,' piped up Kurt. We've only got one more day at sea and then we're home so if I start packing tonight then I can enjoy the Privilege Party tomorrow night without worrying about it. I know the butlers will do it but I'd rather pack my own Calvin Klein undercrackers if you don't mind!'

The group laughed at Kurt's attempt to lighten the mood. 'Don't talk to me about packing. We came with 16 cases and it took Lewis three hours to unpack for us so god knows how long it'll take him to repack as we've had to buy another five cases for Sarah's purchases,' said Jasper.

'Good idea, Kurt. I think I'll ask Lewis and the team to make a start on mine tonight. I do have rather a few trunks which need careful handling, don't I Cosmo?' laughed Mia. Cosmo smiled and rolled his eyes as he agreed with Mia in his own camp style.

'My god, you should see her dressing room. It's got more gowns than Macy's and Bloomingdale's combined.' Again more laughter erupted as discussion took place around the benefits of early packing and what they could look forward to at the Privilege Party.

Commodore Griffiths spent 17 hours straight on the bridge of his ship. In storm force gales like this with swollen seas it would be negligent to rely on the less experienced officers. *Opulence* continued to pitch and toss through the remainder of the day and night. The weather finally took a turn for the better in the early hours of the next morning. The winds dropped and the seas calmed to force 4. The ship picked up speed again and sailed onwards towards the UK.

Louisa and Mia decided at breakfast to go shopping. They had avoided the ship's mall until now but they were aware of the beautiful items and couldn't resist a little retail therapy. They would meet at 10am and blitz the credit cards.

The passengers had all regained full health and any thoughts of sea sickness were put to the back of their minds as they tasked stewards and butlers to pack their cases and trunks and started preparing for the Privilege Party that night.

Sarah awoke feeling much better than she had the day before. Jasper was still distant with her, despite her best efforts to keep her husband on side for a few more days. 'Don't forget we're back in Southampton tomorrow so you'd better start getting your stuff together for packing,' reminded Jasper.

Sarah smiled sweetly and assured him that she would start gathering things together after her shower. Sarah had every intention of visiting the mall again today but would keep this from Jasper as he didn't need to find out.

Kurt and Andy went for a brisk walk on deck after breakfast. The weather wasn't too bad but there was a wind which was good for blowing the cobwebs away. 'So Kurt, you need to check your itinerary. My PA emailed it to you yesterday and shows your schedule for the next eight months. It's pretty full on and you'll have to behave as this is your make or break. Screw this up and you're finished.' Kurt merely nodded but had already seen the schedule and knew that this was it. His playboy days were over. He would have to grow up or he would regret this for the rest of his life.

Andy had secured his future and he was grateful to him for

that. *Perhaps the nagging had finally paid off,* thought Kurt. *Maybe I really have grown up?*

Michael was in his suite busy making a Skype call with his rental agent in the UK. He was making use of his grieving widow celebrity status to secure a six-month rental away from prying eyes where he could mourn the loss of his beloved wife in private. Sommers & Chapman were estate agents to the stars. They respected confidentiality and always came up trumps securing the best accommodation available to meet the client's needs.

Drew Thorpe had found Michael the perfect place. A five-bed mansion house with sea views set in 20 acres of private estate in a little village on the outskirts of Cornwall. A gated quarter-mile drive led up to the house which was walled off from the road by a 12-foot wall. Drew reassured Michael that his privacy would be fully respected and it would be unlikely anybody knew he was there.

The house belonged to an investment banker who was currently living in Dubai and was happy to rent it out to Michael at a much reduced rate after hearing his tragic story. He had been an admirer of TV's golden couple for years.

Michael knew that this was just what he needed to give him some breathing space to sell the London pad and find something else after he sorted Michelle's affairs out.

Michael told Drew to draw the contract up and to leave the keys to the house under a specific planter in the rear garden. He also asked Drew to furlough the housekeeper and gardener for six weeks until he had time to get his head together. He had the code for the electric gate and would make his own way there on disembarkation. Michael asked Drew to do one last thing for him and that was to stock the fridge and cupboards with enough fresh food to last him a couple of weeks. Drew said he would be happy to do so and as Michael ended the call he was smiling to himself.

Rocky and Terry were snuggled up to Chris and Denise in the boys' suite. When the girls first saw The Jackdaws' suite their mouths hung open.

'Oh my god,' said Denise, 'and I thought our penthouse was

phenomenal. This is just gorgeous. I didn't think they could be any nicer than ours but I was wrong.'

Todd and Ed had moved out to their own suite a deck lower and more forward on the ship. The boys hadn't spoken to them since the altercation when they asked them to leave. Terry had poured them all their third vodkas and Chris decided to broach the subject of what happens next. The quieter one of the two, she became brave when she'd had a couple of drinks. She pulled Rocky aside and asked him to go on to the balcony with her. Rocky followed her outside, curious to what she wanted to speak to him about.

Chris didn't waste too much time. She told him she'd had the most amazing time on the holiday, made all the better by meeting him. Rocky took her hand and said he felt the same. He was so glad that Chris and Denise weren't longing for the rock 'n' roll lifestyle most people thought they lived. Chris reminded Rocky that she herself had come from humble beginnings and that she liked him for who he was and not what he had. Rocky pulled Chris towards him and looked into her eyes as he told her that when they get back to the UK, he would like it if Chris would officially become his girlfriend. Chris was reeling. Her heart thumped in her chest and she grinned from ear to ear. She'd been hoping for a reaction similar to this but never dared expect it in case she was disappointed. Chris shrieked and threw herself at Rocky, kissing him all over his face.

'I never thought you'd ask,' she said.

Rocky laughed and kissed her back. 'I have no problem letting the world know I'm in love,' said Rocky as Chris cried tears of happiness. She was officially Rocky Fallon's girlfriend and in just over 24 hours time the whole world would know.

Denise was having a similar conversation with Terry inside the suite. They both said they liked each other lots and would be sad for it to end. 'Denise,' said Terry, 'It doesn't have to end. You could always be my girlfriend and keep me happy for years to come.' Denise laughed at Terry's unromantic suggestion but appreciated the sentiment.

'I suppose I could,' said Denise, pausing before finally agreeing. Her eyes twinkling, she kissed Terry lightly on the lips knowing there would be more to come in the future.

Andy was sitting on a cabana, lost in his thoughts. The last three years had been worth the sacrifice of being away from his lover. It gave him time to build his career and to secure his future. He always knew she was the girl for him and it wouldn't be much longer until they would be together.

Cosmo was packing Mia's clothes. He didn't trust anyone else to touch her couture outfits and was happily humming away to himself as he folded her silk lingerie into the cases. Cosmo was reminiscing on his life. His poor start raised with nothing and his struggle to be somebody. *I've made it,* thought Cosmo. *I may only be dresser and PA extraordinaire to the hottest legendary actress on the planet today but my time is nearing when I will be myself and claim what is rightfully mine.* Cosmo snapped the case shut and made his way to his own suite to choose his outfit for the Privilege Party that evening.

Sarah disappeared to the library with her laptop to finalise her plans to end her sham of a marriage. She typed swiftly and diligently ensuring her plans were in place and that her belongings would be cleared from their home by nightfall. Sarah wanted to ensure her items were being moved into her new home on their last day at sea and so far it seemed like everything was going smoothly. Janie and Sam had her keys and were at the apartment packing all her clothes and accessories as they Skyped. They had ordered a removal van which was due around 2pm UK time to collect all Sarah's favourite furniture and fittings. The apartment would look pretty bare by the time Jasper returned and Sarah giggled to herself when she imagined his face.

'I won't forget what you have done for me, guys,' said Sarah. 'Best you block Jasper's number tonight as I'm sure when he gets back he'll start ringing round my contacts to find out what's happened and I don't want you two taking the brunt of his anger.'

Janie and Sam had worked for Sarah for a couple of years. Janie was her glam squad and did all Sarah's make-up, hair and helped her shop. Sam was Sarah's man Friday. He drove her to her lunches, collected her from nightclubs and was at her beck and call for whatever she wanted. Janie and Sam were paid well and didn't mind their roles. There was a special £20k bonus in this for each of them to help her escape without Jasper knowing so they were more than willing to shut up and clear the apartment out. *It's coming together nicely,* thought Sarah as she fired off her last email to a limousine rental company confirming her disembarkation time and date on Friday for them to pick her up.

The group had arranged to meet for drinks at 3pm in the Champagne Flute. This was their penultimate day on board and they wanted to make the most of it. Tomorrow they would be busy settling their on-board accounts and saying their goodbyes. Their final social event would be the Privilege Party held by the Commodore in the ballroom this evening. A rather special event where old and new money came together to drink champagne, nibble canapes and say goodbye Opulence Style.

Michael arrived in the Champagne Flute where the others were already gathered. The weather was pleasant. The storms of the last 24 hours had given way to blue skies and calmer seas. The temperature had dropped considerably from balmy Caribbean standards, however, for the beginning of September it was still fairly warm.

The group got up to greet Michael. The desperation of the situation was not lost on them. Michael had come on the holiday of a lifetime with his soulmate and she had been tragically taken from him. He would never know what happened to her and they felt so sorry for this gentle soul whose world was shattered in the blink of an eye.

Cosmo beckoned the waiter for another glass of champagne, while Sarah grabbed Michael's arm and ushered him to a space between her and Cosmo on the champagne-coloured velvet sofa. 'Come sit with me, Michael, and I'll tell you all about my packing disasters.' Michael took in her sparkling eyes and smiled at her. A wave of happiness spread through him. *What a lucky guy I am,* he thought. *If only they knew, if only they knew.*

The group drank bottle after bottle of the finest Dom Perignon while Jasper switched to his Chivas Regal fairly quickly. Sarah was animatedly talking with Cosmo and Michael, occasionally throwing the odd dark glare at her husband. This went unnoticed by Jasper as he could barely bring himself to acknowledge Sarah anymore. The incident with the diamond necklace finished him. Jasper was deep in his own thoughts about his new life and how it would pan out. *He'd played it well so far to fall at the final hurdle,* thought Jasper as he finished his fifth Chivas Regal. *I'd better not have too many more as we have just over 42 hours to get through and I can't risk anything going wrong.*

Andy, Louisa and Mia were bellowing with laughter which snapped Jasper out of his thoughts and back to the group. He beamed at them as though he was part of their joke. *Maybe I am*, mused Jasper. *Maybe I am?*

Alcohol and close bonds turned the more sombre gathering to a fun-filled couple of hours on the penultimate day of their voyage.

'Does anyone fancy a dip in the pool,' laughed Mia, as she stood up and wobbled on her unsteady feet.

Louisa and Sarah jumped up giggling like schoolchildren shouting, 'Oh yes, let's go, let's have some fun as we'll be home soon'

Jasper shook his head and muttered that he didn't feel like it but Louisa held out her hand and said, 'Oh come on Jasper, don't be boring.'

Jasper was exasperated. He was being cautious but he also didn't want to stand out for being totally boring. Jasper took Louisa's hand and leapt up grinning.

'Come on then, what are we waiting for? Last one to The Terrace buys us all a Rolex!' With that, Jasper sprinted away pulling a giggling Louisa along behind. Cosmo, Michael and Andy also jumped from their seats and started running after Mia and Sarah who were hot on Jasper's heels. There was lots of shrieking, laughing and yelling which wasn't becoming of their surroundings but it was nearly the end of the voyage and they were having fun. The bar steward smiled as he watched the melee. *At least they are enjoying themselves*, he thought.

Kurt was spending his afternoon relaxing in the spa again. Since Louisa had blown him off, he was finding solace in the spa staff. The girls were hot. Typical youngsters of today. Fake lips, big boobs and slugs for eyebrows but that didn't matter. He wasn't marrying any of them. *I'm having my final fling before I have to grow up,* thought Kurt. *I'd better be pretty careful though,* as he closed the door to the cryotherapy room where Yvette was waiting for him.

Todd and Ed were in their suite. Their set-to with Rocky and Terry hadn't taught them anything. They were more determined to do what they wanted and in their drug-fueled haze they were adamant they would sue Bernie, Rocky and Terry and ruin Rocky and Terry's career.

Their lounge was a mess. Despite it being cleaned and tidied earlier in the day, there was a trolley of half-eaten food, a half-empty bottle of Jack Daniels, an empty bottle of Grey Goose and ashtrays full of smoked joints. When they started this behaviour in The Jackdaws' suite, Rocky was always careful to dispose of any drug evidence. He knew Todd and Ed smoked a bit of weed and did the occasional line of coke but he hadn't realised just how badly hooked they were. Now on their own, they were so wasted that they didn't think to clear up after themselves.

Ed was sprawled out on the blush sofa, his trainers smearing the material with tracks of dirt. He hadn't bothered to use any other footwear so these trainers had been worn to all the destinations and brought the dust and dirt back on board.

'When are the chicks coming?' slurred Ed.

'I told them to be here at 3pm,' said Todd. 'Where the fuck are they?' Todd was lying on the floor staring at the ceiling and holding a half-smoked joint. 'I fancy taking Jess on the balcony,' said Todd. 'I can just imagine her riding me on a sunlounger.'

Ed chuckled and announced that in that case he and Liv would take the jacuzzi. Life was no more than drugs, alcohol and sex to these two. They had reached rock bottom and it was unlikely they would be able to redeem themselves. 'Sex, drugs and rock 'n' roll!' shouted Todd as they both laughed deeply and darkly at their lifestyle described so well by the well-known saying from the Spectator in 1971. It couldn't have described these two more perfectly.

Jess and Olivia were in Chanel, one of the many designer boutiques on board *Opulence*. Jess decided she needed some retail therapy and Daddy had transferred £300k to her account and told her to buy herself something nice.

'What do you think of this, Liv?' shouted Jess as she held up a white skirt and turquoise t-shirt.

'I'm not like sure the t-shirt is your colour,' Liv replied.

'Maybe you're right,' said Jess. 'I like don't think there's much here that I don't, like, already have so let's go and buy some of my best friends.' Liv laughed and agreed that she too needed some more diamonds as they headed off to the store to browse.

'Oh god look at this!' cried Liv as she pointed to a 14-carat gold, 7-carat diamond tennis bracelet. Olivia beckoned to the assistant to get it from the case and show it to her.

'Wow, like that's lush, Liv. Let's see it on you.' Olivia tried the bracelet on and it was stunning. 'You've like definitely got to get it, Liv. It really suits you.'

Olivia danced about happily admiring her wrist as she told the assistant to box it up.

'Certainly ma'am. Shall I have it sent to your suite?'

'Hold on!' snapped Jess, 'I haven't bought anything yet.' Jess asked to see a pair of diamond and Columbian emerald drop earrings. 'What do you, like, think Liv? Do you like these? Do they like, suit me? I like, don't have many emeralds and these are like so pretty.'

'Go for it Jess,' said Olivia.

'OK I'll like, take these and you can get them sent to our suite with my friend's bracelet,' said Jess as she turned her back on the assistant and left the shop.

'I suppose we'd like better go and see the boys,' said Jess. 'I fancy a little bit of afternoon delight.' Liv and Jess both laughed as they hurried their way to see Todd and Ed.

Up on The Terrace, it was pretty lively despite being an area for the more sedate 'A' list passengers.

Jasper, Mia, Cosmo, Louisa, Michael, Andy and Sarah were all three sheets to the wind. They had all dashed from the Champagne Flute to their suites to change into their swimwear and grab their accessories before heading to The Terrace. Sarah was the last one to arrive as usual although she was only a few minutes behind the others. her vanity a priority even when drunk.

They were all in the infinity pool laughing and playing. Louisa was sitting on Andy's shoulders, Jasper was lying on an inflatable with his forever present glass of Chivas Regal watching Mia, Cosmo and Michael doing an impromptu synchronised swimming performance. Sarah was also on an inflatable next to Jasper trying to make small talk with him but to no avail. Jasper had blanked her from his peripheral vision in the same way he was about to blank her from his life. There were smiles and laughter from other passengers sunbathing on The Terrace as they watched the antics of the group.

The impromptu pool party carried on until the sun started to wane. They each wished each other a good night as they all decided that in-suite dining would be the best option that evening. In other words, they were all too pissed to be bothered to get ready.

Opulence herself was lively. The other passengers were enjoying their last couple of days and made the most of every minute. The bars were all lively, dining rooms full and guests happy. Just as *Opulence* was coming alive for the evening, the group were wandering back to their suites worse for wear and looking forward to a quiet night in.

An hour later and back in their suite, Jasper and Sarah were barely on glancing terms. Jasper was on their balcony having ordered room service. He was tucking in to comfort food to soak up some of the alcohol consumed that day. His steak sandwich and truffle fries had done the job and he fired up his laptop to converse with a special person in his life. Sarah was sulking in the oversize bathtub. She wasn't upset that Jasper wasn't speaking to her, she just didn't want to ruin anything so near to her plan coming to fruition. Sarah got up quickly, grabbed her soft robe and made her way to their lounge area where she could see Jasper through the huge glass doors. She fired up her tablet and smiled as she thought, *Only another few hours until it's over but until then I have plans.*

Cosmo had left Mia in her suite lying on her bed, happily mumbling to herself about how great a day it had been. He kissed her on the cheek and told her there were some painkillers and water on her bedside table should she need them and there was a platter of fresh sandwiches and fruit in the lounge if she felt peckish. *This is one lady who will have a hell of a hangover tomorrow,* smiled Cosmo. *It won't be long before she's fast asleep,* he thought as he left his boss's suite and headed to his own to get his laptop out and make a special call.

Louisa, despite having consumed a fair amount, could hold her alcohol quite well. She was mellow but not drunk. Louisa closed her laptop to finish her meal. She had been liaising, planning this evening's entertainment. Louisa had also ordered from room service and had just tucked into confit chicken, salsify, horseradish cream and pickled walnut followed by a vanilla cheesecake with pickled blackberries and almonds. For such a petite girl, Louisa could eat whatever she wanted with no weight gain. *I suppose I'd better freshen myself up,* thought Louisa as she swallowed her last mouthful of cheesecake. I *will be entertaining later and I want to make sure I'm ready.* Louisa smiled to herself as she stepped into the hot shower and raised her head directly into the steaming jets.

Andy hadn't seen Kurt all day and went to check on him, hoping to god that the little shit hadn't done something to ruin his new contract before it had even begun. Kurt answered the door to his suite with a big grin. His hair flopped over his forehead as Andy realised he'd just stepped out of the shower. 'Come on in, mate, what have you been up to today?' Andy explained about the Champagne Flute and impromptu pool party and Kurt laughed at Andy's tales of how the group were when they let their hair down.

Kurt seems sober, thought Andy. Kurt was currently drinking Peroni straight from the bottle and offered Andy one but he declined, admitting he needed to eat and turn in for the night.

'What are you doing tonight, Kurt?' asked Andy.

'Nothing much. Just intending to watch some DVDs and chill. I'm going to order some food and have a night in.' Andy believed Kurt and thought that perhaps the tide really had turned.

'OK mate, have a good night and behave,' said Andy as he left Kurt to make his way to his own suite.

Once safely within his own walls, Andy switched on his laptop and quickly sent a message. A ping alerted an immediate response and he smiled and closed his laptop. He picked up the phone and ordered turbot with steamed vegetables then jumped into the shower to bathe before the food arrived. *I have a date*, grinned Andy.

Michael was alone in his suite. He had ordered a New York strip steak, fries and salad to soak up the alcohol consumed over the last few hours. *I hope I didn't overdo it today,* thought Michael. *I know Michelle has only been missing a few days but I don't want people to think I'm happy about it. I'm sure many of them just think I'm so traumatised that they forgive me for over doing the alcohol and enjoying myself. I also need to ensure the booze doesn't loosen my lips,* thought Michael as he made his way to the bathroom and started running the marble bath ready for some sensual back scrubbing and who knows what else a little later? Michael checked himself out in the mirror. *I am a pretty good looking guy aren't I* as he stripped off his shirt and started to unbutton his trousers.

Jasper finished his cigar then got up and walked into his suite. He could see Sarah on the sofa and ignored her as he went into the bedroom and emerged seconds later with his door key card. Jasper made his way to the door and left, letting it slam behind him.

Sarah was watching her husband from lowered eyes and as soon as he left the suite she breathed a sigh of relief. Sarah darted up and ran to the bathroom. She quickly showered then reapplied her make-up, put on some black lingerie and slipped into a little black Dior sheath. Sarah quickly fastened her Giuseppe Zanotti heels and grabbed her phone and suite card. 'I hope the fucker falls overboard,' muttered Sarah as she made her way along the corridor from her suite.

It was a sight to behold. Every member of the group on their laptops and tablets sending messages and texting. Ping alerts going off in all suites nearly simultaneously. *Opulence* looked as though she was hiding more than one secret.

As the shadows fell and the night drew in whispers of 'I love you' and 'we're nearly there' echoed from some suites. Illicit affairs were about to get real.

Opulence sailed towards the UK at 22 knots. This was the final day of the voyage. In just over 24 hours she would dock at the Neptune Terminal in Southampton to disembark her 600 passengers. Within three hours she would be turned around, suites deep cleaned, communal bars and areas cleaned to pristine standards and tons of fresh seafood, meat and vegetables brought on board ready for her next adventure which was a two-week cruise to the Mediterranean.

Although the final day at sea was usually relatively quiet, as many passengers directed their butlers and maids to pack their trunks and confirm final arrangements for disembarkation, it was a busy day for the pursers and concierges.

The Pursers Office was responsible for invoicing all passengers and having the invoices hand delivered to the suites before 5am to ensure that they were waiting for the passengers when they wakened. The concierges desk was full steam ahead from 6am when it opened. Six-hundred passengers would be disembarking and all 600 had private vehicles and drivers coming to collect them. Timings and parking arrangements had to be sent to the limousine companies to ensure the drivers knew exactly where to go and what time, to ensure a seamless flow of traffic.

Mia woke at 6.30am with a blinding headache. *There's no fool like an old fool,* she thought as she sat up clutching her head. 'Cosmo, Cosmo are you here? I need help!' shouted Mia. Cosmo had risen early knowing full well that Mia would be suffering and needing him to make her better.

'Good morning, darling,' gushed Cosmo as he entered Mia's bedroom. He handed her a glass of water and two painkillers. 'Take these and you will feel better in about half an hour. I have some croissants, oatmeal, yoghurt and fruit coming shortly. Once you have something in your stomach you will feel even better.'

Mia smiled weakly at Cosmo. She was certainly a legendary actress as her performance for 'Women with Hangover' would have won her an Oscar.

'Oh Cosmo, I feel so wretched. What happened, darling? Why did you let me drink so much? Do you think someone spiked my drinks?' cried Mia.

'No one spiked your drinks, Mia, you just drank too much. We met around 3pm in the Champagne Flute and didn't stop drinking until around 8pm last night. It's self-inflicted, my darling girl,' Cosmo said with a smile as he went into her bathroom to run her a bath.

Mia swallowed the painkillers and laid back on her pillows with a sigh. *I'll get up as soon as these start to kick in,* she thought. *It's our last day and I don't want to miss any of it.*

The rest of the group were also in various states of hangovers. Louisa fared best as she could handle her drink. Cosmo was working and on call for Mia 24/7 so he rarely drank too much.

Jasper was in a foul mood as his head was thumping. Jasper arrived back at his suite at 5am and climbed into bed. Sarah was not there. He was livid. He wasn't worried about her, just worried that she would embarrass him on the final hours of the voyage. Jasper was however happy that he'd had a brilliant night of unadulterated sex and knew there was much more to look forward to. This helped him keep his tongue firmly in place until the time was right and it wasn't now. Sarah arrived back at their suite around 5.15am. She didn't realise that Jasper knew she had been out all night. She thought that she would get away with it, with Jasper being a heavy sleeper. He wouldn't know what time she came back. She smiled as she climbed into bed.

Michael sat up in bed drinking fresh coffee and looked lovingly at the crumpled pillows and sheets on Michelle's side of the bed that had been vacated earlier. 'Only another 24 hours, my darling. We're nearly there, babe.'

Andy was bright and alert as he emerged from his shower and opened his laptop. *I'll do a couple of hours' business then enjoy my last day,* he thought. *Just a couple of things to check on before tomorrow.*

Terry and Rocky woke in their own rooms with Denise and Chris snuggled beside them. Rocky kissed Chris on the nose as she nuzzled against his shoulder, making sleepy gurgling sounds. *What an eye-opener this trip has been,* thought Rocky. *We came away single guys as the biggest four-piece rock band on the planet and are going home with girlfriends and The Jackdaws advertising for two new members! Who would have thought it?*

The weather was fine but windy so The Sea Bed was closed on the last day. It was too windy for the parasols and diners. Food would have cooled too quickly. The group did their own thing for the morning then came together in The Oyster at lunchtime to enjoy their final gourmet lunch. Jasper and Sarah could barely look at each other. Michael sat with Mia and Cosmo and Andy, Louisa and Kurt chatted amicably as they dined on wonderful fare.

'If I don't get the chance to speak to you properly before the voyage is over, I'd just like to thank you both for your kindness and for taking me under your wing since Michelle's tragic disappearance.' Tears welled up in Michael's eyes as he dropped his head.

'Oh Michael, you poor man,' cried Mia. 'We are so sorry for what happened, aren't we Cosmo? You must be devastated? We could see how so in love you both were.'

'Absolutely,' said Cosmo, 'We are beside ourselves for your loss. We can't begin to imagine how you must feel.'

Mia took Michael's hand and raised her glass of Chateau Neuf Du Pape. 'To Michelle, forever in our hearts.' Cosmo and Michael raised their glasses, Cosmo repeating Mia's toast while Michael sat quietly with tears in his eyes.

Officer Scott McDonald was sitting behind his desk chewing on the lid of his pen. Since Michelle's disappearance he had been keeping an eye on all the passengers and digging as much as he could into his passengers' backgrounds but to no avail. Michelle Benson was missing presumed dead, at least that was the official version, however, something was niggling him which he couldn't let go. Jenson Jenkins was pretty adamant he witnessed a murder and despite him being a colourful lad there was something about the way in which he recounted the story with earnest that Scott believed him. Unfortunately, all Scott's investigations and limited surveillance hit a brick wall. He believed Jenson Jenkins was telling the truth and had indeed witnessed Michelle Benson being killed. Scott sighed as he signed off the investigation paperwork. *All I can do is give the information to the police when we get back. My work here is done.*

Opulence would forever be party to this most awful secret never to be uncovered. This was her secret and hers alone.

Lunch passed pleasantly. Alcohol was consumed at a social rate, bearing in mind that the Privilege Party was this evening.

Passengers again made their last trips to their favourite bars and special areas of the ship. Video cameras filmed the gorgeous vessel and pictures were taken with celebrities. The shops were busy with credit cards taking a last minute hammering. Everything started to quieten down around 4pm when passengers disappeared for afternoon tea or to their suites for pre-dinner cocktails.

The Privilege Party was starting at 10pm in the Court Ballroom and the dress code was cocktail for the ladies and smart for the men. In other words, short cocktail dresses for the ladies and shirts, trousers, ties and blazers for the men. Most of the packing had already been done and it was not fair to expect passengers to keep their black tie formal outfits out for the last night. When passengers retired to their suites tonight they would throw their outfits into their luggage and the butlers would collect the luggage by 3am to be taken away. The next time passengers would see their luggage after tonight would be in the Neptune Terminal customs hall tomorrow morning. A small handheld holdall was all that was required to put their remaining toiletries and jewellery in to carry off the ship.

'I've left out your teal McQueen cocktail dress with the silver Gucci sandals, Mia!' shouted Cosmo from the dressing room. Mia was in the shower getting ready for dinner and the final party. 'I'll be back to do your hair and make-up in half an hour. I'm just going to put my suit on.'

'OK darling!' shouted Mia over the noise of the jets. 'See you soon.'

Cosmo returned to his suite where he quickly changed into a dark grey Tom Ford three-piece suit with a lavender-coloured silk shirt and matching heather-coloured silk tie. Ever the perfectionist, he had finished his packing earlier and only had to put the suit away after tonight's party ready for his luggage to be collected. He and the other passengers would leave his suitcases outside his suite in the corridor for the crew to collect in the wee small hours.

Sarah was dressing in a white Chanel crystal boat necked dress which showed off her tan. Her look was completed with white Zanotti sandals and her hair pinned in an elegant chignon. Sarah again looked stunning. Jasper too looked great. He wore a navy wool blazer over a crisp white shirt, navy trousers and grey fleurs de lis patterened tie. They were a dynamic couple. No one could ever take that away from them.

Sarah chattered away mindlessly mainly to herself about her evening bag and Jasper just grunted angrily at her. The ice wall was still erect and would forever remain so. They both wished this voyage would be over with. They both had their own reasons and couldn't wait to make their announcements.

Michael met with Kurt, Louisa and Andy in the Mermaid Lounge for pre-dinner drinks. Michael dressed all in charcoal Armani looked so handsome. Kurt made an effort with a linen blazer, trousers and matching blue shirt and tie and Louisa looked drop dead gorgeous in a coral knee-length chiffon off-the-shoulder dress and matching heels. Her hair curled, the curls fell loosely around her face. She was stunning.

'What time are we eating?' asked Louisa.

'8.30pm, I believe,' replied Andy.

'OK, best we drink up and make our way to The Oyster. We don't want to be late on our last night,' replied Louisa.

When they entered the dining room they were escorted to a large round table set for eight people. Mia had suggested that they all dine together for their final night and they all agreed this would be a lovely idea. The table was exquisite with the finest crystal and white floral display as a centrepiece.

Michael, Sarah, Jasper, Mia and Cosmo all arrived shortly after and they excitedly chatted to each other about their memories of the trip. They all ordered from the sumptuous menu with Mia announcing she needed to go on a detox and diet when she got home as she'd gained a few pounds on this vacation.

Their final dinner in The Oyster was delicious as always. They toasted each other and Cosmo made a special toast to Michelle on behalf of the group. At 10.10pm they made their way from The Oyster to the Court Ballroom to enjoy the final party of the voyage.

The ballroom was lit with crystal chandeliers sparkling against the white and purple backdrop of chairs and wall decor. The 12-piece orchestra was playing a variety of easy listening tunes as background music and a few passengers were dancing. Waiters were walking among the guests with trays of champagne and canapes and all of the ship's senior crew, from Commodore Griffiths to the medical and entertainment staff and chefs were mingling with the guests to thank them for vacationing with them. It was always a great opportunity to increase the size of the tip!

The group mingled with other passengers and crew for about an hour then sat down together to say goodbye.

Rocky and Terry arrived in the ballroom with Chris and Denise on their arms. They looked so happy and so right together. Jess and Olivia were there alone. They looked on with envy as Chris and Denise paraded their prizes across the ballroom.

'It's just like, not fair, Liv,' cried Jess. 'That should have like been us not them. We should have like, had Rocky and Terry and not been left with like those two idiots.'

Jessica thought back to earlier that day after they returned from shopping to meet Todd and Ed in their suite. They had just snorted some coke and necked a couple of shots and climbed into bed with the boys when there was a loud banging on the door. Ed stumbled drunkenly to open it and Scott McDonald was there with four of his security staff. Scott entered the room without being invited and in his most authoritative voice told Ed and Todd that they were being placed under maritime arrest for illegal substance misuse on board the vessel.

Jess and Olivia were terrified. They grabbed their clothes to hide their nakedness as Officer McDonald told them to leave now or they would be arrested also. Jess and Olivia all but ran from the suite, their clothes trailing behind them, mortified as they bumped into crew and passengers alike.

Todd started to create a fuss. He was shouting and swearing. Scott McDonald nodded to his team who walked forward and grabbed Todd and Ed. They were restrained with ratchet handcuffs and marched unceremoniously to the security department where a jail-style room awaited them. Lewis had reported the drugs to security and it was decided the boys would be arrested. They would spend their last night on board, sobering up in a simple but basic room in the bowels of the ship with no luxuries. Lewis and his team would pack up their belongings and wouldn't be sorry to see the back of these obnoxious guys.

Jess and Olivia looked on wistfully at the two girls who had bagged two of the most eligible rock stars in the world.

'It's like so unfair!' cried Jess. 'If those two morons talk then our TV careers are like over before they've started.'

'I've had enough, Jess,' said Olivia. 'I'm going back to the suite. My holiday is done.'

'Don't you like want to talk to some of the boys from the Russian family?' said Jess.

'No, I'm out, I'm done,' said Olivia as she turned and flounced out of the room.

Kurt joined the group for the remainder of the evening. He sat quietly and on his best behaviour. He looked at Louisa with sadness thinking about what might have been as he watched her chat with Andy. *Come to think of it, those two have been pretty pally recently,* thought Kurt. *I wonder if that bastard has crossed me?*

Mia was checking with Cosmo that everything was in place for their trip home. They were travelling to London and booked into the Savoy until the Monday when they would fly back to Los Angeles. 'Stop panicking Mia. Everything is sorted. Enjoy your last few hours.'

The group made small talk until midnight when the ballroom started to empty. Passengers were aware they all had an early start the following morning and wanted to travel hangover-free.

The group left together and made their way to their respective suites, stopping to kiss and hug each other goodbye as each person or couple tailed off. They were unsure whether they would see each other at breakfast or disembarkation so numbers were swapped and goodbyes said tonight.

Thank fuck that's over, thought Jasper as he pulled off his tie and poured himself a large tumbler of Chivas Regal. *Just another few hours and it's over*. Jasper made his way to the bedroom, dropping his clothes as he went. Sarah sat on the sofa nursing a straight Grey Goose on the rocks as she went over her last minute plans. The mood was dark in the Teasdales suite and was about to become darker.

Louisa skipped happily from her shower to bed. *Finally*, she thought as she hummed to herself. *Tomorrow is the start of the rest of my life*. She threw herself back on her pillows laughing and wishing the hours away.

Kurt turned in with no issues. He didn't even pour himself another drink. His future was secured thanks to Andy and that film deal but if Andy had crossed him by banging Louisa he wouldn't be happy. *I'll sort that soon*, thought Kurt as he drifted off to sleep.

Cosmo dropped Mia off in her suite and did her final packing. He kissed her goodnight and made his way to his own suite. Once there, Cosmo checked the final arrangements for tomorrow and took himself off to bed satisfied that Mia was happy.

Andy had put all his arrangements in place. He knew the plan and pulled out his phone. Andy sent a text. 'See you soon x'. With that, Andy turned his phone off and made his way to his bedroom.

Rocky and Chris spent the night in Rocky's suite while Denise and Terry stayed in the girls' suite. This would be their last special time alone for a while and they wanted to make the most of it. The boys would be whisked away to seek their replacement band members soon and they may not get to see the girls for a while.

Ed and Todd had sobered up considerably since being held by security a few hours before. They were not happy. Todd was shouting to speak to his solicitor and was told by the on-duty security officer that he would have time enough soon to see his brief. Todd threw himself down on the bed in the secure room and chuntered to himself about the injustice of it all. Ed on the other hand was trying to sleep. He felt awful from the withdrawal of drugs and alcohol and couldn't even think about what had happened and the shame he'd brought to his family. He covered his head with his pillow as he yelled at Todd to shut up.

The voyage was over. Guests awoke to find *Opulence* docked in the Neptune Berth at Southampton. She docked at 5.45am while all the passengers were still asleep. Around 6.30am most passengers were receiving alarm calls. Many had vast distances to travel and they all had to be off the ship by 10am. 'A' list passengers had priority disembarkation from 7am. Those who wanted to leave at 7am dined in-suite from a pre-ordered breakfast menu chosen the night before.

The early departure saw not only around 140 passengers disembark but also Todd and Ed get escorted off the ship via a service gangway on Deck 1. Waiting to greet them was a police van to whisk them away to Southampton Police Station for questioning.

'This is fucking out of order, do you know who we are?' screamed Todd.

The bored looking police officer merely held Todd's arm as he said, 'Mind your head, sir' while helping him into the back. Banging could be hear from the van as it drove off with Todd and Ed in the back. These bad boys of rock would certainly be all over the media but not necessarily for the right reasons and no decent record label would touch them again after this.

In the Teasdale's suite, Jasper was waiting for Sarah in the lounge. 'This is it Sarah,' barked Jasper. 'You're not honestly so stupid that you think I love you, are you?' 'You've been nothing but an embarrassment to me and I'm finished. Take your whining Essex voice, your fake tits and your incessant drivel and fuck off out of my life.' Jasper glared at Sarah as he threw her a buff-coloured envelope. 'I've tied everything up so tight and your settlement is in there so if you dare to try and get more from me you'll be sorry. Do you hear me?'

Sarah had emerged from her dressing room looking every inch a lady. She was dressed unusually in a navy Chanel skirt suit and court shoes, her hair pulled into a messy bun and a pair of Bulgari sunglasses sitting atop her head.

Sarah listened quietly to Jasper. Her dark eyes flashing anger but a confident smile growing from her lips as he launched the envelope towards her. 'If you think you can stitch me up, Jasper Teasdale, you have another thing coming. I've put up with your foul moods and temper tantrums since practically the day we met. Take your settlement and shove it up your arse, you fuckwit' Sarah spat. 'How dare you take me for a fool, did you really think I was so stupid that I didn't know how you felt about me or what you thought of me? Well, I'm not so dumb, Jasper. I've secured a very good future for myself. Our assets, or rather my assets, are listed here.' With that, she opened her Hermes tote and threw a white envelope at Jasper. 'I think you'll find my solicitors have tied up all the loose ends and if you want a fight mate then bring it on. You may have the family name and wealth behind you but your name will be shit if I tell the world what you are really like with all your infidelities and what a sexual deviant you are.'

Jasper leapt towards Sarah but she sidestepped him and ran to the door. Jasper hit his shin on the glass coffee table and stumbled. 'You won't get away with this, you fucking bitch!' shouted Jasper after her. 'I'll ruin you, bitch.'

Jasper's voice trailed off as Sarah hurried along the corridor to the lift. The lift arrived and she entered it. As the door closed, Sarah leaned back against the mirrored wall and let out a huge sigh. Tears welled up in her eyes as she remembered the look on Jasper's face. *I thought he was going to kill me. I really thought I wouldn't make if off this ship.* The lift pinged and the door opened on Deck 2. A bellboy met Sarah as she composed herself and relieved her of her carry-off. He escorted her to the disembarkation point where she flashed her best smile at the waiting crew and walked graciously down the glass-enclosed gangway to the customs area and baggage hall.

Kurt and Andy called to collect Louisa so they could disembark together. They made their way to Deck 2 chatting amicably but sad that such an experience of a lifetime had come to an end. Kurt was unusually quiet. Deep down he was seething that Andy had betrayed him with Louisa.

They got to the baggage hall and Kurt and Andy helped Louisa point out her luggage to the waiting porters. 'So this is it then, Louisa,' said Kurt, as her last suitcase was placed on the trolley and the porter started to wheel it away.

'This is it guys. The end of a chapter and the beginning of a new one. Good luck with your film, Kurt. Look after yourself.' Louisa leaned forward and hugged Kurt. She knew that they would never hook up again. *It was fun while it lasted,* she thought *but there's no going back.*

Louisa turned to Andy as Kurt watched them closely. 'Goodbye Andy. Thanks for everything. I had a blast.' Andy and Louisa embraced and Louisa turned and walked away.

'Best get our luggage now and be on our way, Kurt. We have things to do and people to see. What time is our car collecting us?' said Kurt.

'Your car will be here in about five minutes, mate,' said Andy. 'I'm not going back to London just yet. Something has come up. I'll see you in a week before you fly to the States, OK?'

'What do you mean?' garbled Kurt. Where are you going?' With that, Andy turned and walked away with his porter towards the terminal exit. He raised his hand and waved to Kurt without looking back at him. Kurt's questions still being fired. 'Andy, Andy, Andy mate, where are you going?'

Rocky and Terry disembarked with Chris and Denise. Determined to make every last moment count, they stood outside in the early but weak sunshine saying goodbye. 'We'll facetime tonight when we're settled and when we have something concrete with our schedule, I'll let you know.' Denise and Chris shed a tear as Rocky and Terry got into their chauffeured Range Rover.

'I can't believe they've gone, Chris,' said Denise, wiping the tears from her eyes.

'Neither can I. I wonder when we'll see them again?' Denise and Chris didn't live far from the Neptune Terminal but they had booked a car to collect them and their vast amount of suitcases.

Jasper left his suite just along the corridor from Michael at the same time. They were waiting for the lift to arrive as Mia and Cosmo appeared round the corner.

'Are you sure you've got everything, Cosmo? You haven't forgotten anything?'

'Relax, Mia,' Cosmo said as they approached the lift. 'Our car is already here waiting for us. I've checked, so stop worrying.'

'I don't know what I'd do without you, Cosmo,' gushed Mia. 'I'm such a worrier.'

'Oh hello, darlings,' drawled Mia when she saw Michael and Jasper.' Going our way?'

Michael just smiled as they entered the lift to take them on their final descent of *Opulence*. 'Where's Sarah, Jasper?' 'Jasper smiled and said she'd gone on ahead to the car as she didn't like to hang around when things were over.

They disembarked and made their way to the baggage hall. Jasper summoned a couple of porters who expertly assigned the correct luggage to the trolleys.

The baggage hall was bustling now as the early passengers had left and the bulk of the remaining passengers were now leaving. They stood chatting while their luggage was being managed.

Parked in a car park just a couple of minutes from the terminal sat a stretch limousine. Sarah sat inside tapping away on her mobile. Suddenly the car door opened and Sarah beamed from ear to ear. 'We're ready to go, Josh,' said Sarah.

'Yes ma'am. Exactly where is your new destination, please?'

'Paris,' said Andy as Sarah sank into his arms. 'Paris.'

Jasper was saying goodbye to Mia with all the drama a legendary Hollywood actress could muster. He was engulfed in her embrace when Cosmo shrieked that he thought he'd dropped his wallet in the security area. 'I'll be back in a minute, Mia, I need to run back and find my wallet. Jasper, be a darling and escort Mia to our car. Michael, It was so lovely to meet you. I am desperately sorry about Michelle.'

Michael smiled at Cosmo and shook his hand. 'Take care, Cosmo. I hope life is better to you than it's been to me.' Cosmo gave a gentle smile and ran back towards the security area. 'Come on then, let's go,' said Michael as Mia linked arms with him and Jasper.

They saw Mia safely to her limousine which was parked up in a long line of cars awaiting their clients. Jasper said his goodbyes to Michael and headed along the line of parked cars and around the corner of the building.

Jasper saw his regular driver Barry, standing outside the limo awaiting his master's return.

'Welcome home, Mr Teasdale,' said Barry as he opened the door and Jasper got in and sat down. He felt a hand grab his crotch and his eyes popped.

'Can't you at least wait until we get to yours?' laughed Jasper.

'Not a hope in hell of that,' said Louisa, her eyes sparkling as she unbuttoned her blouse.

'Barry, shut the windows and don't disturb us until we get to Miss Hudson's.'

'Yes sir,' said Barry, smiling as he raised the blackened-out glass partition and switched off the audio speaker.

Michael was standing in an alcoved recess just outside the terminal. Passengers were bustling around looking for their cars.

Suddenly he felt the familiar warm presence next to him. Their fingers brushed and Michael turned subtly. 'I'll be with you in Cornwall later tonight. I'll drop Mia off at the Savoy and then tell her I'm leaving. I told you I loved you and I'd do anything for you. I promised you she'd never hurt you again and I always keep my promises.'

Cosmo gently squeezed Michael's fingers as he looked deep into Michael's soul then turned away and walked towards his awaiting limo.

Michael stood for a minute thinking about his life, Michelle and his new love. There would be some hurdles to face in the coming months but he was happy, happier than he'd ever been before. Michael strode forward, found his car and jumped in.

'Let's go, Mark.'

The car drove slowly out of the terminal, *Opulence* rising up behind them as Michael left his old life behind and contemplated the new one yet to begin.

THE END.

Printed in Great Britain
by Amazon

81502800R00115